The Reb

ISBN: 9781957290140 (eBook)

Print: 9781957290157

This is a work of fiction. Any references to historical events, real people, or real places are used fictitiously. Names, characters, and places are products of the author's imagination. Inclusion of or reference to any Christian elements or themes are used in a fictitious manner and are not meant to be perceived or interpreted as an act of disrespect against such a wonderful and beautiful belief system.

Cover image provided by Envanto Elements

Image created by twenty20photos

The Rebel Christian Publishing LLC

350 Northern Blvd STE 324 - 1390

Albany, NY 12204-1000

Visit us: http://www.therebelchristian.com/

Email us: rebel@therebelchristian.com

Other Books by A. Bean

The End of the World Series (Christian End Times Fiction)
Too Young (Christian Children's Fantasy)
The Scribe (Christian Fantasy)
The Woof Pack (Christian Romantic Suspense)
[Coming 2022]

This one is for the member of the Holy Trinity Who's often overlooked

The Living Water
By A. Bean

A Rebel Christian Publishing Book

A note from the author

Praise Jesus! I appreciate all the love and support; it has truly encouraged me to keep writing. Please know that all church scenes are not in mockery of the faith, rather, they are the very vivid memories of church services when my grandmother used to preach long ago. I want to do nothing but honor the Christ and the church, and my late grandmother.

I hope that you will enjoy this tale of romance and faith. If you'd like to keep up with me, follow me on Instagram **@awritingbean**. Until the next journey begins…

A. Bean
Habakkuk 2:2

Part I

One

The Living Water

When I was eight years old, Reverend Bernie Lee prophesied over me. The sanctuary was full of the usual faces; Mother Murphy, Deacon Jones, Sister Anne, and all the others who made All Saints Temple a home—not just a church building.

As a kid, I'd always enjoyed church. It was exciting. Especially when everyone would get the Holy Ghost and dance around the building. One time, I pretended to have the Holy Ghost, too, so I started toe-tapping and dancing all around the church, throwing my arms up and shouting 'Hallelujah!' That was when Reverend Lee rose from her seat at the back of the pulpit and cut the Spirit.

"Sit down, everybody," she said calmly as she stood at the wooden podium. Reverend Lee paced slowly across the creaky church floor, holding the microphone in her aged hand. "Y'all out here churchin' so hard, y'all don't even see that boy dancing around like he on the dancefloor. That's not what this is about, young man." Her dark brown eyes glared over thick round frames as she stopped pacing to look at me. Swallowing hard, I clutched to my momma, as she went on, shaking her head in disappointment. "Stand to your feet, young man. You gon' learn somethin' today."

I didn't move.

"C'mon now, gittup." Her southern drawl made all her words slur together in a way that made her seem so much more intimidating.

I sat there clutching momma's skirt a little tighter. "Go on, Cameron," Momma said softly. Her skin was as dark as Reverend's. We didn't look anything alike at all. Everyone always said I looked just like my daddy, except I had a little more color, but I'd never met the guy, so I didn't know.

Tanned skin with dark curls, everyone said I was a pretty thang—pretty like a girl—and when I got older, Momma would have to beat the women off with sticks. But I never wanted any problems for Momma, so I kept to myself and tried to avoid trouble as much as I could. She had enough issues, living in a divided town in Alabama with a biracial son who'd never met his father. Sometimes it felt like neither of us belonged. I was too white, and she was too black and in smalltown Alabama, there just wasn't any in-between.

Everyone said they knew my father was John Taylor, an upper-class man from the *other* side of town. Pale skin, bright eyes, and a dangerous smile—which he'd often used on women from *our* side of town. Word around the block was that he liked ladies like Momma, just not enough to marry them.

"I won't ask again," Reverend Lee's voice came out

4

harsher, strong enough to snap me from my reverie.

Nervously, I stood to my feet from the bench.

"Now," Reverend said, slowly making her way back to the podium as her golden robe trailed along the carpeted pulpit. "How old are you, young man?"

I looked back at my mother who had a gentle smile that masked the embarrassment I'd brought her.

"Don't look at her, look at me when I'm talking to ya'. You see, Savannah, you got that boy too spoiled. You gotta make him be a man, let him grow up. Stop smothering him all the time." The cruel words only earned an apologetic nod from my mother.

"I'm eight," I finally said.

Reverend Lee nodded as she placed the mic back on the stand. Her long arms stretched across the podium as she flattened her palms on it and said, "Do you know why I had to stop the service today?"

I shook my head.

"Because you were playing around with the Spirit, and we can't have that."

I was so nervous I wanted to run back to my mother and hide behind her, but I knew that would only make matters worse for me *and* for her. I swallowed the anxiety creeping up my throat and tried to stand still as all eyes were on me. With everyone's attention, it felt like the boiling Alabama heat had intensified, making me melt in the center of the congregation.

"You ain't never been taught not to play with the Spirit, so I'm gonna go easy on you," Reverend Lee said, stopping to take a sip of water. I couldn't believe she considered this 'going easy on me,' but I'd heard being taught something in church was good ol' Baptist love, and good ol' Baptist love was *always* tough love.

"Now, your momma is trying to make somethin' out of you, boy, since ya' father won't help. Bringing you to church is the best thing for you. It'll keep you as you get old, and it's gonna guide you as you mature. But you gotta take it seriously. Can't be no playin' games and runnin' around here dancin' like you ain't got no sense." She paused and peered at the audience behind me. "Can I get an 'Amen,' church?"

"Amen, Reverend!" I heard Mother Murphy say. Others joined in, and a tambourine played in the background. I saw Fat Boy Kenny Joe getting to the keys, as he always did when Reverend was about to preach.

Reverend pointed at me, her voice coming low and serious and preachy. "Ya' momma can only take ya' so far," she heaved, "but *God!*" Her voice came out as a shout, and I nearly jumped. "God will take you the rest of the way … if you let Him."

"Alright now, alright now!" a woman called from behind me.

"God is going to do something in you, something that's gon' change you forever. But you gon' have to go through something to get it." She wiped sweat from her forehead with a cloth. "Y'all don't hear me this morning." Then, without notice, she snatched the mic off the stand and rushed to the edge of the pulpit. "I said, God is gonna do somethin' in him,

6

but he'll have to go through something to get it!" She put her hands on her hips as the church began to cheer and praise God. Fat Boy Kenny Joe hammered the keys to a moaning organ and Ricky Boy had jumped on the drums.

The congregation was wild with excitement, I felt something like an electric charge in the air. It buzzed around me, like the room was suddenly filled to bursting with praise and worship to the Lord. I loved whenever this happened, because it meant the Holy Spirit was present, but I was still nervous, and Reverend was still preaching about me, so I didn't get to jump around with everyone else.

"You may have to go through the valley and face all kinds of death and evil, but *God*," she said dramatically, "is *always* on your side. He will see you through His mission." She paused and stamped her feet in rhythm with the organ and the clapping crowd. "God's mission! His glory! His Grace! And His MERCY!" She shouted as she leaned back. The congregation went quiet, waiting for her to continue. She said in a very serious whisper, "Shall be known."

Fat Boy Kenny Joe played the organ so hard, his sweat poured down his face, and Ricky Boy hit the drums like never before. The people were up dancing again, shouting and screaming in the aisles of the old hot church. I glanced quickly over my shoulder to see Momma clapping her hands and shouting praises.

"Hold on! Hold on!" Reverend Lee said, silencing the congregation again. Fat Boy Kenny Joe played lighter on the keys, and Ricky Boy gently tapped the cymbal. Turning

7

abruptly, Reverend Bernie's robes twirled behind her as she marched across the pulpit and down the steps to me. As she got closer, I could see the sweat drizzling down her neck. She placed a heavy hand on my head. "I hear a word from God. Close your eyes."

I followed her instructions and snapped my eyes shut.

"God said, He's gonna give you His living water. You don't have to look for it, you don't have to try and find it, it's gonna come when God gives it to you. And whatever you see right now, that's where you'll receive that living water."

As I listened with my eyes shut, I was suddenly taken outside, standing before a well. It was deep and wide and almost ethereal. As I approached it, I could see hands reaching out, asking for water. People knelt with cupped hands lifted above their heads as I walked by, moving closer to the well. When I went to look inside and retrieve water for them, the vision disappeared.

I heard Reverend ask, "What do you see now?" She shoved the microphone into my face.

"I ... I see a well," I stammered.

Reverend hummed deeply, as if in thought. "Then that is where you shall find that living water."

Two

New Frames

Years Later…

I walked off the elevator and headed toward my apartment, ignoring the thump of my backpack slung over one shoulder. Down the white halls, I walked, going over my homework assignments in my head. I was studying to become an engineer at the University of Wyndington. It was considered an elite college. Prestigious, with a genuinely good curriculum, which meant UOW was out of my league. It meant I shouldn't be able to afford the tuition. But I was smart enough to snag a scholarship.

I'd gotten interested in robotic engineering when I was young, and everyone at church said it came from John Taylor, my father. He was the CEO and founder of Taylor Robotics. It started as a company that studied technology in the medical field and found ways to make that technology more efficient. But then, right around when I was born, the company branched out its research into other fields, and eventually began producing prototypes, not just blueprints for the tech upgrades. Now, they're a booming tech giant that mass produces for some of the largest companies in the world. Unfortunately, I'm not part of that legacy at all. John and I don't even share the same last name.

"Cameron Frierson," a lady's voice called behind me. I turned around to see Garrith Washington waltzing down the hall. My girlfriend. Her long peachy legs reached out from beneath her skirt that was almost too short. Momma didn't like Garrith very much, but since she was still in Alabama and I was here in Illinois, there was nothing she could do besides give me an earful every day.

Garrith walked over to me, gripping my free hand in hers, and pulling me close to peck my cheek. Another thing my mother didn't like about my girlfriend was the fact that she was not Christian at all, but *I* liked the fact that she at least respected me and my beliefs enough to keep things safe in our relationship. She always played it cool, chaste kisses, no sleeping over at my apartment, I'd never even been to hers.

But it wasn't like Garrith wasn't willing to take the next step. She never missed an opportunity to remind that the choice was mine. Whenever I was ready, we could ... um ... do it. But I told her I wouldn't be ready before marriage— she'd only laughed in response, and I had only smiled. But inside, I felt worried.

"Are you working today?" Garrith asked, adjusting her new glasses. Green eyes smiled behind the black square frames as I said, "Just got off, actually. I was coming in to call Mom and get some homework done." I paused and then followed up with a compliment, "I like those new frames."

She blushed. "Thanks, Cammy. I was hoping you'd notice."

"Of course," I said, squeezing her hand. "You're done today, right?"

She nodded as we began down the hall to my apartment. "Why don't you skip the phone call to Mom today and let's go grab dinner at that spot I've been telling you about?"

She'd been nagging me about going to this upscale seafood bar and grill, but I wasn't sure how I felt about it yet. I'd been putting the place off because it seemed like more of a bar than a grill and I wasn't comfortable with that.

"I don't know, Garrith, you know how Momma gets when I don't call her, and Cray-On is a little," I paused, raising a single shoulder, "not my style."

"C'mon, Cammy," she said, turning and stepping in front of me. Her eyes whined through her frames, making me sigh.

"Alright, fine, but we'll have to go now before it gets too late."

"Yes!" she squealed, jumping up and down.

I rolled my eyes and pushed past her to reach my door.

"I'm so excited!" she said behind me. "But that place is kind of expensive."

"I know. But don't worry, I've got it."

We entered my small apartment and Garrith went for my couch as she always did. The small space was all I could afford

11

on a scholarship and the parttime job I was working, however, I was sure Momma would think I was living like a king. At least I did when I first moved to UOW. I thought they'd somehow gotten my place mixed up, I even called the company that rented to my school, but they simply confirmed I was at the right place.

There was a short hallway that gave way to a common area where my couch sat across from the television. There was a kitchen area off to the side, and a few storage spaces while big windows lined the entire place. But, in the middle of the apartment was a case of spiral stairs that lead up to my bedroom, which I split into a working area, and there was a full bathroom up there. But even though my apartment was nice to me, it wasn't to Garrith and her group of friends when they came by for the first time about a year ago. They teased me and told me that Garrith's mother would use my place as a walk-in closet.

"I'm going to get changed, and then we can go. Are you going like that?"

Garrith looked down at herself, and then said, "You're totally right, I can't wear this. It's too trashy." She stood and slung her bag over her shoulder. "Pick me up in an hour?" It came out as more of a command than a question, and I sighed, agreeing to her terms, despite not having a car to pick her up in.

I didn't have a car because everything was in walking distance to my apartment. My job was only fifteen minutes away, and I caught the university's shuttle to and from classes.

Whenever I went somewhere else, I took public transportation. So, when Garrith said to pick her up, she really meant to meet her outside her place, and she would have someone drive us there.

I didn't mind Garrith's fortune, it was a little tiring to always be teased about my *mis*fortune, but I believed that God had better for me, too. I just had to keep going until it manifested, at least that's what Momma said.

As soon as Garrith left, I jogged up my staircase to call Momma. I dialed her number and tossed my phone on the bed as I undressed.

"Hello?" Her voice came through the speakerphone.

"Hey, Momma," I said as I crossed the floor to my drawers.

"Hey, baby."

"I'm taking Garrith out today to that seafood place she's been asking about."

"The expensive one?"

"Yeah," I said, rolling my eyes. I pulled my shirt off and slipped on a t-shirt.

"Mmm," was all she responded with.

I frowned. "Come on, Momma, don't be like that. She's been asking since it opened." I tucked my arm into the sleeve of my white button down.

"I'm just saying, I don't like that girl. Something ain't right about her; she won't never go to church with you. I don't know why you're with her."

"Momma," I stepped out of my jeans and into my slacks, "she'll eventually come. It takes time for people to change."

13

"Yeah, it takes time for people to change *themselves*. But it doesn't take God very long at all. There are some people He's changed instantly." She harrumphed and I knew a nugget sermon was coming. "When people wanna live righteously, they start making changes the instant their mind is made up," she said sassily. "The problem isn't that it takes time to change, it's that she hasn't taken the first step in changing to begin with."

"And what's the first step?" I asked, tucking my shirt into my pants and zipping them closed. I already knew the answer, Momma and I had this conversation every other week. I mouthed her reply as she said, "The first step is *deciding* to change. And Garrith clearly hasn't done that."

I covered my mouth so she wouldn't hear me sigh over the speakerphone. Then I said, "Well, Momma, I don't know what to tell you. I like Garrith. We get along well. And she's cool. One day she'll decide to change. And then she *will* change. Until then…" I trailed off.

Momma's voice was tired. "I can't make you do anything, but I know that when you bump into a real woman of God, you're gonna have a change of *heart*. You're gonna wanna go after her, but good ol' Garrith will be right there with her prissy little hand around your heart."

"Momma, you worry too much," I said as I buttoned a cuff on my sleeve.

"No, Cameron, you don't worry enough."

I figured this was as good a time as any to change the subject. "How are you, Momma? How ya' holding up? I mailed

14

you a check yesterday, it should be there soon."

"Cam, I told you not to send me money. You need that for you."

"Maybe, but it helps me sleep at night knowing you've got a little extra money in your pocket. Besides," I sat on the bed beside my phone, "one day you won't get a couple hundred dollars a month, you'll be getting millions."

Momma laughed. "I know that's right."

As I pulled my socks on, I saw a flyer I'd gotten from the campus bulletin sitting on the floor. *It must've fallen out of my pocket*, I thought as I reached to grab it. Looking it over, I said, "Momma, I need some advice."

"Alright," she said cheerfully, "what's going on, Cam?"

"You remember that trip I signed Garrith and I up for?"

"The one sponsored by the Christian group on your campus?"

"Yeah, that's the one," I said, staring at the flyer.

"What about it?"

I didn't answer.

Momma said, "Cam, you haven't told her yet, have you? Baby, when are you gonna tell her? The semester will be finished, and the trip will be here."

"I know. I just didn't have the opportunity, but I think I can tell her tonight. What do you think?" I asked nervously. I set the flyer down and checked my watch. I had a few minutes before I'd have to leave to get to Garrith's place.

"I think that's a very good plan, Cam. Make sure you don't just come right out and say it, though. Be straight, but be," she paused, "*smooth* with it."

I let out a laugh. "Alright, I'll be smooth."

Momma laughed a little and then her voice was low and serious. "Cameron, this is a big decision to make. Taking someone across the world with you, that's a big step in the relationship. Are you sure you want to do this?"

I inhaled deeply, rubbing a hand over my face. "I want to do it. I think this might really change her perspective of the faith, especially going with a Christian group. We'll have separate rooms, and everything. It'll be good."

"Well, maybe. You won't know until you get there."

We stayed silent for a moment as I tucked my wallet into my pocket and gathered my keys from my desk. "I've gotta get going now, Momma, but I'll give you a call tomorrow, alright? I love you."

"I love you too, Cameron. Bye now."

Three
Dinner Date

Garrith looked stunning sitting across the table from me. She wore a single-shoulder black dress and let her cascade of dark chocolate waves sit elegantly on her shoulders. She looked different without her glasses; they made her look young and nerdy, but without them she looked like a woman of great stature. I watched her as she gently lifted the martini glass to her lips, taking a small sip before setting it back down. Cray-On was packed when we'd arrived, so we decided to go to a different place up the street, somewhere quieter and better suited for Garrith's attire. She always over dressed, but tonight, her seductive black dress was fitting for our change of location.

I took a sip of water, feeling more nervous than ever to tell her about the trip I'd booked for us. I'd have to hurry, though, since she was on her second martini, and she wouldn't be remembering much after a third one. I hated that Garrith drank, but it was only on occasions, so I let it slide, despite how guilty I always felt about it. It was times like these I wished

Momma's nagging wasn't running amuck in my head. Telling me all the right things about a Christian woman, and how I'd let myself become unequally yoked. I knew that, but I didn't know how to become *un*yoked, and sometimes, when I'm honest with myself, I had to admit I didn't want to be. I've gotten used to being with Garrith; I knew her well, and I didn't want to be alone again even though I knew being with her wasn't right.

Garrith wasn't a Christian, but I knew that when the relationship had started. She was so pretty and kind, she seemed like she understood me, and I understood her, and then one day we kissed. At the ripe age of twenty-three, I'd never kissed a girl before. So I was really nervous. But Garrith said I'd done fine. Even with her compliment, I'd promised I wouldn't kiss her again until our sixth month anniversary.

Now, she says I'm a good kisser, and hopes for more than kisses one day, but I'm not ready for that. She's been asking about taking our relationship to the next level a lot lately. Sometimes Garrith could be a little upfront about what she wanted, and it had become increasingly clear that she wanted me. Sexually.

I wanted her, too. But I also wanted to do what was right by God, and I believed this trip would change things for her. For both of us. I was hoping it would get her mind off of sex and steer it toward my faith.

"Garrith," I finally said. Big green eyes looked up at me from her plate of pasta and I swallowed nervously. "I was thinking about what you've been saying. About taking our relationship to the next level." She stopped chewing for a moment, and then set her fork down. Dabbing her mouth with her napkin first, she sipped more of her martini and watched me with sultry eyes that almost made me lose my train of thought. "I've given it a lot of thought, and I think I've found a way to take a big step in our relationship." Her eyes glowed with excitement and for a moment, I felt myself feeling confident. "I want to take a trip with you."

"A trip?" she asked, mechanically turning her head sideways.

"Yeah." I dug into my pocket for the crumpled flyer and set it on the table for her to look at.

Perfectly manicured nails lifted the flyer from the table, and she read it aloud. "Come reignite your fire for Christ in the wonderful land of Peru. See how a country grounded in Christianity takes their faith seriously. From the practices of Roman Catholicism to Christian services, we will explore the way Peruvians stay rooted in God despite the challenges they face." She looked up at me, and my confidence was washed away at the sight of her expression. She wasn't angry, but she looked like I'd betrayed her somehow.

"Cam, you know how I feel about this," she said slowly.

"I know." I adjusted in my seat. "But I think it'd be good for us. It's two weeks away from everyone and everything. It'll be just us and God." I reached for her hand, but she pulled it away.

"I don't want it to just be us and God. I want to have *fun* this summer, not be stuck in the hot deserts of Peru, climbing the Indian pyramids. Are you kidding me?" She crumpled the paper and tossed it back on the table. "We're not going."

The Indian Pyramids... I thought correcting her might sour the mood even more, so I sighed and uncrumpled the paper. "Come on, Gary, it's not that bad. Sure, Peru might be hot, and seeing Machu Picchu might not be something on your bucket list, but it's such a great experience. I thought—"

"No!" she fired at me.

I bit my lip and glanced around the room as everyone was staring at us now. "Can you keep your voice down?" I whispered.

"Can *you* stop pestering me about God and this stupid trip? I said we're not going. I've already made other plans for us anyway."

I leaned back in my chair and tossed a hand up. "So, we have to do your plans but not mine? Don't we always do your plans?"

"No." She squinted as she folded her arms. "You're so selfish, Cameron. All you do is try to get me to go to some church every Sunday and Wednesday. Newsflash," she held up her hands, "it's not happening!"

I nodded just as a waiter came over and said nervously, "I'm sorry, you're going to have to keep your voices down, or we'll have to ask you to leave."

"It's fine," I said, looking at a glaring Garrith. "I was just leaving."

"So, you're leaving? Someone finally tells you 'No' and you can't handle it?"

"I've *been* handling it!" I said sharply. "I've been asking you to give church a try since we first started dating and you've never even considered it. You call me selfish, but it's you who's the selfish one." I stood abruptly and dug through my wallet, tossing a wad of cash onto the table. "Goodnight, Garrith," I said, turning to leave the restaurant.

"Cameron!" she shouted behind me. "Cameron!"

I picked up the pace, pushing open the door and jogging down the street until I tired. I neared a bus stop and sat down in the booth as tears blurred the world around me. I pulled my phone from my pocket, dialing Mom's number before I knew it.

"Hello?" she answered, confused.

"Momma," I said shakily.

"Oh, baby, what happened?" Her voice was full of concern.

"She said no. She said no to everything! To the trip, to church, to God! She said," I choked, "she didn't want to be with me or God in Peru. She wanted to do something else. And … and …" I stammered as I cried. "She said she was never going to church. But I love her. I wanted things to work out. Even though I knew it wasn't right, I wanted it to be."

"I'm so sorry, Cameron," she said gently. "I know it hurts to have your heart broken like that. But, listen to me, you go home and get some rest. When you wake up tomorrow, I want you to pray and then send her a text; tell her you want to try and talk about everything again. And if she doesn't respond, then all you can do is cut your losses. I'm so sorry this

21

happened."

"I could barely hold it together. And we were in a fancy restaurant."

"You didn't go to uh," she paused, "Cray-On?"

"No, it was so crowded, and she didn't want to go anymore."

"Oh, I see. Well, until you get a definite sign that you guys aren't together anymore, I would say give it another chance. Don't feel defeated."

"Momma, she called me selfish." I shook my head, choking on my tears. It was hurting so much more because Momma wouldn't say it. She wouldn't say 'I told you so,' and her voice didn't carry an ounce of sarcasm or pride in it.

"Now I know if I've done one thing right, I know I raised a giving boy. Not a boy who is selfish in the slightest bit." Her sass made me chuckle as I wiped at my tears. "Cameron, I'm so sorry," she spoke again, and it almost made the waterworks start all over.

"Don't be. I can still give it a try in the morning, and if I don't hear from her then that's it. A year down the drain."

"And the trip?" she asked. "What will you do about that?"

I looked up to see a bus stopped down the street at a red light. "I'm still going to go," I told her. "I'll take those two weeks, maybe longer, to get my head straight and come back to start prepping for the next semester. I've got a few extra courses I'm taking, so I can complete my masters this year instead of taking a third year to finish it."

"That sounds like a good plan to me," she responded

happily.

"Maybe I'll come home to see you for a little while instead of waiting until Christmas," I said, watching the bus come closer. "I miss you, Momma."

"I miss you too, son. I'd be more than happy to see you a little early this year."

I smiled and took a deep breath, exhaling all the frustration. "Thanks for everything. I'm heading home now, so I'll give you a call tomorrow."

"Alright, Cameron. Now don't you stress tonight. You give this over to God and let His will be done in this situation. You understand?"

"Yes, I understand," I said as the bus came to a screeching halt before me.

Four

What is it to Gain the Whole World?

Garrith didn't answer for two days after I texted her. And when she did answer, she said she was sorry, but we needed space. I agreed, but there was no date on when we'd had enough space, and I had a feeling that 'needing space' was just a weak way of saying we'd broken up.

I ran into one of her friends who didn't even know we were technically still together. For the past three months, Garrith had been seeing some guy in her astronomy program and, apparently, their relationship had gone to the *next level* almost immediately.

I was barely able to pull myself together for exams. I would spend all day on the phone with my mother, or at work. I wanted to do anything to get away from anywhere that Garrith might've been. I'd never had a broken heart before, and I promised myself I'd never have another one because I didn't want to love anyone again.

When classes were over and the trip rolled around, I could

hardly wait to leave. I'd been on edge since everything with Garrith unfolded, I just wanted to get away and relax. The morning of my flight, I gave my mother a call, she was awake because I told her I wasn't sure if I'd be able to call her often in Peru. She said she'd miss me a lot, and she couldn't wait until I returned to tell her all that I'd seen. Pathetically, I wished Momma could've gone with me, but I had a feeling that going alone was what God wanted me to do. I needed to take time to rebuild a relationship with Him, and I was hoping my time in Peru would do that for us.

After I hung up from Momma, I got a text from Garrith. She asked if I was free today, because the space was driving a wedge between us, and she wanted to clear up the rumors I'd heard about Astro boy. I almost left the airport. I wanted to run to Garrith and tell her I didn't care about any of the rumors, even if there was truth to them. I'd blame myself for forcing my faith onto her, and I would tell her that I would try to work up the courage to take our relationship in the direction she wanted … but I realized that I was broken.

I realized I'd let someone have so much control over me that I was willing to compromise the only thing I'd held onto all this time: My faith.

I'd become desperate. Lonely. But I always had been, even in the relationship, I just didn't know it. It wasn't apparent until I realized I'd do anything just for Garrith to come back and allow her to treat me the way she always had. Control me, tell me what I should do, and make fun of me. But as I waited in the airport, listening to the announcements from the flight crew, watching people pass by and others line up for priority boarding, I prayed.

I remembered a scripture Momma told me about one day when I was angry that we were so poor, but my father was so rich. She'd patted the lumpy grey couch beside her as she sewed up the hole in my pants. Bitterness and resentment swelled within me as I climbed onto the sofa. *My mother*, I thought, *was too kind or too prideful to ask for help. But my father was no man at all.*

"Sometimes, Cameron," Momma had said, "it's better to leave things as they are. There are other factors at play here."

I crossed my arms quickly and said, "What kind of factors? Everyone at school says I'm poor, and everyone at school says that if Martin Luther King couldn't end racism, then what made you think you could end it by dating a white man?" I bit my lip as tears burned in my eyes. "What does that even mean?"

Momma's tired hands stopped sewing. Mist gathered in her eyes and, suddenly, the anger I'd been feeling melted as I watched her try to hold it together. "Well," she said, forcing a smile onto her smooth, dark skin. "I know kids poke fun, but they're just kids, Cameron. They don't know any better." She took a deep breath. "You have to forgive them and keep going. If you don't forgive," she paused and waited for me to finish her statement.

I sighed, unfolding my arms. "Then God won't forgive me. I know that, Momma. But it still hurts. Why does it hurt so bad?"

"Because you want them to like you," she said simply. "It hurts when you seek people's approval. You put yourself in situations that bring you pain because of desperation." She chuckled. "Sorry, Cam, you got that from ya' momma."

"I did?" I asked, looking up at her.

She leaned down and kissed my head. "Yes, you did." Her gaze flitted through the small apartment, a somber look in her eyes. "It's not much, but this is our home, Cameron. We're here because of a bad decision I made, but the most beautiful blessing came from that mistake, and I'll do anything to protect that blessing."

I looked around at the apartment and wondered if this was all God had to offer us. A laugh escaped Momma's full lips and as if she'd heard my thoughts, she said, "God has more in store for us than this. This place is just a steppingstone, baby. We'll get out of here and when we do, you'll see what God is really made of."

She was smiling genuinely now. There was no pain, no hurt. Momma loved God so passionately, it was hard to be around her and not believe. She wasn't forceful with her beliefs, but the Light of Christ rolled off her shoulders every day, letting others feel God's warmth through her.

"Momma," I asked as she began sewing again, "why do you want to protect this place?" She had called it her 'blessing.'

She glanced down at me. "No, Cameron, the blessing God gave me is you."

I jerked back into the couch, completely amazed that she'd said *I* was a blessing.

"But I thought blessings were special gifts from God?"

Her smile only widened and sparkling white teeth shined as she said, "You're exactly right."

I'm special, I thought. I was a gift from God for Momma, which meant I was supposed to bring her happiness.

I hopped off the couch and turned to face her. "When I get older, I'm gonna take care of us. Don't worry!"

Momma set my pants beside her and leaned down to hug me. "I know you will, Cameron. You're special, remember?"

I nodded as she held me, but I couldn't help but notice how tired she looked up close. Heavy circles around her eyes, lines of premature aging. Momma was exhausted, and I was heartbroken.

"What's wrong?" Her brows furrowed and her warm smile began to fade.

"It's just, I won't be older for a long time. What will we do until then? Why won't he just help us? Can't Dad see we're in desperate need?" Tears came from my eyes and before I knew it, I was angry again. Hard hands from working all day rubbed my back as she tried to soothe me.

"Cameron," Momma knelt beside me, "what is it to gain the whole world, but to lose your soul?"

I'd heard that scripture before in church. Reverend Lee preached about that often. She told us on our journey called life, we couldn't let the cares of the world sweep us away or else we'd never truly be with God.

"I don't know what you mean," I said.

"Sometimes, it's better not to ask for help. Because that

help may come at a price that will cost you more than you realize." She paused. "Especially when you're desperate. That's the devil's playground, putting you into a situation where it looks like God has forsaken you, you're alone and there's no way out. But, baby boy, that's just smoke and mirrors. God is always right there, and if you let Him, He'll come to your rescue." She turned me to look at the apartment and said, "It's small, and it's not the fanciest place, but I've got Christ and you, and that's all I need. If I'd asked your father for help, it would've come at a price that would've caused us to be separated and for you to lose your salvation. I couldn't have that." She kissed my cheek, and I kind of understood what she meant then. But it wasn't until I was older that the conversation we'd had would mean something every day.

I held onto my ticket as the airline called my boarding section. I looked between the ticket and my phone as I stood to my feet. I asked myself, *What is it to gain the whole world, but to lose your soul? What is it in this desperation to go after one woman, but to lose the One True God?*

I couldn't do it. I deleted the message from Garrith and took my place in line to board the plane.

Five

Peru

It took four flights to get from Illinois to Peru. On each flight, I drifted off and had the same dream. I could see myself walking towards a well, and just before I looked in, my eyes would open and I was sandwiched between two men, much larger than me, or gazing out the small plane window.

It was a familiar dream; I'd had it before. The first time I'd ever seen that well was when Reverend Lee called me out for dancing in church. From time to time, I'd have a dream of the vision God showed me when I was only eight years old. It was like He didn't want me to forget it. And after having the same dream on every plane ride, I had high hopes that while I was in Peru, I'd find the meaning of that vision.

I followed the group out of the airport and to the bus we'd be traveling in. The group featured thirteen people, and some of them didn't seem too savory. I didn't even know if they went to our college, but the campus was so massive, there was no telling.

Walking out into the blistering heat of Peru, I nearly fainted. The sun sat high in the sky, tossing violent rays through the thick clouds, creating a damp heat that stuck to you with every movement. I wasn't a fan of the heat, but it was only two weeks, and I was determined to stick it out.

We gathered onto the bus, and I picked a seat by the window. I watched as the rest of the group got on. There was a couple in the back of the line, holding hands and talking. The girl was clearly in love with the guy, and his heart was strung out for her too. They ogled at each other as they spoke. She flipped a lock of chestnut brown hair over her shoulder and giggled at something he said. He was beet red, laughing, embarrassed, and getting scorched by the sun.

I raised one corner of my mouth, trying to ignore the burning tears in my eyes. It was hard watching the couple, but I'd have to see them for two weeks, so I had to suck it up. I sighed and looked away, sitting back in my seat so I could dig through my bag for my headphones. Powering on my phone, I saw that Garrith had sent me two more texts. I wouldn't look at them. I deleted them, and sent Momma a text, letting her know I'd finally made it.

"I should send her a picture," I said, lifting my phone to get a picture of the airport.

"Taking pictures already?"

I turned and found a woman sitting across from me. She had dusty blonde hair and a pin that read, *President*, clipped to her shirt.

"Yeah," I nodded as I turned back to snap another photo.

31

"Sending them to anyone special?" she asked as she fumbled with her things.

I chuckled. "Just my mom."

"What? Is your mom not special enough?"

"She is." I grabbed the back of my neck and let out another chuckle. "I just thought you meant, like, a girlfriend or something."

She shrugged. "I guess I can see that." She pulled out a camera, one of those professional ones and screwed on a lens. "I'm here as the president, and to take pictures for the club *and* my little sister, or she'll kill me." She laughed.

"Seems serious," I said.

"Oh," she leaned over the seat. I could see her freckles smattered across her nose. "You have no idea." We shared a laugh and then she asked, "Can I take a picture of you?"

"Me?"

She nodded. "You're pretty cute, and it'll bring in more girls to our group."

I raised a brow. "So, you're using me?"

She blushed. "Maybe a little."

"Well, I guess so. Do I look all right?"

"As handsome as it gets." She winked.

Now I was blushing, and I could feel my ears burning. I sat back against the window, and let my arms sink into my lap. She raised a brow as she looked at me through the camera lens.

"You look right at home."

I heard the camera shutter flicking at rapid speed as she snapped a few photos of me. When she lowered the camera, I exhaled finally. "Was I all right?"

She grinned as she said, "Better than all right! You did great. What's your name?"

"Cameron."

"Lydia." She reached across the seats to shake hands. "Well, Cameron, it was nice to meet you. I've got to get to the front to start rollcall so we can get out of here."

"Sounds good," I said.

She waved as she made her way to the front of the bus; it gave a huff and a cough to get its engine started.

Traveling through the beautiful city of Lima, we got to see much of the wonderful capital district. Important buildings, historical statues, houses of their government officials. It was amazing. I took as many pictures as I could while we rode. The bus driver doubled as our tour guide, and he told us of many of the wonders of this beautiful country. I enjoyed all the colors, and the funny shapes of the buildings. Palm trees scraped the sky, and green grass and crystal blue waters shimmered. We were taken around the tourist area briefly, but our driver said it was best to tour on foot, rather than by bus.

As we reached the hotel, Lydia stepped off and went inside a tall building covered in glass windows. There was black awning where men stood in uniforms, welcoming Lydia and the vice president as they went inside the hotel. People were walking down the street, taking pictures, holding hands, pointing. The city of Lima bustled with action. I was beginning to think this trip wouldn't be as bad as Garrith thought. The beautiful hotel, and the rustling of the city, Lima seemed like a place she would've enjoyed. Garrith was a night owl, and she loved to have a good time. With the many restaurants and bars we'd passed, I know she would've enjoyed her stay.

Frowning, I scolded myself as I realized I was doing it again—making things all about Garrith. If Garrith had come, I would've only had as much fun as Garrith did. I wouldn't have enjoyed the tour because Garrith hated tours. I would've spent the whole time trying to entertain her. I was suddenly relieved that she didn't come, even though I missed her a little.

As I saw Lydia exit the hotel with a folder, I pushed thoughts of Garrith away with a sigh. We were each given a room, men shared rooms and women shared rooms. Except, I ended up alone since three people didn't show up, one of which was Garrith, and apparently another one was my roommate.

Dragging my luggage through the lobby, I stared at the quartz pink floors, and the red leather chairs sitting on a swirling pink and white rug. The lobby looked expensive, and I remembered that UOW was the one responsible for choosing this hotel. We were only given the price—that was significantly reduced for us students—and told what the price covered. I should've expected luxury from a university like mine.

Reaching the room, I was amazed. Two queen sized beds sat in my bedroom, along with a living room, dining room, and even a laundry closet. I'd only stayed in a standard hotel once, and that was when I was on my way to Illinois. My flight got cancelled and the airline paid for a room for me. I thought that was nice, but I'd never been in a suite before. There was a jacuzzi tub, and a walk-in shower with three big showerheads. I fell onto the cushiony bed, bouncing for a moment before it finally settled. Whipping my phone out, I called Momma to tell her all about the trip.

"Hey, Cameron!"

"Hey, Momma, you sound excited, what's going on?"

"I'm happy you called. I wanted to hear about your trip!"

I laughed hard, delighted that she was excited, as if *she* was here on the trip and not me. "Well," I said, "we took a tour of the city and it's beautiful here. I've never seen such richness before. The colors are so vibrant, the people are all smiling. I wish you could see it."

"You took pictures, didn't you?"

"Yeah, but it's not the same, Momma. So, I've decided I'm going to bring you back here sometime soon. Maybe I'll save what I was going to use to come see you and put that towards a trip for us to visit Peru together."

"Oh, Cameron, that sounds wonderful," Momma said joyfully. But there was something off about her response. She was happy, but I don't think she liked the idea of me not coming to visit for Christmas.

Sitting up off the bed, I held the phone to my ear. "You sound upset."

"No, I'm happy."

"Momma," I said sternly. "I'm going to come visit you. But I think this trip would be better for us. It'll be fun." I placed my elbows on my knees and stared forward as I listened for her response.

35

"It's not that, Cameron," she said. Her voice was low and sad. "I just wish you didn't have to work so hard. I wish I could help more."

"Momma, it's fine. I'm only a junior engineer because I need a masters degree to get the higher pay and work fulltime. Once I get my masters, I'll have all the money I need, and I can take care of you. It'll be just like we planned."

Silence echoed on the airwaves before she said, "Yes, but that was before I got injured at work. Now I've got disability and you work so hard, and all I do is—"

"Keep my head on straight," I interrupted. "You keep my head on straight, and I'll never make enough money in the world to pay that back. I'll never make enough money to pay *you* back for all the hard work you did when I was just a kid. And I'll never have enough money to express the value of salvation. You've done your part, now let me do mine, okay?"

She exhaled heavily into the phone. "Fine, Cameron. I'm sorry, I know you don't like me talking about this stuff."

"It's okay, Momma. Listen, I'm going to shower and get some rest. I'll send you the pictures and we can talk about it sometime tomorrow. Sound good?"

"Yeah, that sounds really good."

"Get some rest. A check in the mail should be arriving soon, I dropped one off before I left."

"Thank you, baby, I love you so much."

I smiled. "I love you too, goodnight."

The next day, Lydia gave us a wakeup call around eight in the morning and told us that breakfast would be served in an hour. It consisted of freshly baked bread that could be topped with jam or cheese. There was ham available, but not the deli kind, it was the kind you eat during the holidays, and there were sweet potatoes too.

Lydia read from a fact sheet as we ate in one of the private dining halls, telling us that the traditional Peruvian breakfast consisted of hardy foods when in a family setting. But most Peruvians had busy mornings—no different than any other culture—so they would usually make simple sandwiches from the items we had for breakfast, or they'd eat tamales.

After breakfast, we met for another bus tour. We were going to visit a tribe who lived on the waters of Lake Titicaca. They were apparently a very Christian group, and they loved to teach tourists about the culture of their floating tribe. I stared at the pamphlet in my hand as the bus rocked and swayed. Peru was full of indigenous people. There was a list of tribes in the pamphlet that went over the tribal breakdown, detailing where each tribe derived from. There were a few tribes mentioned in the pamphlet that were wiped out, but some of their roots influenced other tribes that still existed today.

As I read over the pamphlet, I heard our driver say over the speaker that he was going to take a detour and then a shortcut to the drop off.

Riding along, Lydia sat in the seat across from me, going through her pictures when she said, "Are you excited for today?"

I shrugged, trying to be nonchalant. "A little." I was lying. I was very excited to meet this lake tribe.

Lydia nodded without looking up at me, "I'm a little excited, too. I've never heard of a tribe on the lake. Sounds neat. It'll at least make for some good pictures."

"I think so, too," I agreed. Flipping open another pamphlet from the hotel, a loud popping noise made me jump.

"What was that?" Lydia asked.

"I don't know," I said, turning to look out the window. Our bus began to bumble along, and I could hear the bus driver complaining loudly.

"What's going on?" someone shouted to the driver.

Lydia passed me a worried look. "I better get to the front."

I nodded but as she stood, another popping noise came and the bus dropped, raking the bottom of the great vehicle against the ground. We spun out of control to the sounds of panicked cries from everyone inside. The bus turned violently, trying to keep us on the road. Lydia's body smashed into the seats hard before she hit the floor and remained still. Unconscious.

"Lydia!" I screamed. But there was more chaos erupting. The bus was spinning now, and there were screams so loud, I couldn't hear anything else. "Please, God!" I hollered out. "Save me!"

Suddenly, I was thrown against the window as the bus slid across the road, dragging us over a small cliff and tumbling to the ground.

"You are breaking every tradition we stand for," an elderly woman's voice hissed me into consciousness.

"Awila," a younger voice spoke, "please, I could not just leave him out there."

"An outsider's problem is his own! We cannot help him. Take him back to where he came from."

Outsider? I thought. *Are they ... are they talking about me? Who are these people? Where am I?*

"I do not know where he came from! He was the only one there," the voice paused, one sentence away from trembling. "We are not like them, Grandmother. We are different. That is what our tradition is."

The only one? Where? What happened?

"No, Saloso! You are not like them, and you are bringing shame to our tribe!"

The room fell to a hush as I lay there. Each breath I took felt rough and rigid, like something was wrong with me. I wanted to sit up, but every part of me ached. I felt like I'd been beaten all over—aggressively, angrily. I wanted to drift off again if it meant the pain would disappear, but my eyes fluttered open instead.

Drowsily, I was pulled into reality. As I blinked away the blurriness in my vision, I could see I was in a hot and dry tent. I could hear the shuffling of people around me, and then a voice came, "The outsider, he is awake!"

39

Six

The Cry of the Wild Goose

"He's awake!"

A woman leaned over me, her buttery golden skin glowing the way the harvest moon does when it's full and the night is its darkest. Her kind eyes were a striking blue, like the chasm separating us from God. She was beautiful to say the least. I didn't think I would mind waking up to a face like that, except I didn't know whose face this was.

Why is she looking over me as if something is wrong?

Is *something wrong with me?*

I couldn't even panic because a throbbing pain in my arm erupted while the rest of my body ached as well. I thought I was going to pass out from the pain when the voice of an elderly woman sharply snapped me back from the unconsciousness I was drifting into.

"Do not get so close to that outsider! He cannot stay here, and you will do well by staying away from him, Saloso."

"But, Awila!" Saloso cried.

"No!"

Saloso's eyes studied mine for a moment before she left my side and scurried away.

What is going on? I wondered in my weakness. I couldn't get myself to ask any questions as the blaring pain radiated all over my body.

"What do we do, Chief?"

"Leave me and the outsider to speak."

I could hear the steps of those who'd been gawking over me leaving the room. All that was left was the elderly woman they referred to as 'Chief,' as I lay on display before her.

"Outsider, do you know where you are?"

I wanted to speak, but my voice wouldn't come. I was barely managing consciousness and was too groggy to form words.

"Very well," she said. "I am Grey Hawk, Chief of the forgotten tribe of the Sand Ribbon."

Sand Ribbon? I thought. I'd heard that name before. *Television?* No, it was a book of some sort. *No!* An article. *Where have I heard of these people from?*

"We are the last of the Sand Ribbon people, along with our kindred who live hidden in the Andean Mountains. Your presence here is tainting the very beauty of our forgotten history."

I could hear her pacing behind me. It sounded like she had three legs, but I figured the extra *thud* was coming from some sort of walking stick.

"We do not let outsiders in," she stated firmly. "Our

41

ancestors did long ago, and all it did was bring our great people to near extension. I will not let that happen again." Her voice was serious and low. "Because of Saloso, my foolish granddaughter," she spoke harshly of the beautiful girl, "you are here. But you cannot stay. You will have one week of recovery, at the request of Saloso, and if the healers reason that you are safe for travel, you will leave. We will care for you while you are here, but as soon as you are well, you must leave and never return. And you must *never*," she emphasized loudly, "breathe a word of our existence here."

With that, she left and I lay there, thinking over what was happening. *Where am I? What happened to the bus? And Lydia, she passed out...* The memories of the bus ride began to flood into my mind when I heard someone enter through what sounded like tent flaps.

"You still have not risen yet?"

Risen?

"Come now, you will never get any better if you do not at least try." The voice was similar to Saloso's, but it was more girly, and sounded younger.

"My sister rescued you. She hauled you all the way back here by herself."

Taking a deep breath, I used all my energy to force out a scratchy, "From where?"

"So, you do speak?" The girl came around and knelt beside me with a pail of water. Her face was bronze with gentle red undertones, and her eyes were nut brown, the opposite of Saloso's. But they resembled each other in that family way,

42

same sharp cheekbones, and polished skin, not a single impurity touched their faces.

Saloso's sister looked me over, perkily twisting a cloth in her wooden pail. The water rushed from the cloth as she shook it a few times. She reached over and lifted my left arm to dab it with the damp cloth. I jerked away, sending a rippling pain through the rest of me, and she blinked at me.

"This was far easier when you were asleep."

"Do you," I tried speaking again, "know what happened?"

She shrugged as she reached for my arm again. She held it by the wrist, dabbing more gently this time. There were burns and torn flesh along my arm, going up to my shoulder. I didn't know what the rest of me looked like, but I was sure I was tattered, at least that's how I felt.

"Saloso was out hunting, and there was an explosion nearby that drove all of the animals away. She, of course, went to find the source, since no one is usually out this far. She said she found a tour bus on fire." She wrung out the cloth and reached for my arm again. "The fire was too big to put out, but she heard someone coughing, so she dived in and rescued you. Grandmother was very upset, but Saloso is too kind to leave anyone behind." She set my arm back down and dropped the cloth into the water. I closed my eyes, letting my heart sink out of my body and through the ground as I realized I was stranded.

I was stranded in a hot, dry tent, injured and sore, being cared for by angry tribesmen and women who enjoyed being stranded and forgotten. And, as if it couldn't get any worse, I could assume I was the only survivor of the bus crash, and I could barely even remember how it happened.

"God spared you," the young girl said beside me. She was holding a stone bowl now, and with a smooth oblong rock in her hand, she crushed leaves together inside of the bowl. "Saloso said God spared you as a sign for us to start learning about the outside world. But that is just Saloso talking. She has been wanting to reach the outside world for so long, but Grandmother will not let her. She says it would soil what little aptitude Saloso has as the next chief."

"Where am I?" I asked, ignoring her chatter.

She looked up from the bowl and said, "Grandmother did not tell you?"

I squinted, unsure of who her grandmother was. "Chief Grew Hawk mentioned something about the Sand Ribbon people."

She nodded and set the bowl down beside her before grabbing a big green leaf. "That's right. We are the lost tribe of the Sand Ribbon. We are very small, but we have existed throughout the years here in this part of our homeland for many generations. We practice the ancient farming techniques with the *puquios*."

"What's that?"

It was almost coming to me where I'd heard of the Sand Ribbon people and the puquios—I knew it was a word for something I couldn't remember.

"Sorry," she giggled, "that is our old tongue. You will know them as aqueducts, or springs," she said, reaching over and

44

retrieving my arm again.

That's it! I thought. The Sand Ribbon people were known for their farming and their way of life. I'd read about their tribe in a pamphlet. But the pamphlet said they died out ages ago with no descendants. Here I was, lying on the ground of the people who technically didn't exist. I didn't know if I should feel sorry for myself or rejoice that I would end up in a place where history had no records. I felt more bitterness than sweetness as I laid there trying to keep my composure.

The Sand Ribbon were so special because they lived in the desert lands, where nothing usually grows. But these people found some way to draw water to their land, and fertilize it enough to create soil, and grow food. They took on the name, 'Sand Ribbon,' because they lived in the desert and the streams of water that flowed through the sand made it look like ribbons. All that I'd read was coming back to me, and I was feeling more stranded than ever now. I had a sudden resentment in my heart for the stupid Saloso. She rescued me, and now I was stuck and injured, trapped by these people who didn't want to be known.

I exhaled angrily, but the young girl didn't pay me any attention. She continued to talk as she used her makeshift mortar and pestle. "Our tribe was preserved long ago. A woman ran away during the raiding of what was left of our tribe after a storm. She took a small group of people with her and rushed to the Andes Mountains where she found another group from a lost tribe there and merged with them." She dipped her hand into the bowl, lifting the bright green paste into to the light to examine it. I wasn't sure what she was examining it for, but it smelled as bitter as anise seed. After another moment, she nodded and spread the paste onto my arm.

"Eventually," she continued, "the tribes split because of disagreements. The woman left and some people followed her here, where they began their life as a small tribe all over again."

As I listened, I found the origins of the Sand Ribbon quite interesting. And even though I was stuck here until I was better, it *was* a privilege to arrive at such a secluded village. One that wanted to be forgotten and thought it was beautiful to be left out of history for the preservation of their culture. This story was one no person could confirm or deny except for the ones who lived here.

As she spread the paste on my arm, it felt cool against my skin, soothing the pain that was wreaking havoc on my arm. The young girl reached across me again and placed the corn leaf onto my flesh. "So, Outsider, what is your name?"

I didn't really want to talk, but I didn't want to be rude since they were doing me a huge favor and taking care of me; despite them not wanting me here and I didn't want to be there. Swallowing thickly, I said, "My name is Cameron."

"Cameron?" she asked as she stood to her bare feet, "that is a very strange name, Outsider."

I cleared my throat. "What's your name?"

"My name is Kateri. I was named by my grandmother, chief Grey Hawk."

Ahh, I thought, *the old hag who wanted me to die in the fire is this sweet girl's grandmother.*

Kateri returned to my side, holding a liquid. She sat it down and scooped the rest of the paste into the liquid, stirring it with a thin stick.

"You have a pretty name," I mustered.

She smiled delicately at me and said, "It is a beautiful name with a dark story. Would you like to hear it?"

I sighed internally, but I had nothing better to do. I tried to nod, and it made Kateri laugh.

"Kateri is of the Mohawk tongue," she explained. "It does not belong to my people, but to a tribe somewhere distant from here."

"How'd you get that name, then?"

"You see, Outsider, names mean something here in our tribe. Each name is carefully chosen, and its meaning and destiny is woven into our lives." She paused her stirring to scrape the small bit of paste left in the bottom of the bowl into the clumpy liquid. "As we are villagers," she continued, "we also sell in the markets to prepare for the new cold we've been experiencing. There are things our animals cannot provide that others who sell in the markets can give us." The liquid and paste mixed together as she continued to stir. "My father fell in love with an outsider." She paused. "He fell in love with her while our mother was pregnant with Saloso. He sold in the markets for our tribe and had secretly been meeting with a woman who brought him into her bed. It would have stayed a secret, I suppose, since they only saw each other once a year during our winter preparation. But she became pregnant with me sometime later and their secret was uncovered."

I tried not to react, but I could see how torn Kateri was. Her smiling face had darkened to a soft frown, and she'd begun to absently stir the paste as she retold the story. It was an odd story to tell a stranger, but I think Kateri needed someone to talk to. I guess I was the perfect choice. One day I'll forget I was even here, and her story would be forgotten as well.

"I am the product of the pleasure of my father," Kateri hissed. "And the demise of one of the greatest chiefs in our history; the mother of Saloso, Chief Nunca de Achille. She was a strong and fierce, mighty woman who they say resembled the first woman who began our tribe. Grande Chief Zasca. Some say her only weakness was our father. She'd loved him since they were young. But my father did not love her, and when I was born, their world fell apart." Lifting the now thick green liquid, Kateri smelled it deeply, before producing a smile. "It is ready," she said, lowering the bowl to ground. Leaning over me, her brown shawl shifted as she lifted my head close to her chest. Rocking back a little on her knees, she held up a wooden bowl with the swirling green liquid.

"Drink this, it will make the rest of you feel better, and probably put you to sleep, so I can finish patching you up."

The strong aroma of anise raged against my nostrils, and I wanted to resist, but it worked so well on my arm, I was somewhat interested in trying this green drink. Sipping it, the smell betrayed its flavor. There was something savory about it that lingered for a moment before a hint of something citrusy dazzled your taste buds, leaving the fresh feeling of mint on your tongue.

"As you sleep, I will finish my story," she said.

I inhaled, suddenly feeling a rush of freshness rolling over me. The drink seemed to work instantly, and I was beginning to fade when Kateri said, "My father left me with Chief Nunca and his mother, Grey Hawk, and he never returned. Chief Nunca stepped down and passed the chiefhood to Saloso with the promise that she would return someday to reclaim her place as chief with her husband. I am now sixteen, and Saloso is twenty, still too young to be acting Chief, and Chief Nunca has not returned. It is quite funny, though," she said, sitting on her bottom. She tucked her dress beneath her legs as she pulled her knees to her chest. "My name is Kateri, I was named after my mother, who went by the English calling, Catherine, instead of the Mohawk calling of Kateri. It was a punishment on me as the impurity in the village. My name was to remind every man who would like to wed me that I am not of the Sand Ribbon people, I am only partially Sand Ribbon." She looked embarrassed when she spoke, as if I would somehow want to punish her as well.

"However," she began again with her chin sitting on her knees, "it is not I who Grandmother criticizes the hardest. It is Saloso. Her name was changed after I was born. She was not always Saloso, she was once Sunstar de Achille, next in line for chief. But Grandmother wanted to take the chiefhood from her since Chief Nunca had left the village. She could not, since Saloso is a direct descendant of the Grande Chief and the chiefhood cannot be shed from them. So, Grandmother

49

stripped Sunstar of her name instead. She gave her a name of embarrassment, one that no great chief could ever wear proudly." She chewed her lip, staring off at the ground as the room began to blur, and unconsciousness began to fog my mind. "But Saloso is determined to prove grandmother wrong despite the meaning of her name."

I snapped my eyes open, trying to fight the strength of the medicine she'd given me.

"She carries the weight of the tale of our father on her head," Kateri laughed weakly. "Did you know that geese are hard to catch? You are to never attempt to catch one unless you have been trained by the chief. Well," she squeezed her knees to her chest a little tighter. "When you catch a wild goose, it will release a cry to warn others that it has been caught and that it needs help. But it was not father who cried or was caught. It was Chief Nunca who cried many tears as she was ensnared by the clutches of a broken heart. So, in a tongue that only Grandmother knows, the name of the next chief was changed from Sunstar to Saloso. And Saloso means, the cry of the wild goose."

Seven

There is Much to Learn

Locusts buzzed loudly, fluttering me from my slumber. That was the first time I'd heard the locusts. The other times I'd briefly gained consciousness, it was silent or humming coming from Kateri. I'd catch glimpses of her applying paste to me, and sometimes when I was livelier than other days, she'd force me to drink the left-over paste. When I woke up today, Kateri was there again. She was dressed in her usual brown shawl and a tunic with fringes that were different colors.

"Good morning, Cameron. Today is day seven that you have been here. I must report to Grandmother that you will require a longer stay. You are not well enough to leave, you have not even stood in a week, let alone really eaten anything. Today we will start your recovery process, which may not take long; maybe another week or two, and you will be fine."

Shaking my head, I asked, "Have I been out for seven days?"

She nodded. "You have been sleeping and groaning for

seven days. You are not well yet."

"But I don't even feel much pain." I lifted my injured arm. "I'm feeling a lot better."

"As you should." She stood, placed her hands on her hips, and smiled down at me. "I am one of the best healers here in the tribe. Do not worry, Grandmother does not want you here any longer than you have to be. So, we will not be holding you as a ..." She paused, glancing at the ground.

I suggested, "As a hostage?"

"That is it! Hostage!"

Why couldn't she think of the word 'hostage'?

"Outsider Cameron, I will be back; I am going to give my report to Grandmother. When I return, I will get you on your feet." She raced from the tent, leaving me there to think.

I'd been out for seven days, not including how long I might've been out before I woke up the very first time when Kateri told me about her name. Hopefully by now, someone had come searching for me ... but maybe not.

"If I was out seven days," I paused, piecing my memories together, "and our college group was only on day two of the fourteen-day trip, that means only nine or possibly ten days have passed." Staring up at the ceiling of the tent, I sighed. "No one is going to be looking for me yet. Maybe the hotel, but that probably won't be until checkout, which is on day fourteen. I'm actually stranded."

"Well, Outsider, I have heard it is impolite to believe one is stranded when they are in a foreign place." The voice belonged to Saloso, the one who glowed like the moon. She came in, dressed similarly to her sister, except her shawl was black with an elaborately stitched white pattern along the hem. She wore a tunic dress, the same cream color as Kateri's, but her fringes were not multicolored. They followed a pattern; a black fringe, then a white fringe, then a mixture of black and white fringes, and the pattern continued around the entire dress that stopped just below the knee.

"I'm sorry," I said nervously. "I didn't know anyone was here."

"It is alright, Outsider, you are free to feel that way." She sat beside me. "This place is unfamiliar to you, just as you are unfamiliar to us."

I nodded.

"My name is Saloso, heir to the chiefhood."

I lowered my brows. Kateri had said the same thing about her, and here she was saying it too, that she was going to be the next chief. It really hadn't made a difference to me until I saw her sitting before me. She was a young woman, not much younger than me with a brilliant smile and wonderous eyes. I couldn't pass judgement on whether she was fit for chief, but I was certain that in every textbook I'd read, and basically every book, a chief was never a …

"Woman?" I thought aloud. I instantly tried to recant the statement, but a ridiculous laugh exploded from her, and a flurry of giggles from Kateri, before Saloso said, "Dear Outsider, you have much to learn about our tribe. Our chiefs have always been women since the Grande Chief Zasca. She was the one who reestablished our tribe, and as her descendant, it is my duty to take the throne in three years." She spoke proudly, holding her head high.

I glanced over at Kateri who was sitting not directly beside Saloso, just a little further back from her, as if she was her sister's own servant. If I'd blinked, I would've missed her shaking her head at me. The subtle movement was my cue, and I knew that Saloso had no idea Kateri had told me the tribe's history or anything about their names.

I cleared my throat, glancing back at Saloso, who was still sitting proudly. "Really?" was the most convincing thing I was able to come up with.

"Truly, I am," Saloso said, patting her chest twice. "Well, Outsider, my sister says that the name given to you is Cameron. Is that so?"

"Yes." I nodded.

"What a funny name," she snickered. "Cameron, I believe in your tongue they say, 'the pleasure is all mine.'"

"My tongue? You mean you don't speak English?"

She nodded. "We have learned English through the many generations who have traveled and returned. We also learned through literature we have gathered, as well as trading in the marketplace."

I wanted to ask if they were still allowed to go to the market, but instead, I focused on their travels. "You guys travel?"

"Everyone of age is given twelve months to live outside of our tribe. If they do not return by the end of the twelfth month, they are prohibited from returning. If they return before the twelfth month, they are welcomed back but are not allowed to bring anything from the outside world into the village."

Curiosity and a twinge of annoyance forced me to ask her, "Why not? What's wrong with the outside world?" Chief Grey Hawk was so adamant about nothing coming in, but I wondered if it was because of what'd happened with Chief Nunca.

Saloso sighed heavily. "I have been trying to get Chief Grey Hawk to understand that it may be well for us to reach the outside world. But she is against it." She paused, pulling her ocean blue eyes from mine to stare at the ground. "It is a rather long story. I cannot get into it now, Outsider. But we must get you up now and on your feet."

"Saloso!" Chief Grey Hawk called as she stormed into the tent. "I told you to stay away from this outsider did I not?"

"Yes, Grandmother, but this outsider knows very much and we—"

"No! I do not want to hear what he knows. I want you to listen. How can you ever be chief if you cannot listen to simple instructions?"

"Because your instructions are unreasonable!" Saloso yelled as she got to her feet and stormed out of the tent.

Grey Hawk sighed, and I heard her walking across the tent to me. My eyes finally met hers. She was an older woman with brown skin. And she had a head full of white hair. Necklaces, and jewels sat heavily around her neck, and she wore a deep rouge shawl over a tunic that swept the ground.

"Outsider," she spoke, "she is easily influenced. Kateri says you are still not well, and this is what I was afraid of, that your wounds would prolong your stay, and your stay may impact Saloso negatively. As long as you are here," she frowned down at me, "you must stay away from Saloso. She cannot have her head crowded with the ideas of a world she can never reach and will never accept her." I wanted to protest because I knew she was wrong. I could name at least five people who would love Saloso—

My thoughts stopped and I didn't hear anything else Chief Grey Hawk said to me. I began drowning in my thoughts when suddenly Garrith popped into my head. Garrith, Momma, school, Lydia, it all seemed like yesterday despite how long I'd actually been trapped in the hot and humid tent. I wanted out of here as soon as possible. I missed everyone, even Garrith. I'd do anything to see her again. I'd do anything to see anyone except for these isolated people.

Feeling indignant, I asked abruptly, "How much longer do I have to stay here?" I glanced over at Kateri, and her eyes were as wide as the moon. When I looked back at Chief Grey Hawk, she was fuming.

"How dare you interrupt me?" she asked, leaning forward over her stick.

"I—I," I stumbled over my words as anxiety caused the anger I'd felt to suddenly diffuse. "I'm sorry, Chief," I apologized. "I didn't mean to interrupt you."

She stared at me, and then without another word turned to leave, letting her long tunic dance along the ground behind her.

Kateri scrambled to my side and burst into laughter.

"Outsider!" she exclaimed. "No one has ever spoken over Chief Grey Hawk like that before! I am surprised she did not beat you with her tawna!"

I was cringing at her shrieking laughter, and at how embarrassed I was. But the word 'tawna' caught my attention and I asked, "What's a tawna?"

Kateri said, "It is her staff. Each chief is given one, handcrafted by the previous chief."

I nodded, thinking that her walking-stick probably belonged to Saloso's mother. "Even though I don't particularly like your grandmother, it was rude of me to interrupt her. She's the leader of your tribe."

Kateri threw her hand and said, "My grandmother has a sharp tongue, and although she is chief, she certainly does not have to treat us as if she does not like us. It is not fair that we cannot defend ourselves. But we assume she knows best, and we hold our tongues. An outsider like you is the perfect challenge for her."

Kateri made me feel a little better. *To be fair,* I said to myself, *I wasn't paying attention—which I guess is still rude.*

Kateri finally began my recovery. As she rubbed me over in oils that would help prevent me from getting scorched by the sun, she told me I'd been battling an infection I'd caught from a large burn on my abdomen. I also had other scrapes that were only a little infected. Other than that, there were some minor burns and cuts, but I walked away from a bus accident basically untouched. It was a miracle that I barely had anything wrong with me. But it was an even bigger miracle that Saloso had found me, and the infections didn't get any worse because of the kindness of the people here.

I was incredibly grateful to God and to the tribe for rescuing me after hearing that report. I felt bad for being angry with Saloso; previously wishing for death rather than being here was a little dramatic. Despite my gratitude, I still wanted to go home. As I lay there, I wondered if I would ever return. *Am I stuck here? Why here, God?* A well flashed in my mind and I gasped, jerking away from Kateri.

"Come on, Outsider, you have to eat something," she said, trying to feed me. Holding a spoon carved neatly from wood, there was a thick brown liquid on it. I hadn't even noticed she'd finished the oils and had moved on to food.

"What is it?" I asked, blinking at her.

She didn't seem fazed that I'd jerked away from her, she simply continued to try to feed me. "Are you alright, Cameron? You are sweating." She lowered the spoon.

I had only noticed a little before since I was being covered in that green paste which helped keep me cool, but it was excruciatingly hot. I was sweating—not because I was sick, but because the extreme heat in the tent was smothering me.

"Can I have a little water?"

Kateri traded the spoon and bowl for a pouch from her hip and passed it to me. I turned over and adjusted slowly onto my elbow. The movements felt incredibly forced, like my body didn't want to recover or move. Slowly, I pulled the small cork out of the pouch, and I took a few sips of the water. The freshness of the water made it taste sweet, and I threw my head back and chugged the rest of the pouch, winning myself a bout of nausea.

"You were very thirsty," Kateri said, taking the pouch from me. "I forgot an outsider like you is no match for this heat."

"How do I get out of here?" I asked suddenly. The bout of nausea brought on annoyance, and a strong desire to go home. I didn't want to be hot and sticky anymore. Lying in that heat, I watched Kateri's smile fade and she said, "We will take you to the edge of the land when it's time for you to leave. We cannot take you now."

"Why not?" I asked, feeling impatient.

"Because God has not told us to take you yet."

"What do you mean?"

She laughed, stirring the brown soup. "God is always very clear about these things."

"And He told you I need to stay?" I leaned forward. Surely, we weren't talking about the same God. I thought He'd be getting me out of here, not *keeping* me here.

"He said the time for you to return has not yet come," Kateri explained. "You can only become a healer if you can interpret the tongue of the Spirit. It means you understand the language of God and will be able to ask and receive answers from Him for our tribe."

I squinted, trying to understand.

"A healer knows what is best for the body because God tells us what is wrong with it. Then He gives us the ingredients we should use for the healing and recovery process."

"You're kidding me," I said, folding my arms. "There's no way God answers all the time." I paused and looked down at the speckled animal skin pelt I was sitting on. "He doesn't answer me all the time."

"You simply are not asking through dependency. We have nothing here but God, therefore our prayers and requests from Him are earnest. God does not always answer quickly, there have been many times I have seen healers lose people because God did not answer. He chooses when to respond, and in times when He does not, we must choose to continue to believe in Him." She spoke so confidently about God, I felt like all this time I hadn't known Him very well. If I was honest with myself, it was true that I had stopped getting closer to God since I'd started dating Garrith. *I lost my way a little*, I admitted to myself, *maybe this is why I'm here.*

"Come now, Cameron." Kateri raised the soup bowl. "You need to eat so that you may leave this tent."

I sighed, wanting to think longer on why exactly I was here, whether there was a way to get home. But if I wanted answers, I'd need to leave this tent and see where exactly I was. And if I wanted to ever leave, I basically had to prove that I wasn't sick anymore, and that started with eating.

"What is this?" I asked Kateri.

"It is called *Caldo de Gallina*," she said as she stirred the steaming liquid. The aroma coming from the bowl smelled oddly familiar.

I reached for the bowl. "What does that mean?" My arms

were sore, but they were functioning and that was good. Kateri hadn't removed the corn leaves from my left arm or right shoulder, but they seemed to work like bandages. They were flexible, bending with each of my movements, and they stayed put.

"It means Peruvian Hen Soup. It is something the oldest healer in the tribe makes for those in recovery. She has only taught a small bunch the recipe. It is one she discovered after a trip to the market and finding these odd twistings." She raised an egg noodle. Setting the noodle back into the soup she passed me the bowl as I tried not to laugh. Glaring at me, she asked, "What is so funny, Outsider Cameron?"

"Odd twistings," I muttered, stirring the steaming soup. "These are called noodles." I held one up to her.

She turned her head sideways like a cat and stared intently at the noodle on my spoon. "A *noodle*? I am still learning many words. We call them twistings."

"Well, you shouldn't," I said, "because there are other kinds of noodles. They're not all shaped like this one."

"Really?"

"Of course. And this soup is actually identical to the soup my mother used to make me. We call ours 'chicken noodle soup.'"

She stared at me, her eyes opened as wide as possible, and then she pointed, "It is the same thing! You use a young bird while we use older birds. And you too have the twistings—I mean noodles."

I laughed, "That's right."

61

"Well then taste it, Outsider, and tell me if it tastes like it is from your world."

I nodded, getting a spoonful of noodles and hen. I raised the soup to my lips and slurped the broth first. There was an earthy taste, like they'd somehow managed to make a stock from the ground. The smothering earthiness was broken by the strength of the ginger and, eventually, there was a bright burst of the freshest vegetables I'd ever tasted. An onion so ripe, it could make you cry even after being cooked. Carrots that produced a flavor of richness, and other herbs that swirled together, delighting your tastebuds. Putting the noodle and hen into my mouth with the rest of the broth, the Caldo de Gallina gave momma's chicken soup a run for its money.

"It's really good," I said after swallowing the spoonful. My stomach immediately felt queasy, but it wasn't the food; I just hadn't eaten anything solid in a week.

"That is very wonderful to hear!" Kateri said with all the giddiness of a child in her voice. "I will have to have Saloso teach me. She made this pot for you while I said a special healing prayer over it."

I stopped slurping for a moment, and I felt myself smile for the first time since I arrived. "Thank you," I said.

She nodded.

"I'm going to get Saloso, so stay right there."

I nodded as if I could go anywhere else. The soup was very good, but it made me homesick. *Momma,* I thought, *how will I get back home? These people are kind, but I can't stay here. I've got to leave as soon as I can.* I glanced around the tent for the first time as I ate the hen soup. I found there was a wooden shelf on one side that held jars of herbs and liquids and spices. The rest of the tent was like any other. There was some kind of animal skin stretched over wooden poles as wide as a small tree trunk in the center, while pegs held down the skirt of the tent.

"Cameron, we are back," Kateri said as she entered the tent. Saloso followed in behind her, looking more troubled than I'd ever seen her.

"Are you alright?" I asked, setting down the empty bowl of soup.

She looked surprised as she knelt beside me and said, "You are concerned for my wellbeing? It should not bother you, Cameron."

Kateri folded her arms. "Grandmother was awfully harsh on Saloso this morning, but she still came to visit you. She thinks Saloso will not want to be chief anymore if she learns too much about the outside world."

I nodded, understanding Chief Grey's hesitancy. "The rest of the world would surprise you both," I said, glancing between the sisters. "I can tell you about it if you want."

Kateri and Saloso looked so excited, I thought they would explode from happiness. But Kateri's smile quickly turned into a hard frown, and she said, "But I still have healing studies to do, which will take up a lot of my time. You will be gone before I even learn anything."

"It is alright, Kateri," Saloso said, grabbing her sister's hands. "I will learn all that I can from Cameron and then I will teach you." The two girls looked so much like sisters as they held hands, squealing in excitement. Kateri was a little bolder, and more rambunctious than Saloso, but she always played the role of a servant. While Saloso carried the heavy burden of being the next chief. Watching the two girls laugh with each other seemed to make this place less stifling.

"Really?" Kateri jumped into her sister's lap, squeezing her until Saloso begged her to stop.

"But first," Saloso said, "we have to get the outsider on his feet."

Standing to her own feet, she marched around and grabbed my left hand while Kateri grabbed my right. I adjusted to stand, bracing myself for the dizziness I was certain I would feel. The girls pulled me to my knees first, letting me get my feet under myself, and then pulled me up. Dizziness, nausea, exhaustion, and heat was all I felt as I stood there. The two sisters suddenly shrank before me, and I realized they were short, and I think they realized I was taller than they thought initially.

Gazing at my shirtless body, Kateri blushed. "He is better looking standing, and he is far better looking than Catskill."

Saloso nodded. "I believe you are correct."

"Uh." I raised a hand to my neck and felt a wave of embarrassment wash over me as the two sisters giggled and pulled me outside of the tent.

Eight
I Am Responsible

The sun glared down at us as we stepped out of the tent. The scene around me looked like a campsite which, technically speaking, it was; but this place wasn't a mere camp to Saloso and Kateri—it was their home.

Tents like the one I was in were far and few, most of the structures scattered throughout the village were houses made of packed clay and straw. Shirtless men carrying logs walked through the site while women carried large sticks with pots hanging on each side. There was an array of colors as we walked forward. Shawls decorated with intricate designs and patterns, beaded tunics, and tribal tattoos of complex motifs decorating smooth skin of various shades. Bronze, brown, pale, and tanned skin—it was an incredibly diverse family.

"Catskill!" Saloso called.

I didn't know Catskill was a person. He approached us, shirtless and pants-less. He only wore his angled hip shawl that didn't look feminine at all on him. Every step he took, the ground seemed to shake—he was so bulky and lean with muscles so large I almost felt rude for staring at him. Like I was watching a dirty movie every time my gaze found his shoulders or arms.

His intimidation only went so far, as Catskill spoke, a surprisingly soft voice filled the air. "Saloso," he said, taking her hand in his and kissing it.

Just from the way he gazed at her, I could tell he was a man in love. But Saloso didn't look like a woman in love. She gave him an awkward smile, retracted her hand, and said, "The outsider is going to need work and clothes. Do you think you can help us?"

His eyes shot over to me, and he looked over my frame, making me feel small and exposed. "Did not Chief Grey Hawk say you should have no dealings with him, Saloso?"

"Chief Grey does not understand the bridge this outsider can build for us. I thought you would."

Kateri stepped forward. "As a healer, I am requesting your service, Catskill."

He sighed. "You know we cannot refuse the request of a healer."

"Exactly." Kateri smirked and crossed her arms. "He needs work to help him get back on his feet. And he will need clothes. He will be your project for the next week or so. Understood?"

"A week or so? He will slow us down," Catskill complained.

"I won't," I finally spoke up. The three of them looked over at me, and I cowered a little. "I won't slow you down. I'm a hard worker. I want to get out of here as much as you guys want me gone. So, help me get stable and then I'll be gone forever."

Catskill looked like he was going to pummel me just for speaking, but he lifted a hand and said, "You are right, Outsider. We want you gone, so I will help. But I will not go easy on you, got it?"

I swallowed thickly and nodded at him.

"Follow me." Catskill turned from the sisters and headed back into the busy campsite. I followed him, but Saloso grabbed my hand and said, "Be careful, Cameron. Now go." She pushed me forward, and I stumbled into a woman carrying a large pot.

"Hey!" she screamed.

"Sorry!" I said, waving my hands frantically at her. I could hear Saloso and Kateri chuckling behind me, but I didn't look back at them. I smiled shyly at the angry, sweaty woman and moved through the crowd to find Catskill.

"Alright," Catskill said as we approached a small, wooded area away from the bustling campsite. "You are going to chop wood." He picked up a thick piece of wood and set it down on the tree stump, then he grabbed his axe. "Just do as I do." He raised the axe above his head and chopped the wood in one swift motion. "You want to hit it right on the top, Outsider. It will make splitting easier." He collected the split pieces and then pointed to a pile nearby. "After you split the rest of that pile, you will strip about half of them. The stripped wood is used for weapons, shelter, whatever. The other half will just be firewood. Understand?"

"Yeah, I think so. But, uh." I glanced around. "Do you peel this wood by hand?"

He squinted. "Do you think we are barbaric? Use the axe head, it is not hard." A frustrated sigh blew from his lips. "I told them you would slow me down."

"I just need time to get the hang of it."

"Then I will leave this to you. I will retrieve you before dinner."

I guess lunch was out of the question.

"If you get hungry before then, eat berries of the fruit bushes you will find through that trail. Our God has provided plenty for us." Catskill turned to leave.

I was left there with a pile of wood to chop and half a pile to strip. I'd never even heard of stripping wood! I glanced over at the path and wondered how far I could get if I ran away now. But I figured not very far since I had no idea where I was or where I would end up. I chased the idea away as I turned to the large pile of wood I'd need to finish before dinner.

Setting a piece onto the stump, I lifted the axe to split it. With one heavy slug, the axe slammed into the wood, and that was it. No splitting, no breaking, not even splintering, the wood held the axe captive, and wouldn't let it go. I tried pulling on it, but it wouldn't come out. Letting go of the axe, I stepped back and stared at it.

"Come on," I said, wiping away my sweat. "I can't do this. There's no way. I'll never be able to split wood as easily as Catskill." The statement made me think for a moment; if I didn't get this wood chopped, I couldn't leave because the others would assume I was still too weak.

I groaned, rubbing my hand over my face. "It's a pretty high standard to ask someone to split wood evenly *and* peel the wood." I chewed my lip with my hands on my hips. "Alright, let's try this again."

With renewed inspiration, I gripped the axe with both hands and put one foot on the wood where the blade was still stuck. My jaw clenched as I pulled back on the weapon, violently tugging until it sprang loose. Momentum sent me tripping to the ground with a thud, and the axe fell beside me. Even though I was panting, I found the strength to rejoice a little in my head, ignoring the fact that I still hadn't chopped a single piece of wood yet.

I stood and rolled my shoulders out. *I can do this*, I told myself. Then I lifted the axe, but I stopped when I heard a voice speak, "Wow, Outsider, you haven't even chopped one piece yet."

I was frozen in place when Saloso stepped from behind the bushes. "Don't scare me like that," I said, lowering the axe to grab my chest.

Saloso laughed lightly as she approached and boldly took the weapon from my hand. "I'll show you how it's done," she said.

I took a step back. "There's no way you can hack that."

She held the axe like a bat and smirked at me. "Are you kidding? I taught Catskill everything he knows."

"Really?" I teased. "Then chop this wood."

She shrugged.   "I was going to anyway."

She smiled, and I felt a rush of nerves attack me, but I didn't have time to sort out my emotions. The next second, Saloso gripped the axe in both hands and, just as swiftly as Catskill had cut the wood, she swung the blade and split the log like it was nothing.

I stared at the perfect halves of wood and said, "How?"

A cute laugh escaped her, and she waved me over. "Take the axe," she said, passing it to me.

I took it.

"Now let me see your stance."

"My stance?"

"Mmhmm. Your stance."

I shook my shoulders out and grabbed the axe, placing one hand on the lowest part of the handle and the other up high near the blade. Then I raised it above my head, rotated my shoulder, and took a swing at the stump.

Saloso said, "No, Cameron! You swing like that, and it will get stuck every time. Take your stance again, but do not swing."

I huffed and lifted the axe.

"I see your problem." Saloso walked over; she was shorter than me, her head only at my chest, but she was just as strong as Catskill which was strange and intriguing.

"Your strength," she said, resting a gentle hand on my stomach, "comes from here." Her small hand traced up my abdomen, to my chest. "Not from here." When she looked up at me, I couldn't look away. Beautiful honey-crisp skin, with foreign blue eyes, and chocolate tresses that spilled down her back. Her thick lashes fluttered, and I was sweating so hard I thought I'd have a stroke. She smiled, patted my chest. "I will teach you how to hold the axe."

I nodded, trying not to sweat even more as I felt her hands on my arms, and then on my shoulders. "Relax," she said as she pressed her hands into my shoulders. It felt good, *really good*. I chewed my lip, trying to push away the hot thoughts that were aiding in the heat exhaustion I was feeling.

"Now," she whispered, reaching up and touching my hand. "Bring this hand here," she guided my hand down the axe handle, "and place this one here. And when you swing this time, pull from your core, not your chest or your shoulders."

She backed away, coming around and placing a piece of wood on the stump. I nervously adjusted my grip on the handle and took a deep breath. Her instructions replayed in my head as I lifted the axe; I squeezed my abdomen as I pulled the blade down.

It crashed into the wood.

It didn't split, but it did splinter.

"Excellent, Cameron!" Saloso squealed. "Now just push back on that handle, and it will come out."

I did as Saloso said, and the axe came out.

"I did it!" I shouted to her.

"You did! Now, try it again."

I nodded and raised the axe, feeling a sudden shock of pain jolt through my arm. I dropped the axe and fell to my knees.

I heard Saloso cry, "Cameron!" as she ran over to me.

71

"What is it?"

"My arm, it just started hurting again."

"Then you must return to the tent. This task it too hard—
"

"No!" I cut her off. "I want to go home! I don't want to be stuck here forever! You guys don't even want me here. What is the point in making sure I'm alright if you're still going to put me out? Just let me go!" Tears pricked my eyes as they rushed forward. I kept my face to the ground as the beaming sun beat down on my back. My jaw ached as I clenched it tightly, my tears hitting the dry ground. "Sorry," I said bitterly.

Saloso was quiet for a while. "Cameron, I will escort you back tonight if that is what you wish."

When I looked up from the ground, I was greeted with a look of sorrow. She didn't pity me, but she was sorry that I was so angry, and so was I. I didn't mean any harm by what I'd said, but how could I tell her that?

"Returning you to the real world as healthy as possible is my way of showing you gratitude," she continued. "Because I hoped to learn from you while you were here. In exchange for half of my traveling time, I asked Grandmother if you could stay until you are healthy enough to return to your world."

I stared at her, feeling my heart sink into the ground. She'd given up six of her traveling months just for a few weeks to learn what she could from me. Learning was important to Saloso, so much so she was willing to do anything for this chance. It was a bad bargain, but I felt a little responsible since I technically took half a year of her life away.

"I will take you at once if that is what you wish, Outsider," Saloso said into my thoughts. She was forcing a small smile, and she blinked away tears as our eyes connected. "I have already learned so much, just from the way you speak. I will cherish these memories."

"I'm sorry, Saloso. I want to go home." I paused, remembering what Kateri told me about God wanting me here. "But I don't think I can go yet."

She gasped, drawing my gaze back to her. Tears had sprung from her eyes, rolling down her cheeks. "You mean, you will stay a while longer?"

I nodded. "I will, but then I must go home. I have a mother who will be worried if I don't return."

Saloso rushed into my chest, wrapping her arms around my neck. "Oh, thank you, Cameron! This means so much to me." She clung to me a little longer and, awkwardly, I wrapped my arms around her small frame. I wanted to go home, but I knew I'd never be able to live with myself if I left right now, knowing Saloso's chances of experiencing the real world were just slashed because of me. It was the most annoying thing, but I couldn't stop feeling responsible. And, for some reason, God wanted me here, and I was curious to know why.

Nine
Fulfill

"Alright," I said, lifting the axe over my head, "noodles are what?"

"Pasta," Saloso answered.

"Good." I hacked into a piece of wood.

It'd been eight days since I agreed to stay a little longer for Saloso's sake. I wish I hadn't, I should've let her take me into the city, but I felt responsible for her missing six of her twelve months of freedom. And even though the tribe isn't *so* bad, I didn't have much longer until someone started looking for me.

When I emerged from the tent eight days ago and began chopping wood, there was only four or five days left until the group I was traveling with was supposed to return to UOW. That meant someone would start looking for our group soon. I planned to tell Saloso tonight at dinner that someone would be coming soon for me, even though the last time I'd told a woman something serious over dinner, things got out of hand.

Despite the hot sun, I've enjoyed being here. The food is

74

good, and it's always something I've never had before. I've spent most of my days chopping wood, but Kateri wanted me to give my body a rest for the next two days, so I'll be visiting the farming area of the tribe. I'm excited to see this new area and learn how they managed to get water out here in this almost desert land.

Saloso was also enjoying her lessons about the outside world. I've been telling her about schools, and jobs, how things are different from here in her small tribe. She always arrived for lessons during her free time, when she wasn't under her grandmother's thumb, and could have Kateri or Catskill take over her load for the time she was gone. She would come and sit with me for a while—I have no idea for how long since I had no way to tell time—in the shade of a tree, while I chopped firewood.

"And pasta is usually made up of what?' I asked, wiping the sweat from my brow. I hadn't improved very much at chopping wood, but my left arm seemed better after Kateri gave me a new bandage and paste.

"Pasta is usually made of flour, and flour is made from," she paused, looking away at the ground. I picked up another piece of wood and set it on the stump, giving her time to think.

"Flour is usually made out of …"

"Wheat," I finally answered.

She looked up me with a deep scowl. "You did not give me a fair chance! I would have remembered if you would have just given me more time."

"Calm down," I said, slinging the axe over my shoulder.

75

"What are you so antsy for? We've got time for you to figure it out."

"No, we don't! I have to remember it all now!" Her scowl suddenly softened, and I pulled the axe from my shoulder. She was right, we didn't have much time. I'd have to go home soon, and this would be it for Saloso. She wouldn't have another chance to learn about the rest of the world after I left, not until she was allowed to leave the tribe for six months.

I heard her clear her throat. "I am sorry, Cameron. I should not have raised my voice. Please forgive me."

"No," I shook my head. "I shouldn't have made light of the situation. It's a very serious one. I'm sorry, too."

She smiled a little, and I raised my axe and brought it down the way Saloso had taught me—using my core and not my chest. The wood split into two jagged halves. I stared at them, and then my eyes shot to Saloso's.

"I did it!" I screamed.

"You finally did it!" Saloso yelled as she jumped to her feet.

I rushed over and hugged her, lifting her from the ground and spinning as she giggled. I wanted to explode from excitement. I'd finally chopped the wood in half, and that meant I was one step closer to going home.

"So, this is why you have been asking me to cover for you?"

I stopped spinning to find Catskill standing with his large arms crossed against his wide chest. His hard cheek bones made his frown more intimidating as he blinked from me to Saloso while I set her down.

"Catskill," she said, walking briskly to him, "I am sorry.

76

Cameron had just—"

"Cameron? You speak to him by his name? I thought he was just an outsider, Saloso, someone you wanted to learn from?"

"He is." She turned to look at me. "Cameron—I mean—the outsider is just helping me learn more. It is nothing more than that."

"Yeah, well maybe you should tell that to Chief Grey Hawk when we get back."

"No," she said, backing up. "You cannot tell her of this!"

"You should have thought about that before you started sneaking off to meet with this outsider. When he leaves, he will forget about us and never return! Why waste your time?"

"That is not true! Cameron is not one with low water in his rivers! He is one who is a spring of life!" Saloso was standing right in Catskill's face now. He was hulking over her, but she did not back down.

"Saloso is right," I said behind them.

Catskill moved Saloso out of the way and stepped to me. "What did you say, Outsider?"

"Stop it, Catskill, this is between you and I!" Saloso yelled behind him.

"I said I'm not going to forget you guys. I appreciate your hospitality. I could never forget the people who nursed me—" flames burned my face as my nose crunched beneath Catskill's heavy fist. I stumbled to the ground, holding my bleeding nose. Before I could react, another punch landed on my face, whipping my head so hard, I felt my neck crack. I gasped, as I rolled over. Slowly, I got onto my hands and knees, trying to make the pain and blurring stop when I heard Catskill grunt and Saloso scream, "Stop it!" but it was too late. My ribs felt a crushing blow and I toppled over to my side.

Heaving now, I heard another voice say, "That is enough, Catskill. Healer's orders."

He was hovering over me, ready to pummel me some more when the woman's voice interrupted. I held my side, wheezing as I blinked lazily at a tall woman who didn't wear a shawl. She wore a sleeveless white tunic that ran to the ground. The rim of her tunic was covered in black designs, and the slits up the side gave way to legs as mighty as Catskill's. She looked like she could take him in an arm-wrestling match, and it'd be no problem for her. Her skin was as dark as Momma's, and she had chocolate waves that peeked from a black scarf atop her head. She dressed like a member of the tribe, but she was not one of them.

Taking a step forward, she said, "You dare challenge me? Let the outsider go, now."

Just then, Kateri showed up and was panting wildly as she watched our interactions. *Why is Kateri here?* Catskill withdrew his fist and stepped away, muttering darkly, "I see where your loyalty lies, O Great Mist of the Sea."

The woman standing there in all white said, "My loyalty is to the tribe, not to anyone else."

"And this—this is for the tribe?" he yelled as he pointed at me.

"His presence here enlightens the next chief. I only want

what is best for this tribe, and the chiefhood."

"You cannot be serious, Misty? How can an outsider enlighten us? His ways will only do more harm than good."

"Only a fool could believe that," she said forcefully.

Catskill tried to control his temper as he yelled, "I am trying to protect this place!"

"You, our current chief, and anyone who thinks like you will end this tribe! Our land is changing, and there is no way we can ignore this any further! We must do something or the very place Grande Chief Zasca fought for will be nothing but dust."

Catskill shook his head. "I am going to see what Chief Grey Hawk has to say." He pushed through the group of women, storming off towards the village.

"Priest Misty, please, Grandmother will never allow this," Saloso cried as she ran to the tall woman's side.

Misty's face was gentler now as she turned to Saloso and said, "I will deal with Chief Grey Hawk. She and I will talk. For now, take care of this boy, and cause no more problems. Understood, Saloso?"

She blubbered a shy 'okay', and Priest Misty turned to me, a single brow raised. "There is purpose for you here, despite what you think or feel. The God who sees all has said so. There will be an interruption in your development, but the plan God has for you here will be fulfilled." She turned on her heels and left Kateri and Saloso to rush to my side.

I stared ahead at the woman as she walked off, disappearing into the bushes, my mind swirling with questions about what she'd meant.

"Cameron," Saloso was kneeling in front of me now. "Are you alright?"

"Take this," Kateri said calmly. "Put this on your nose, it will help stop the bleeding." She handed me a big brown leaf from a satchel she was wearing. I took the rubbery leaf and held it to my nose. The pain blaring from it made my eyes water, but I held in the tears.

"I'm sorry," I said finally.

Kateri stopped digging through her satchel and said, "It is not your fault, Outsider. Catskill is to wed Saloso, at least that is what Grey Hawk wants."

I looked over at a sullen Saloso.

"It is true," she said, patting her chest twice. I remembered her doing that before, but a bolt of pain shot through me when Kateri pressed a hand to my ribs, cutting my thoughts.

"Sorry," Kateri said as I groaned. "I wanted to see if anything was broken. You are fine, but you will probably bruise and be very sore. Now help me raise him, Saloso. We will take him to a healing tent."

As quickly as I'd been released from the healing tent, I was back. Kateri left after she and Saloso guided me back. She had other work to do, but Saloso decided to stay with me to avoid her grandmother's fury. This time I didn't lie down, I sat on the pelt in the center of the tent as Saloso picked herbs for my nose and face. Catskill was strong, and my face was still burning from his punch. I kind of admired his strength. Of course, I'd been in fights before. Growing up in Alabama, there were things that people expected of you. They wanted you to look and act a certain way because of the color of your skin, and because I didn't, I ran into a number of problems.

My kin were supportive of me, but they didn't like that I wanted to be an engineer and not a schoolteacher like every other person in my family. They thought I was trying to be like my father, and not like my mother, but that just wasn't true. I was interested in different things, and sometimes that put you in difficult situations that the only way out was to fight. I wasn't allowed to lose when I was a kid, and I wondered what Momma would think when I told her I'd lost my first fight out here.

"Cameron," Saloso called. Her voice jerked me out of my thoughts, and I was met with piercing blue eyes that seemed saddened.

"Yes," I responded.

"I am going to apply this paste to your eye. It is for swelling and will help reduce the pain."

I nodded and closed my eyes. Gently, I felt Saloso patting the paste onto my skin. She was much better at this than Kateri who was always a little rougher. Saloso was softer, using delicate pressure when applying the paste.

"I am sorry, Outsider," she said quietly.

Keeping my eyes closed I asked, "What for?"

"For this. For Catskill. He is such a brute of a man, I do not care for him on a deeper level, but he is a good friend. He means well, he is just…" she trailed off.

"He's not your type."

She chuckled. "You are correct. He is not the type of man that interests me." Since she was being so open, I started to ask what kind of man she was looking for, but it didn't seem appropriate. She filled the awkward silence and said, "Kateri is far better at this than I am. I have only learned very little from Priest Misty."

"That woman," I said, "she told me that God has a purpose for me here. Is that true?"

Saloso replied, "If Priest Misty said it, then it is true."

I opened my eyes to find Saloso rubbing her hands into the ground, and then sticking them into a bucket of water. "She's the leading priest here. We are all brought before her when we are young, and she can see the calling on our lives. If it is so that one bears a flame over their head, they will be a healer. Once they begin to interpret the tongue of God, she takes them under her wing."

"I see," I said, feeling the paste begin to harden. "So she's very close to God and that's why her word is law for the tribe?"

"Correct." Saloso offered a weak smile. "She is known as the Great Mist of the Sea, because God visits with her the way he did with Moses. A cloud of smoke fills her tent, and encompasses the outside, signaling us not to draw near."

I stared at her, surprised that God still did things like that. "Are you serious?" I asked.

She nodded. "It is a marvel to wonder at."

I dropped my head, sulking now, because I was *actually*

stuck here. There was no way I could leave until my purpose was fulfilled, but what did that even mean? What could my purpose even be? And what did she mean by an interruption to my development? The amounting questions left me feeling dizzy for a moment. When the dizziness passed, an idea popped into my head and I asked, "If Priest Misty is super close to God, then I can just ask her to get some clarity from God about this, right?"

"Perhaps." Saloso shrugged. "But Priest Misty only receives messages from God concerning our tribe as a whole. Individually, God still expects us to come to Him."

I dropped my head, feeling hopeless. But Saloso said, "It is better to receive an answer from God personally than for someone else to receive the message for you."

"Why?"

"Because God can speak to all of us directly. But if the only way He ever sends you word is through someone else, then He is only instructing you. It means you have no relationship with God. You must dive deeper to receive His messages yourself, instead of depending on others to do it for you."

"I guess that's true." I offered her a weak smile.

"Do not feel sad, Cameron. Surely if you take time to spend with God, He will answer you. Like when I show you the farming fields, it is a beautiful sight to see. You will see the true beauty of God there, and maybe it will help you reconnect with Him."

I glanced at the ground for a moment. "Do you really think so?"

Saloso patted her chest twice. "I am certain."

Ten

O Great Mist of the Sea

Kateri was strict about me resting my body which was alright
with me. I needed more time to accept that I was stuck here,
and in the two extra days I spent in the hot tent, I got to teach
Saloso more things about the rest of the world. The
conversations would sometimes get intense, forcing Saloso to
blink dumbly in awe and wonder of the world she wished she
could experience. She loved learning, and she loved what she
learned. Even things she didn't agree with, like racism, which
left her angry and confused, but she still loved learning about
the efforts of Dr. Martin Luther King Jr., and all the other
activists during the Civil Rights Movement. She'd also never
heard of women needing rights. As far as Saloso knew, women
ruled every nation.

"So women do not lead your tribes?" She knew the world
beyond her borders weren't full of tribes like her own, but for
teaching purposes, I let her refer to families as tribes since to
her, tribes and families were synonymous.

85

"Well, no one really *leads* anyone," I explained, taking a sip of water from a pouch. "Like the way Chief Grey Hawk makes all the final decisions for the tribe, it's not like that for everyone else. We have leaders, but even they must answer to someone else."

Her eyes widened with shock, and she blinked at me for a moment before shaking her head. "How do you all live, then?"

"We all live together. And the husband and wife make decisions together, each one equal to the other. No one decides for the other or forces the other to do what that person wants without..." I paused, realizing I wasn't suited to teach about leadership or relationships. I'd let Garrith walk all over me with no consideration of my own feelings. I'd let her disrespect me and my faith. And it wasn't because she was a woman, it was because I was a weak man.

It was shameful how awkward and desperate I was for her. I guess being on this trip, despite its sudden turn of events, was still doing the job of getting Garrith out of my head.

"That seems awfully complicated," Saloso said softly.

I looked over at her, and with delicate hands, she brushed a loose wave of hair behind her ear. Saloso had pretty hair, chestnut waves sat all over her when she wore it free. Although she was just as strong as Catskill, she was frighteningly gentle. Soft spoken and meek would be words I'd use to describe her.

We sat there in silence for a moment. I looked her over as she stared at the ground. I could see the mounting confusion in her tightened jaw and furrowed brows. Suddenly, she looked up and caught me staring. I tried to look off, but she said,

"What is it, Outsider?"

"Nothing," I said shortly.

She bit her bottom lip, making her expression melt from confusion to innocence. Her gentleness made her cute, but her face was stunning. The last two days I'd been in my tent with her, giving her more lessons, I could see why Catskill would like her. She had a small nose and cheekbones that were as fierce as her blue eyes. But her glowing skin looked like it was drizzled over her, like honey on your favorite treat.

"So, Saloso," I called.

She raised her eyes to meet mine and nodded.

"Why don't you tell me a little about you and your culture?"

She perked up, pulling her shoulders back. "You are interested in knowing things about my tribe?"

"Of course, since I'm going to be here a while."

"That is true. It would serve you well to learn our ways."

"First things first," I said, adjusting on the pelt, "why do you pat your chest sometimes after you say things?"

Raising her hand to her chest, she patted it twice and asked, "Like so?"

"Yeah."

"It is a sign of truth-telling. If one pats their chest twice, that means there is no lie or false information in what they say. Their word can be trusted."

"Really? Why don't you guys do it more often then?"

"Because it is only used to encourage a statement." She frowned, and I laughed and said, "Do you mean emphasize?"

She nodded. "Yes, Cameron. I believe that is the word. To

emphasize."

"Can you remember the definition?"

"Hmm." Placing a finger to her chin, she lifted her blue marble eyes to the sky and then said, "It is to give stress to your statement or word ... I believe."

"Very good." I smiled.

She clapped her hands. "I am so glad I was able to remember that!" She smiled at me, genuinely, and it was hard to look away.

Clearing my throat, I said, "So, tell me something else—"

"Good afternoon, teacher and student," Kateri interrupted as she entered the tent. "I am going to make lunch now, would either of you like to join me?"

I shrugged and Saloso said, "Come, Cameron, you should join us. It will be fun."

"I will even let you help me." Kateri leaned forward with her hands on her hips, and I sighed at the smiling girl.

"Fine, it beats sitting around in this hot tent."

"Sorry that I could not provide better company, Outsider," Saloso spat at me.

Waving frantically, I said, "No! Saloso, you are good company. *Very* good company. I really like you."

Kateri and Saloso both stared at me with wide eyes and then I realized I'd said something weird and cried, "No! Not like that! I mean you are a very beautiful woman, but you are going to marry Catskill—" Kateri burst into laughter, and Saloso covered her mouth and laughed quietly.

"So, if Catskill was not to wed my sister, I see now that you would. Very nice, Outsider!" Kateri exclaimed.

"No!" I yelled.

"So, you do not like me?" Saloso asked. I couldn't tell if she was playing into this or if I'd really hurt her feelings. Sweating, I said, "That's not true, either. I do like you, Saloso. Really, I mean that. But I—" Saloso couldn't hold it together, and she began laughing loudly. I stared at the two sisters as they laughed at me. I could feel the embarrassment burning my ears when Priest Misty stepped into the tent. She smiled at the sisters, who both tried to quiet their laughter into muffled snickers.

Misty said, "Now, ladies, that is quite enough toying with the outsider. Go prepare lunch, I need to speak to Cameron alone."

Composing themselves, the sisters nodded, each one offering me a gentle wave and a quiet goodbye as they left the tent. I sighed, trying to regain my own composure when Priest Misty said, "Follow me, Cameron."

We walked through the buzzing village; I caught a glimpse of Catskill walking Saloso someplace. Neither of them saw me, but I watched them for as far as I could before bumping into a man carrying water. I apologized quickly and stepped around the big meaty man. Most of the men of the tribe were fit and strong like Catskill, but there were others like the meatball of a man I'd bumped into who wore the angled hip cloth, and no shirt, letting their sweaty bellies hang heavily over the cloth.

I walked by the Chief's hut. It was grand, made of three huts with one big one in the middle and two small ones on each side. As we passed the Chief's hut, we went into an area of the camp that was new for me. I had only seen very little of the tribe thus far, and I was excited and nervous to be seeing a new part of it. Misty pushed aside tree branches and bushes as we walked into the forested area. Giant trees, so tall and so wide, they looked like they'd been growing for centuries. The vines on the ground were so thick and coarse, the bristles along them scratched my ankles and I was afraid I'd start bleeding. Misty, who walked barefoot, just like everyone else—I wore sandals Kateri had made for me since she was afraid my feet would be too sensitive—walked over the thick vines as if it were sand mushing beneath her feet.

The further away from the tribe we got, the cooler it got, and the shadier. The trees locked in all the moisture on the ground, causing me to sink with every step I took. The forested area looked like one that had never been explored before. I was afraid I'd get lost if I admired anything for too long, so I kept my eyes focused on Misty until we arrived at her small hut. It was made of wood, and clay, and it looked like a small house rather than the huts everyone else lived in. It had a sliding door, and windows—the kind that had a latch and two sides you pushed open. It looked like a castle even compared to the Chief's hut.

Misty called, "Cameron, are you alright?"

I stared with no regards to my momma's upbringing. My head would've been smacked and my arm pinched twice by now if Momma saw me staring the way I was. Gathering myself, I asked, "Why do you have that?"

Misty squinted and then looked over her shoulder at the house. Her neatly pinned hair, her long white robes, she looked like an advocate for peace on a missionary trip, not a tribal healer.

"My house? Are you asking why I live here and not amongst the tribe?"

"Well, yes, but I'm asking why your house looks like this and not like," I paused, trying to pick the right words.

Misty crossed her strong arms and smirked, "The blood of my ancestors runs through me. The Sand Ribbon tribe that exists today is different from the original tribe. The tribe you see today reflects two tribes coming together." As she spoke, I glanced her over. She was different from the rest of the tribe, appearing more like an African American woman with hair like Saloso's and clothes from the tribeswomen. She looked like an outsider who'd eventually gotten accepted by these people.

"I am only partially Ribbon," Misty admitted. "My ancestors were from the tribe that followed Grande Chief Zasca ages ago, and we have kept our bloodline pure for the most part. Some of us have intermingled with the Ribbon and that is why we do not possess all of the attributes of our greatest ancestors."

"So your ancestors, they were from that mountain tribe then?" I asked.

She nodded and turned back to the wooden house, gazing over it. "El Antiguo Clan del Puño de Piedra." Her words rolled off her tongue.

"What does that mean?"

"It means The Ancient Clan of the Stone Fist. That is the name of the clan my bloodline traces back to. My people were builders. They could turn stones into anything, but they were forced out of their land and into hiding on the mountaintops. Then Grande Chief Zasca showed up, and my clan took another chance at life. They began again with Zasca and the Sand Ribbon people." She shrugged. "Building is in my blood. There are not many stones here, so I build with what supplies I have. That is why this house is different from the others." She strolled for a moment and stopped in front of the door. "It was one of the first houses built on this land. Preserved by the sticky mud, and the hovering trees, the wood does not dry and rot. But each baby born to our clan will make changes to the standing houses and build their own as a way to preserve our culture while intermingling it with that of the Sand Ribbon tribe once they are of age."

"I take it you worked on this one?"

She nodded, keeping her eyes on the house. "I have done some internal work, fixing floorboards, and reinforcing things. This house holds the whispers of my people from many generations. But now, it has been dedicated to God, and only the high priest can stay here." Finally, she turned back to face me. "I was asked by God to bring you here. To help guide you onto the path He wants you on."

"He couldn't have just told me back in the camp?" I said angrily. God seemed to be doing a lot of taking me way out of the way to tell me simple things. Feeling indignant, I snapped, "He had to drag me all the way out here? Is being stuck in the hot wildlands of Peru not enough for Him?" I don't know why, but all the anger I'd been holding in began pouring out.

Misty looked concern, her brows coming together, and her smile fading. "This land is holy. It brings out the truth in one's heart to purify you. In your heart, you are very angry at God."

I rolled my eyes. "Yes, that's obvious. He's got me stuck out here and won't even tell me why!" I yelled. It was true I was angry at God. I didn't want to admit it, but I was frustrated with Him and this situation.

"Who are you that God must answer when you speak?" The words caught me off guard, and suddenly my anger seemed foolish. Misty stepped forward through the bushes towards me, but her posture was straight, and her face was intimidating now. I took a nervous step back, but I couldn't look away from her.

"You dare believe that you are the equivalent to God, and He must answer you instead of you answering Him? Do you think that God is beneath you?"

"No! I don't, not at all," my voice cracked as I spoke, but Misty took another step forward, her white garments shifting along the grass with every step. I glanced down at her feet, wanting to look away from her fiery eyes when I noticed something like a cloud around her ankles. I blinked and it was still there.

"Then why?" Misty yelled, her voice didn't sound like her own anymore, it thundered and clapped heavily at me, making me jump. "Why do you question Me? Why do you question the path I have set for you and resent it? Have you conquered death and tamed the sea? Have you stopped the storms and blocked out the sun? Can you feed an entire multitude or nation?"

The clouds grew heavier and before I knew it, I'd backed myself into a tree. The raging clouds turned into a mist along the ground, rolling forward as if waves trembled beneath it. I pulled my eyes from the ground and found Misty to be missing. Instead, there was a lion standing there. I wanted to react, but before I could, the lion roared so loudly, I thought my ear drums shattered.

Falling to my feet, I frantically covered my ears. I squeezed my eyes closed, hoping this was all a dream, when suddenly the world went silent. The cooing of a gull forced my eyes open. Panting heavily, I stared down at my reflection. My hands were over my ears, and tears dripped into the water beneath me. *Am I dreaming? Where am I?*

I looked up and found a lamb sitting in the arms of a lion. It was bleeding into the waters, and the lion licked the wounds of the dying animal. It was frightening to see, but without thinking, I found myself standing and walking toward the animals. I felt like the lion wouldn't attack if I neared it, there was something calm about the beast that invited me over to it. As I approached the lion and the lamb, the lion finally pulled its gaze from the bleeding lamb and looked me over.

"There are things that happen in the lives of my children that they have no control over. Some choose to resent Me, while others choose to trust Me. You have chosen both, young Cameron, but you are full of anger and confusion. You trust

Me because you were taught to, but you don't know what it truly means to put your full trust in Me."

"Father." I recognized the Voice that came from the lion as He sat there looking at me. His mouth didn't move, and He never blinked, He just looked at me. Glowing eyes seemed to penetrate my inner being. His gaze kept me from being afraid and kept me from disbelief. As long as I looked into the eyes of the lion, I couldn't feel anything negative.

"I am..." I answered weakly. "I am angry about a lot of things. I've been hurt and betrayed by the first woman I loved. I was thrown away by my father, and my mother struggled for so long. Now I'm stuck in Peru with no way home. How is any of this fair?"

"I chose you for every situation you are in. You were the only one strong enough to bear this cross without failing. I am proud of you, Cameron, you have not failed Me."

I didn't look away. I didn't move. I couldn't. It wasn't fear that was gripping me, it was sheer power. Tears swelled in my eyes, and I said, "How haven't I failed You, Father? I've been so angry at You, and I let Garrith..."

"Children get angry at their parents quite often. But just as you are strong enough to carry your cross, I am strong enough to carry the weight of your anger." His words were comforting, and I could feel all the resentment in my body seeping from my feet into the water I stood on.

"I know it all hurts, Cameron. I know that being here in Peru doesn't make sense. But you must learn to trust Me in all ways, not just the ones that are easy for you. This is where your mission begins, because I have known the plans I've had for you since before I knit you in your mother's womb. My plans for you, Cameron, are good, but you must trust Me."

"How can I? It just feels like You've never come through for me before."

"Precious one, I have come through for you when you had not yet known. Each tough lesson you've learned has only made you stronger. For the battles I fight for you are ones you cannot see because you have not seen through the eyes of My Spirit."

"Oh." I couldn't feel embarrassed, but there was a hint of shock resonating within me.

"Your lack of faith has kept My Spirit from you and has blinded you to the Truth. The dirt from the world's lack of knowledge has sullied your understanding of My protection and My ways. You believe because things have not gone the way you wanted, that I have failed you. But I am unable to fail, and thus unable to fail you."

Tears sprung down my cheeks as I stood in awe of the lion. There were things I hadn't known, and things I didn't understand. But being here now before God made me want to weep because of my ignorance. Weep because my ignorance kept me from reaching my full potential in Christ. I wanted to weep because when you lack faith, you lack trust. If you do not trust God, it is because you do not know Him well enough to trust Him. And without God, we are nothing.

I just learned that all this time, I was nothing, but God was still so proud of me.

"The journey I have you on will bring you to the living water I told you about when you were still small. Choose to trust Me, and I will release you from this place. And in your release, you will bring life to others through My Son."

"But how," I cried, "how do I find this well?"

"You must search for Me. Now, close your eyes."

I obeyed and felt the slick wetness of the tongue of the lion grazing my head.

"Open them now," He said.

I shot my eyes open, and the lion was still sitting there looking at me. "I have covered you in My Son's Blood. Go forth now," was the last thing He said to me before I began to sink.

Eleven

The Insider is an Outsider

I jerked my eyes open and heaved a deep breath. Panting heavily, I glanced around the room to find Saloso asleep in the corner. There was a small fire burning, and I realized I wasn't in a healer's tent, I was in what looked like someone's shack. Peering around the room, I wondered if I'd only been dreaming, or if I really met God. How did I get from the forest and into this shack?

"Cameron?" Saloso said.

I blinked at her, trying to put everything together.

"Cameron, are you alright?"

"What happened to me?"

"You passed out and Misty brought you back here. You have been out for a few hours, and Kateri was here watching you. But I came to visit you not too long ago."

"So, it was real?" I whispered as I looked at the fire. The flames crackled and danced, casting strange shadows on the walls.

"Yes, whatever you experienced, and whoever you encountered was real," Saloso confirmed.

Pressing a hand to my chest, I felt like crying. "Then why do I still feel frustrated? I thought I wouldn't feel like this anymore."

"Your situation did not change, Cameron, you are still here—"

"No kidding! I'm still stuck here! Even though I know this is God's plan I'm still so," I paused, trying to find a word more intense than angry, and shouted, "Irritated!"

Panting, I looked up from the flames that were casting shadows onto Saloso's pretty face. Her saddened eyes drifted away from mine. "It is not always easy to accept the plan of God. Sometimes, all you feel is stuck." She gave a half smile and shrugged. "But trusting that this plan of His is not to torture you, or to make you feel bad, it is always to enlighten you and to uplift you, can be difficult. But that is all we have; all I have always had." She looked up at me, and it was as if she wanted to cry. I could feel my anger soothing as Saloso spoke just as quietly as the flickering flames. "You are not the only one who is an outsider, Cameron."

My chest tightened, and immediately, I remembered. "The cry of the wild goose."

Saloso laughed lightly. "Kateri told you."

I smiled a little and nodded.

"Well, now you know that you do not have to be foreign to be an outsider. You can be one within your own tribe. You feel stuck, like there is no way to escape this tragedy. You want to get out, but you carry the burden of chiefhood and can never truly be free." She wiped her nose. "And even though I have accepted my fate, I have come to learn that my life is no punishment. My life is what I make it, and I choose to make the most of it, not see myself as a captive."

"That's why you love learning," I responded. "It makes sense."

She smiled, and I wasn't sure if my chest could get any tighter. But it didn't tighten because I was sad, or even angry, her smile made me nervous, it made me anxious.

"When I felt like I was stuck here," she said as she leaned forward and tended the fire, "I decided to seek God for answers. And in looking for Him, I fell in love with learning new things. I read the scrolls, and I prayed, but I wanted to do more. So, I began trying to learn about the outside world, and how it reflected the image of God." Setting the stick down, she sat back against the shack wall. "Each new thing I learned taught me more about God, His personality, His thoughts, His creativity as well as the world around me. Learning about other tribes, learning about travelers, and trying to read. It all helped me learn about who God is, and that His plans are always good." She smiled warmly at the flames. "God is so fascinating, is He not?"

"He is. Especially because He's so patient. So forgiving." I choked. Tears I didn't know I had, began to pour, and I whispered to Saloso, "I've been so angry at God, at the tribe, and even at you for rescuing me. But I'm trying to believe this is all for the better. I know it is, it's just hard, and it's embarrassing that I've been resenting the people who have been taking care of me. I feel so stupid."

"Oh, Cameron," Saloso said, moving closer to me. "Do not feel that way. You have been nothing but kind to me. Even if you have resented us and God, you no longer do, and we can keep moving forward from here."

I wiped at my tears, but they wouldn't stop. Saloso didn't judge me, and she wasn't angry at me for my resentment because she's been in my shoes. And she's found people who have accepted her, and she has accepted God. Now she was doing the same for me; she accepted me, despite my pinned-up frustration. Saloso was still here beside me, and I was overwhelmed with emotion.

Throwing her arms around me, Saloso held me tight, but it wasn't tight enough. I pulled her small frame into my lap and squeezed her as tightly as I could without hurting her, and I wept. There was a smell of honey and fresh flowers that rested on her. Tresses of chocolate skirted down her back as I held her. In that moment, I realized, Saloso was there for me, there like no one had been except for my mother. She was genuine and kind, and Saloso understood me. She didn't want anything from me, except to learn from me. She was wonderful, but I had been horrible to her. I wanted nothing more than my chance to get out of here, selfishly ignoring all that her tribe had done for me, all she'd done for me. I wished I could take it all back, that I could change my reaction to her tribe, and to Saloso. But I couldn't. All I could do was hold her close and hope that she felt the things that were stirring within me.

101

"Cameron, it is alright," she whispered into my ear. I felt her hand run through my hair. "You do not have to cry anymore; you will be fine."

Sniffling, I sighed and said, "Thank you, Saloso, for everything."

She pulled away, still smiling the kind way she always did. "Give the glory to God, He is the one who rescued you. I am just here on this journey with you until He says your time here is done."

I gave her a broken smile, and she giggled, slowly reaching up and caressing my face before wiping a tear away. The silence between us made my heart thump quickly. There was a beautiful woman sitting in my lap, wiping my tears away, but all I managed to do was stare at her all starry eyed. But she was no different. Her wide eyes studied mine, and I wondered what she was thinking.

A branch cracked, and Saloso blinked. Dropping her hand from my face, she exhaled heavily and said, "Sorry, I will move now."

"No," I said. She looked me over and I fumbled with my words. "No, I meant, you can stay." She raised a brow. "I just meant that you didn't have to apologize. I'm sorry."

Saloso grinned, climbing off my lap. "It is alright, Cameron, I understood what you meant. I just wanted to give you a hard time."

I shook my head and laughed. "I'm not usually like this. Sorry."

"No, no, it is alright."

I chewed my lip, feeling an intense heat radiating on my cheeks when I heard the shack's curtain move. "I see the outsider has returned to the land of the living."

"He did not die, Kateri, you know that," Saloso said, eyeing her sister as she handed us bowls.

There was a leg of meat sticking out of the bowl. It looked like some kind of roasted animal with yellow potatoes sitting on a pile of dark brown beans. Atop the potatoes was something I'd seen before, "Is that... cassava?" I asked.

Kateri smiled. "You have eaten cassava before, Outsider?"

I nodded. "There was an African woman at my church who used to make it for us. I thought it was something only Ghanaians ate?"

Saloso shook her head. "Our tribe only began eating it when we merged with the mountain people. They had a ritual where they worked the cassava down into a drink. But our tribe used it differently."

Kateri pulled on the sticky ball of dough in her bowl. "We eat it with our hands!"

I watched as she used a bit of tacky dough to scoop her food. "We do, too." I pulled on my own sticky ball, but then I paused, staring into the bowl. The animal leg in my food was smaller than a chicken's but it still had its feet ... and its claws.

Blinking, I asked, "What kind of animal is this?"

"It's cuy," Kateri said. She pulled a small animal out of her bowl and held it up to me. "I did not want to waste a whole cuy on you, so I just gave you something small of it."

I stared at the animal a little longer as Saloso asked,

"What is it?"

"That's a rat, isn't it?"

Kateri frowned. "A rat? This is our favorite meal! We do not always get to eat this, but Catskill and the others had some very fine wool to trade, and we got a deal for them."

"I should give Catskill my regards," Saloso said.

"We let little Rocko keep one since it was so small. But just until it is fat enough to eat, then we will kill it." Kateri bit into the meat. "Go on," she said, munching, "try it."

Pulling the small animal leg out of the soup, I bit into it. The skin had a crispy, smoky flavor, but the texture and taste of the animal was that of gamey chicken. The meat was spicy and tangy, seasoned with herbs I'd never heard of before. I took another bite, just to be sure I liked it, and I glanced up from my bowl to find Saloso and Kateri silently watching me.

I swallowed quickly and cleared my throat. "It's good."

"How wonderful!" Saloso exclaimed.

"I should have given you more then. Would you like a full one?"

I shook my head. "No, I'm fine. I still have the rest of the food to enjoy."

Kateri set her bowl down and began eating her cuy, as did Saloso, while I tried the rest of the dish. So far, I'd tried several ways to make potatoes, and I'd had my fill of corn. But the staples of this place were corn and potatoes, so it only made sense that nearly every meal featured them.

Tomorrow, Saloso and I would be visiting the farming fields so she could begin teaching me the way of the farmer.

Catskill was supposed to teach me, but since he and I aren't speaking, Saloso volunteered. I wasn't opposed to her teaching me the field, but I had intended to apologize to Catskill. Hopefully I'd get another chance sometime soon.

The next day, Kateri came and woke me very early. The coolness of the morning was heavy with dew; I'd never known the early mornings of Peru could be so cool. I moved around the small shack, chewing a mint leaf to freshen my breath. When my airways were completely cleared, I spit out the chewed plant and rinsed my mouth using the fresh pail of water Kateri delivered daily. Using that same water, I also rinsed my face, and patted it dry with whatever cloth I found lying around. Kateri also brought me a new pair of pants this morning that I changed into and a beautifully woven tunic. I hadn't worn a shirt in a while, but I was happy to wear the new clothes.

Pulling the shirt on over my head, I let the tunic fall to my knees, and I liked the eggshell white color. As I stepped into my shoes, I made a mental note to ask Kateri for something to shave with. My facial hair was growing in, and it was beginning to itch.

Kateri was sitting outside the door holding a water pouch when I stepped out.

"Morning, Kateri," I said.

She smiled and passed me the pouch. "Good morning,

Outsider. Today is your first day in the fields. I think you will really enjoy this."

"Your sister said something similar. These fields must be pretty impressive."

She nodded and looked off at the rest of the camp blanketed in the morning's darkness. "I am glad you are still here with us, Outsider. It really makes it seem like our worlds are not so different."

"I'm glad I'm here, too."

Grabbing my wrist, she pulled me along and said, "Come now! You will only have a little time with Saloso today. Misty has made it known to Grandmother that we are not to send you off yet. And since Grandmother cannot go against God's will, she will do everything she can to keep Saloso so busy she will not have time to spare or spend with you."

Tripping along as Kateri pulled me, I remembered when Priest Misty first told me I had a purpose here. I still hadn't found it, but I was hoping I'd figure it out soon.

We walked for a while in silence, and I thought over everything Priest Misty had said, and how she and Kateri had shown up the day Catskill and I were fighting out of nowhere. I'd absently wondered how they'd known to come when they had, and with Kateri beside me now, I decided to ask.

"How did you and Misty know about the fight I had with Catskill?"

She stopped walking abruptly, and I stumbled. "God warned me. I had a dream the camp was covered in a great darkness, and everyone lay asleep. But then there was an animal

I have never seen before suddenly walking around in our camp." She paused to swallow. "The animal was harmless, in fact, it was helpful. It was carrying a lamp, which brought light into the camp, and we were beginning to reawaken from a slumber. We woke up thirsty, and the foreign animal gave us water." She stopped, like she was searching for the right way to describe her dream to me. "It was as if the whole tribe had fallen asleep and was fine with disappearing into the darkness. However, that strange animal brought a light so bright none of us could ignore it, and water so sweet, we wanted more. But Catskill, the only hunter to rival Saloso, stepped to the animal and tried to tame it. Beating it wildly, the animal was nearly dead when Chief Grey Hawk appeared. She stepped forward but she would not come into the light, only to the edge of darkness."

Kateri shook her head as she held back tears and I understood why. Although Grey Hawk could be a grouch, it was scary to think that someone had the opportunity to come into the light but wouldn't. The light that brought life and water, she willingly stayed away from and that was hurting Kateri more than she cared to mention.

"She told Catskill," Kateri continued, wiping at her tears. "She told him to kill the animal. And just as he raised his spear to kill it, I woke up. I went to Misty right away, and she had a surprisingly similar dream some time ago. She said she was going to find you that day anyway since God had spoken to her about you. But she said it was urgent to find you and Catskill right away."

I stared at the ground, realizing God had protected me when He'd sent Misty and Kateri after me. They had arrived right before things had gotten really bad. "I can't believe this," I whispered.

Kateri nodded. "You are very special and important to this tribe, Cameron. I wonder what it is you will bring us that will awaken us and quench our thirst."

"Hold on, you're saying it like I'm that strange animal."

Her eyes narrowed and she stepped towards me. "You are and you know it. You just don't understand it yet."

"How could I know that?" I snapped. "I came here by accident." She quirked a brow, and I dropped my shoulders. I was supporting the case of a wandering animal coming into their camp.

"You wandered into this camp to bring us light and water."

My gaze fell from hers. I couldn't help but wonder if that was my purpose here. *But how do I bring them light and water?*

Water … the well.

"God often speaks in riddles to us," Kateri said. "However, those riddles can be solved by the power of the Holy Spirit. It is up to us to allow Him to solve the riddles and reveal the meaning behind them. Dreams are riddles. Allow the Spirit to reveal whatever riddle you have hidden in your heart."

I wanted to protest and ask how she'd known I'd been secretly confused about the well dream I'd been having since I was eight, but Kateri was second in line to Priest Misty. I'm sure God had whispered something to her.

"Let us continue," she said, walking away. "So you will not

miss any more time with Saloso."

"Alright," Kateri said as we walked to the top of a hill, "this is where I leave you. Just follow the path down, and you will see Saloso at the end of it." She skirted away before I could say anything more.

Sighing, I took a step forward. "God, let this be what I need it to be. I want to reconnect with You. Please hear me, in Jesus' name."

There was a small dirt path that looked like it'd been used by animals dragging carts. The road was a little lumpy, but the route outlined the path of wheels. Walking down the dirt, I could see small footsteps and the tracks of animal hooves. The footprints could've belonged to anyone, but I knew they belonged to Saloso, or maybe I was just hoping they did. *No, I told myself, Kateri said she's at the bottom, that's all there is to it.*

Glancing up from the path, I stopped walking. There was a field of corn that looked like a sea of green waving and bending in the morning wind. The rustling of the stalks chattered as the wind gave it's morning wave. Splitting the sky from the corn below, the sun rose, greeting the world with its warm rays and vibrant color. A rich red stretched across, fading into pinks and oranges. The moon gave its goodbye in the background, as the sun rose to begin our day.

I realized this was what the sisters meant. This was the beauty they'd been wanting me to see. It was serene watching the sun in all its glory rise to the occasion. It did the same thing every day, but I'd never watched the sunrise. Buildings and the world around me were so consuming, I'd never stopped to look. But standing there before the glistening stalks of corn, I wanted to weep. I understood why someone could reconnect with God or believe in Him when they saw a sight like this. His wonderous artwork, how skillfully He designed the world. We were privy to see an intimate part of the mind of God, something that would easily remind us that the same God who delicately painted the mornings and gave color to the world, is the same God who is our potter. His designs are beautiful, and His plans for His workmanship are intimately fashioned for each one of us. It reminded me that everything would be okay.

I couldn't get my legs moving for a while, but eventually, I began my journey down the dirt path and I found Saloso. She was standing there, letting the wind rush around her, lifting her hair wildly behind her. She wasn't wearing a shawl today. Just a red tunic dress that reached her ankles. But it mimicked Priest Misty's, with slits up the side, giving glimpses of her strong legs. Her tunic had sleeves, unlike Misty's. They were quarter length and there were all kinds of colors roping the end of the garment. Walking forward, I found myself excited to see Saloso. I was happy she was waiting for me; I'd secretly wanted to see her.

"Saloso," I called, jogging the rest of the way down the path to her. She turned around, holding her hair back, and her vibrant blue eyes chilled me. I slowed my pace, just to look at her a little longer. Saloso looked more stunning than I'd ever seen her.

"Good morning, Cameron," she said with a smile.

I grinned foolishly and made my way to her, stopping just a few feet short. "Sorry I kept you waiting."

"Oh, it is no worry, Cameron. I love this place. I could stay here forever."

"It is beautiful," I said, pulling my eyes from hers to look over the land.

"Unfortunately, Outsider, we cannot waste any time. We must begin our work early, as I only have very little time."

I dropped my shoulders and sighed. I knew I was responsible for the new workload she had, so I decided I wouldn't complain. Instead, I forced a smile and said, "I guess I've got to start doing something around here."

"Indeed. Come, let us begin."

We walked into the forest of corn, and Saloso picked up some tools from a bucket tied to a tent pole. "Here." She passed me a flimsy rake.

"What is this?"

"It is a weeding rake. You will use it to rake the ground beside each stalk to ensure there are no weeds growing up. You must rake all the way down an entire row."

I tore my eyes from the rake and stared at the field. "No way, I can't even see the end."

Saloso began to giggle, and then she burst into laughter. "I am just joking, Outsider! There are many in this field. All cover various sections. You will know when you can stop and collect your raking."

"I really believed you for second."

"There is no way any single human can take care of the entire field. We are a tribe, we do it together. Now, try some raking."

Leaning over, I tossed the rake into the ground and dragged it backwards.

"Almost," Saloso said, "but don't be so rough with it. Try easing up on it."

"Got it," I said as I tossed the rake down again and dragged it back—this time in a gentler manner.

"Perfect!" she squealed.

I resisted the urge to smile dumbly and settled for a nod of approval. "Well, what's next?"

"My plan was to take you to the potatoes as well, but the maize always needs the most hands. So, I think this work is suitable for you."

I shrugged. "Is this it? I just do this until the sun goes down?"

She nodded.

"What if I get hungry?"

Saloso smiled and pulled an ear of corn free. "It is full of sweetness." Peeling the corn, she bit into it, then she smiled and extended the piece to me. "Try it! It is very good. We grow our maize all year round, so there is always some ripe ears in the field."

I took the corn and bit it. There was a sweetness to the yellow and brown kernels I'd never tasted before. They were bright and firm, crunching with every bite.

"It's sweet," I said, squinting.

"It is ripe, so it is sweet."

"I didn't know corn could be sweet."

"Have you ever had fresh maize?" she asked.

"No. I usually eat canned corn. Or sometimes I buy the kind from the big display in the store. But there's been a ton of pesticides sprayed on them or whatever else."

"I have never heard of such a thing as a pesticide," she said. "But I am certain that different places grow different kinds of maize—or *corn*, as you and those in the market call it. I believe this is the truth since the maize we raise is sweeter than that in the market."

Passing her the corn, I said, "I never thought about that."

Saloso took a big bite and then goofily covered her mouth. "Do not watch me! The bite was too big, and I am chewing like our paquchas!"

"Paquchas?"

She nodded. "I believe they are Alpacas in your tongue."

"They've got curly hair and long necks with a tight face, right?"

Laughing, she held up a hand as she managed to swallow her corn. "Yes, they do indeed have a tight face, as you say."

We laughed and she extended the ear to me. I ate the rest of it. "Kateri gave me some water if you'd like some," I offered.

"Sure." Saloso took the pouch and enjoyed a few sips before passing it back to me.

When it was my turn, I took a big gulp, but an air bubble got caught in chest. I squeezed my eyes shut and hunched over, holding my chest.

"Ooh! Ooh!" Saloso cried. "Move around, Cameron. If you move, the air might move, too."

I couldn't move though. I stood there holding my chest until the bubble passed and I was finally able to swallow the water. Saloso had moved over to me and was rubbing my back as I struggled to swallow the water and air bubble.

Heaving a great breath, I said, "Sorry, I couldn't move."

She waved a hand. "It is alright. I am just glad you are okay."

I forced a smile onto my face, trying to push past the embarrassment I felt.

"Come on, Cameron, there is much work to be done today, and I will have to leave you soon. But Kateri will return to help you and bring you back to the tribe."

"Right." I pushed the cork back into the water pouch. "You have to leave."

"Do not be sad, Cameron, or you will make me sad."

"Sorry."

She sighed and took my hand. "Do not worry about me. I worked like this before you arrived. I will of course miss our lessons, but it is alright. I still have a duty to this tribe as the next chief, and I must uphold that. And you, my fellow outsider," she squeezed my hand, "you still need to find out what God has in store for you here."

I tightened my grip on her hand. "As you work towards chiefhood, I will work on my relationship with God."

"That sounds like a good plan, Cameron."

Twelve
A New Side

The past three weeks have been grueling. Tending to the plants of the farm were difficult and tiring since the fields were so vast. Covering a whole field took hours. Although you never did it alone, you never saw the others in the field. At some point, you ran into a stalk of maize that had either been picked or raked, and you knew the work from that point forward was finished, and so were you. But despite the back-breaking work, I found myself feeling lonelier than usual. I'd gotten used to Saloso and Kateri always being around, it was a little boring without them.

Kateri came around more often than Saloso, and she was good company, but I was beginning to miss teaching Saloso. The way she always looked starry eyed when she remembered something. Sometimes she'd tell me she was getting goosebumps from learning so much. Her girlish smile and gentleness, it was embarrassing how much I actually missed her. I was seeing her in passing, seeing her following behind

Chief Grey Hawk, or walking beside Priest Misty and Kateri, even occasionally on the arm of Catskill. But she always passed me a saddened nod, or a stiff wave. Her smile didn't glimmer the way it had before, and I wished things could be different.

Kateri was right; if Chief Grey Hawk could not make me leave the tribe, then she would force Saloso into a work life that took all her spare time. Even during mealtime, Saloso sat in a tent away from everyone. Most days Kateri gave me updates on Saloso's training. She'd tell me how bored Saloso was, and she even mentioned a few times that Saloso had asked about me. That was always the best news. Hearing that Saloso wondered about me kept me motivated. I wanted Kateri to tell her that I was doing well, and she didn't have anything to worry about. Although, internally, I was still a little worried about finding the purpose that God had for me here.

I was praying more now that I was alone. I even recited scriptures aloud. The tribe had a weekly service that I went to. I stayed hidden in the back, mostly just listening to their songs of praise and teachings without muttering a word. But as I tended to the fields, I'd recite the scriptures, or remember the messages, and I'd try to imagine the way Reverend Lee would have preached the sermon.

The evening came, and the workday was over. Packing up my rake and clippers, I slung my water pouch over my shoulder and headed home. Tromping through the fields of the sweet corn, I walked to the edge of the field like I did every day, turning back to admire the sunset before returning to the tribe. I inhaled deeply, letting the fresh smell of the earth rush through me. Then I turned on my heels and screamed.

"Did I scare you, Cameron?"

"Yes! You were standing there quietly." I frowned.

"You were looking at the sky and the field. I did not want to interrupt you," Saloso said, slipping a loose lock of hair behind her ear. The gentle action calmed me, and I couldn't help but smile. Getting myself under control again, my eyes finally connected with hers and I felt my heart pick up the pace. The glimmering sun poured over her shoulder, making Saloso gleam in the evening light. Pink and orange and yellow hues skirted all around her, engulfing the beautiful woman before me. I wanted the moment to last forever, for Saloso to never be busy again. But a sudden wind came and blew the whispers of the harsh reality over me. One day I'd have to return home, I'd have to leave this place. And one day, I'd forget Saloso. But I didn't want to.

At least for now, I reasoned within, *I can enjoy this moment with her.*

"You have some free time today?" I asked.

Saloso said, "Not exactly. But Kateri did, and she took over for me at the healers' tent."

"I see." *I've got to thank Kateri.*

"Tomorrow I'm going hunting. You should join me."

"You're going hunting alone?"

She giggled, and the laughter made my heart stir. "I always do. The chief must be the strongest and most skilled. We always hunt alone. But I get two whole days to myself. No one is over my shoulder, no one is telling me what to do, and what not to do." She sighed. "So will you come? It will be an early start just like your workdays."

"I want to, but what about the fields?"

"The field is immense, Cameron, no one will notice a day or so of incomplete work. And since you are only an outsider, no one will come looking for you."

"Ouch." I chuckled.

She laughed. "I always look for you, if that means anything."

"It means a lot to me." The air swirled between us, and her timid smile almost made my knees weak. "We should go, before it gets too dark," I suggested.

With the sunset in our rearview, Saloso and I walked to the path that would lead us back to the tribe. "How was your day?" I asked.

"The chief duties are tiring; however, I have no choice except to endure. But things will change once I am chief."

I raised a brow, although she didn't see it. "Like what?"

"Like the meetings which take hours to discuss topics concerning the safety of our tribe. While we are not entirely in danger, it is down the road from us."

"What kind of danger?" I remembered Priest Misty saying something about Catskill and Chief Grey Hawk letting the tribe suffer if something wasn't done.

"Well, our resources are vast, but our tribe is tired. Our water sources are growing weaker, and the heat we are experiencing at the end of the year has been scorching at least twenty percent of our crops. And although our fields are producing food all year round, that is not good for the land, and it doesn't always recover what was lost." She sighed as we hiked the hill. "Land needs time to recuperate, but we have not given the land a break in nearly nine years. Our plants seem weaker, but with this new heat, we cannot afford to let the land break. What was once a surplus is now stashed away for when we lose crops."

I nodded in silence. Saloso seemed somewhat worried, but not so much about the loss of their crops as she was of the unnatural heat waves they'd been experiencing.

"You know," I said, catching her attention, "the whole world is actually experiencing a rise in temperatures."

She stopped walking, and when I turned to face her, she was shocked. "Are you telling the truth?"

I smiled and patted my chest twice. Her eyes widened and she walked up to me quickly. "The whole world is on fire, then?"

That was a funny way of putting it, but I shrugged and said, "Seems so. We've done what we could, but the world is slowly getting warmer. Glaciers are melting, uncovering old diseases trapped within the frozen layers. Wildfires are starting more often and lasting longer. Water is drying up from lakes and rivers, forcing people to drain dams and water supply around the world."

Saloso was awestruck, but her tightened brows softened, and her crooked smile formed into genuine happiness.

"Why," I stuttered, "W-why are you smiling?"

She looked up at me, her eyes glistening with the fading

119

light. "Because we are not so different after all." Her words took me by surprise, and now I was awestruck. I stared at the wonderful woman, thinking that for her, this was a learning moment, a connecting moment. Saloso found her tribe was experiencing things like the rest of the world, and to her, that made it seem like they weren't so secluded. It made things seem closer, like there really was a need to connect with the rest of the world.

"Come on," I finally said, "let's go before someone comes looking for you."

"I'm going ahead," Saloso said. "I cannot be caught with an outsider who really is not so outside, is he?"

I smiled and stepped into her space. She looked up at me with a nervous expression and I brushed her hair from her face. "No. We're closer than you think."

She blushed, sinking into herself, but not away from the caress of my hand. A cool breeze pulled Saloso's gaze from mine, and I dropped my hand. "Tomorrow morning," she murmured, still looking off at the setting sun, "meet me at the axe post. Where you learned to chop wood."

"I'll be there."

Saloso shyly passed me one more look before turning on her heels to return to the tribe before me. I stood there, letting the wind dance all around me and I sighed loudly. "Cam, what are you doing?" I said to myself, rubbing my hands over my face. "She's Catskill's woman and you're not going to be here forever. Stop it." I was stern with myself. I couldn't afford to get mixed up with Saloso. *I'll go with her tomorrow because I already promised I would, but after that, I won't let myself get caught up with her anymore.* I nodded, and finally left the fields.

The next morning, I sat on the tree stump where we cut firewood and waited for Saloso. The trees waved good morning as I sat there admiring them. The leaves were surprisingly green for how hot it could get. But their thick leaves shaded the ground, keeping it cool and moist. It had been a while since I stopped and admired the world before I got stranded. School, Garrith, Momma, work, everything seemed so much more important when I was there. But being here, all of my problems seemed trivial compared to the beauty of the earth.

Problems with a controlling girlfriend, trying to make my mother proud, and make ends meet, getting good grades while working late nights. It all kept my attention away from anything that wasn't right in front of me. But being here, seeing the green grass, smelling the fresh fruits and vegetables, I promised myself that when I returned home, I would not forget to take in the beauty of the world, and I would not forget where I learned to admire that beauty.

"Good morning, Cameron," Saloso called over my shoulder. She was dressed totally different today. Half of her hair was pulled into a high ponytail, while the rest of the brown waves sat over her shoulders. She looked like a warrior. Resting over her shoulders was an animal pelt of some kind, held in place by a trophy necklace. A large fang sat charmingly against the hide shirt she wore over her brown under-suit.

I couldn't help but notice the animal tail hanging around her waist. It had the colors of a hyena acting as a belt, with small leather bags, and a quiver on her right hip. Wide, toned arms were sleeveless, and her forearms were covered in bracers as well as one of her knees. Each was made of leather that wrapped around her arms with a hard shell on top. The shell had been carved to hold what looked like some type of knife on one arm, and a small rope on the other. Leather boots ran up to her knees and affixed to her shins, over her boots, were more pieces of thick hide and animal fur.

Stumbling on my words, I couldn't manage to say good morning. I didn't expect to see Saloso like this. She was always so gentle but seeing her in all her gear made her look less like a gentle flower, and more like a thorny rose.

The large bow on her back caught my attention, and I finally managed to say, "You're going hunting today?"

A single shoulder bounced as she stood right before me. I couldn't stop staring at the warrior of a woman. There was no doubt in my mind Saloso could kill me with her bare hands if she wanted. Her gentleness was so betraying that I almost felt like she was pretending all this time. But her familiar giggle forced me to accept that a gentle woman was not necessarily a weak woman.

"I told you we are going hunting. Did you forget?" She reached up and tapped on my head, like she was knocking on a door.

I chuckled, rubbing the spot she'd tapped. "Sorry, I just

really wasn't—"

"Expecting me to wear my hunting gear? Did you think I would wear my shawl and dress to hunt?" Through a bit of laughter, she waved me on and said, "Come now, we must get going."

I nodded stiffly as Saloso marched off towards the tribe.

"We will grab our paqucha and we will leave," she announced over her shoulder.

Thirteen
The Huntress

Saloso and I took a donkey with a small cart as we left the village. She rode the donkey while I sat in the cart, reading a book to her. She told me her village didn't have much literature, mostly books she traded for at the market that some traveler had left behind—map guides, sometimes children's books, sometimes there were good books left by a bookworm. Saloso was the only one reading the books no matter what they were. At least, she was *trying* to read them.

Her reading comprehension wasn't great; she'd taught herself very little from a lesson Misty gave her once. The tribal members were mostly taught the language of the tribe and the surrounding languages. But they weren't taught how to read or write. It's not needed when everyone is doing physical labor. The only person good at reading was Priest Misty, since she read the Word of God from the scrolls for the people.

As we rode, I read aloud to Saloso. It was an interesting book about a young woman pretending to be a historical figure. The story follows the journey of the young woman who is gifted with the ability to read while no one else can. She travels the world to share her abilities with others, although many don't want her to.

When I told Saloso what the book was about, she was extremely excited. She'd only made out a few words and hadn't gotten past the first page when she attempted to read it once before. But she liked the cover. She said the woman on the front reminded her of herself. Even though they didn't look the same, she was working hard not to be an outsider, just like Saloso.

"The girl is brave for journeying away from her home to make a better life for her family," Saloso said as she tied the donkey to a tree. We would walk the rest of the way—in the sweltering heat as the sun had risen high—and return to the donkey this evening to find a place to set up camp.

"You think so?" I asked as I pulled a bushel of hay from the cart. I flopped it down in front of Taki, and he began biting at it.

"Yeah," Saloso called as she sat a pail of water beside the donkey. "Leaving your tribe with no definite return, it seems scary."

"You think you'd ever want to leave your tribe? For more than the twelve months?"

She came around the donkey to me and folded her arms. "I am not sure, Cameron. To never see Kateri or Misty again, even Grandmother. I do not know if I could do something like that."

"It's a big decision."

Her eyes flicked up from the grass to meet mine. A part of me was incredibly sad because I knew when I left, I'd probably never see Saloso again. Even though we weren't family in the traditional way, this tribe had become something of a home to me, and every day I remained was another day I struggled with returning home.

"Are we ready to go?" I asked.

"We'll need to bring a few things with us." She hopped onto the stair of the cart and pulled out a long stick and two pails—one of which had a spare change of clothes in it for her.

"Is that everything?"

"Just needed to grab this." She pulled her bow from the cart.

"Are you any good with that?" I teased.

"Just you wait, Outsider, you will see how good I am."

"You seem pretty confident."

"I am," she said, walking beside me into the grassy fields. "I have been hunting for five years now, and I am very good at it."

"Because you had to be."

"Because I am," she corrected. "My responsibility does not make me good. I walk in the same strength and confidence as King David. The same God who protected him against the bears and lions is the same God who protects me."

I admired her faith, but I didn't respond. I really didn't know what to say. People I was around didn't talk like that; they didn't believe like the people of this tribe.

126

As we walked further along, Saloso led me to what looked like the edge of Peru, where the Pacific Ocean sat, and the ground began to turn into mush. There were wide trees sitting on the water banks, while floating grass and moss made the water a thick and vibrant green.

"We are going to start our hunting here."

"Are we going fishing?" I stared down at the filthy water, but Saloso's answer sent a wave of relief over me.

"No," she said as she removed one of her boots, "we are going duck hunting."

"Duck hunting?" I followed her lead and set the pails and stick down to remove my shoes and roll my pants up.

"That is correct, Cameron, we are going to catch some ducks. Teals, specifically."

"Teals? Is that their color?"

She nodded as she removed her knee brace. "On the wings of the male bird, there is a very distinct greenish strip of feathers on their shoulders. It is barely visible when they are resting on the water, but when they are soaring above, the green strip is beautiful."

"I've never heard of a bird like that."

"Then I will show you one today." She smiled and then walked into the filthy green waters. "I will be teaching you."

"Really?" I moved behind her into the waters and immediately, a shock of coolness went up my spine. "This water is freezing, Saloso!"

"Shush or you will send all of our prey away! If you cannot get into the water, surely you cannot become a hunter."

I rolled my eyes, sighing heavily as I stepped back in. Saloso moved slowly through the water, standing still behind tall blades of grass. The quiver on her hip was filled with different colored arrows. I wondered what each one meant as I slowly and quietly made my way to her.

"Saloso," I whispered.

She held her hand up, signaling me to be quiet, then she pulled out an arrow with red feathers attached to the end, notched it to her bow, and pulled back. She was concentrating, focusing. I'd never seen Saloso so serious. Her eyes were lowered, and her jaw was hardened.

Breathing slowly, I watched her chest rise and fall as she stood perfectly still. She may not have been as big as Catskill, but she looked like every bit the strong leader, a real chief. The way her blue eyes shimmered as she took steady breaths, the fang hanging on her necklace reminding any onlookers that this wasn't her first hunting trip.

The long-speckled bow was incredible to look at in her small hands. It was made of what looked like a collection of antlers and wood, while the string was made of some flexible material. Staring at the woman before me, I couldn't help but admire her when, suddenly, she released her arrow.

A flurry of honking erupted from the ducks. Saloso pushed past me and took off towards the west side of the bay. I stood there, dumbly watching as she raced to the side, whipping arrows out and releasing them one behind the other. Each arrow brought down a bird. It yelped and fell from the sky, spinning out of control until it hit the waters.

"That was incredible!" I shouted as she made her way back over to me.

"That was risky," she corrected. "Usually, one does not move from their hiding place to shoot. However, shooting at the birds that are passing is more difficult than standing behind the flock and simply aiming at them. It is almost like they are not moving targets the way they would be as they flew by you."

"Wow," I said, trying to take it all in. "I never knew that."

She smiled. "We will retrieve what we caught, and then we will move along to catch more."

As Saloso went to change out of her wet clothes, I took the pails and stick and headed to the eastern side of the bank where the birds fell from the sky. Although she'd shot them from the west, they landed in the opposite direction since they were flying away. Stepping back into the cold waters, I walked as far as I could before getting my pants wet and found two birds floating in the yucky green waters with arrows sitting out of them. I pulled both in by their arrows, admiring the brownish red feathers on both birds. When I'd gotten them both in the pail, I took them to land to inspect them.

"These are the cinnamon teals I was telling you about," Saloso said.

I looked up from the bucket to find her standing in the dress she'd brought along to change into. It was just a sleeveless off-white tunic that stopped at her knees, she even had all her hair tied up, but I couldn't stop gazing at her. She was totally different from the warrior she had just been, but I didn't mind.

"What?" she said nervously.

I couldn't speak. I dropped my eyes back to the ducks as she explained, "These are two male birds, they are the ones who have the striped, green feathers."

I lifted the wing of one of the birds and immediately understood why the animal got its name. The feathers of its belly resembled the burning red cinnamon color while its eyes were a fire engine red. The beautiful green stripe made the bird quite handsome, and the fluffy black feathers down it's back could make it look intimidating.

"I've never seen a duck like this before."

"I am glad I can teach you today," she said chirpily.

"You taught me a lot, and I am grateful. Thank you, Saloso."

Her cheeks flushed as she grinned widely. "Let us fill the bottom of the pails with grass and water. It will help keep our ducks cool, and then we will put a little dirt on top of them."

"You want me to carry that?" I asked as Saloso lifted her stick with a pail on each side.

"No." She adjusted the stick on her shoulders "I have got it. I would do this alone if you were not here, Outsider."

"Well," I took the heavy stick in my hand, "I am here, so I'll carry it." I lifted the pails off her shoulders with one arm and rested the stick on only one of my shoulders. Saloso stared at me. I gave her a smirk before turning and walking away. I was no Catskill or any of the other tribal members, but I was strong. Standing at six foot three, I was two hundred and thirty pounds of muscle. Well, I wasn't completely muscle, but I've been physically fit my entire life. Before I started working at Golden's System as a junior robotic engineer, I worked at a gym as a physical trainer. We were required to have an average body mass index, and to be physically capable of doing whatever training program we created for clients. Although Catskill was raised with the brute strength of the wildlands, if given a fair chance, I think our fight might've ended differently.

I carried the pails over my shoulder the entire way to the cart without breaking a sweat. Saloso was pleasantly surprised as I caught her passing me girlish glances and giggling to herself. Her secret flattery was cute, and I tried to ignore it while we walked back. When we reached the cart, I loaded it and hooked it back onto Taki while Saloso changed back into her hunting gear. She told me she only changed into her tunic dress to get in the water, because she didn't want the green moss of the waters to stain her hunting clothes.

As I saddled up our donkey with the cart, I tightened the leather straps to be sure the cart wouldn't loosen. Pulling down on the strap, I heard Saloso scream, "Cameron, get into the cart!"

I glanced around to find her. "Salo—"

"Get into the cart!" she bellowed. Her voice seemed more anxious and without a second thought, I let go of the straps and climbed into the cart as quickly as I could.

"Saloso, where are you!?" The donkey began to move,

kicking and stomping and I knew something wasn't right. He was still tied to the tree so he couldn't move. I tried to quiet Taki when a whistling noise ripped through the air, followed by something that sounded like a shovel diving into the earth.

Silence.

"Saloso?" I called, too afraid to get out of the cart.

I heard the bushes move, and Saloso stepped out. My heart dropped in relief, and I clutched my chest. "Can I get out now?"

"Not yet," Saloso said, placing the bow on her back. I watched as she walked up to the cart and leaned down; she pulled the knife from her bracer and slammed it into the grass. "There," she said, after cutting into the grass. She lifted the head of a snake. "One bite from this guy and you will never breathe again. Highly poisonous and erratic. They attack randomly, and today you were the target, Outsider."

I stared at the snake's head, trying not to vomit from disgust and fear. Blood dripped down Saloso's arm, and it didn't seem to bother her.

Examining the head, she said, "We usually douse our arrows and spearheads in the Bothrop's venom, but they are dangerous to fight. I would rather fight a jaguar than one of these." She knelt to study the rest of the body. "Her body will make good soup, and her skin will be used. I shall use her venom as well, to apply to new arrows."

"Are the red feathers your venomous arrows?"

She shook her head. "My red feathered arrows are nonpoisonous. You would not want to eat something that has been poisoned."

"That makes sense," I said, finally climbing from the cart.

She pulled a green feathered arrow from her quiver and held it out to me. "These are my poisonous arrows. I use these to defend myself."

"Against what?"

"The forest of Peru can be quite scary."

I believed her.

"I have an extra pail in the cart, can you get that for me?"

"You're seriously taking this snake?" I asked, pulling the pail out of the cart.

"Come, I will show you what to make of this."

I knelt beside Saloso; she pulled out a small jar from one of her pouches and opened it before taking the head of the snake in her hand. Jabbing the knife into it, she cut down the head, maneuvering her knife with steady hands. "I will carve out the gland and put it into the jar."

"The gland? Does that hold the venom?"

"Correct, Outsider."

Blood oozed from the creature as she cut away at tendons and muscles to remove the venom pouch.

"Doesn't this scare you? I mean, what if you accidentally cut the gland?"

"That is why only the best hunters extract them," she replied confidently. Slipping the edge of her knife beneath the gland, she lifted it to see if it was still connected. "Alright. I will now transfer the gland into the jar. Watch closely." She smiled. I couldn't even force a smile onto my face. I stared as she turned the snake's head upside down, letting the gland dangle from the bleeding head. Lowering it into the jar, she cut the bit of the gland still attached to the snake's head. With a disgusting flop, it fell into the jar, and she tossed the head away.

Saloso stabbed her knife into the ground and with bloody hands, pulled a piece of hide from a pouch on her leg. I watched as she placed the animal skin over the jar and secured it with the string from her bracer.

She lifted the jar. "Now we have ourselves some valuable venom. I will take it right to Killa, he will be able to get the venom out and into our stash. This is a very good finding, surely Chief Grey Hawk will look past your disappearance for this."

"Wait a second!" I shot to my feet. "You said no one would notice me gone!"

She came around the cart grinning and drying her hands on a thin rag.

"You can't be serious," I whined. I wiped the sweat from my head, feeling the heat of worry thrashing all over me.

Saloso stepped forward and placed a hand on my chest. "You will give yourself a heart attack if you do not calm down, Outsider. Everything will be fine."

My breathing began to slow, and I watched as her small hand retracted from chest, but I caught it before it fell to her side. I don't know why I caught her hand, but I was holding it now, and she was only blinking up at me.

"Sorry." I released her hand and she stared at it.

"My heart felt so unsettled when you held my hand."

"Oh." I paused. "I won't—"

"Will you hold it again?"

I blinked. "What?"

"Will you hold my hand again?" She extended it to me, and I stared at it for a second before taking her delicate hand in mine.

"What do you feel now?"

"I cannot describe it, but I have never felt like this before."

If I was honest, I had never felt like this before, either. These feelings had been mimicked by Garrith. But it never quite felt this real.

"Do you feel the same?"

My mouth suddenly felt dry. "I think so."

Fourteen
The One Who Guides the Lost

I finally let her hand go, and we spent the rest of the time in a crying silence. Saloso dismembered the snake, cutting it up and passing the pieces of the disgusting body to me. I was squeamish the very first time I watched an animal get butchered here, however, after spending so much time here, it didn't seem to bother me as much anymore. I placed the pieces into the pail, filling as much as we could. Its thick body felt like one scaley muscle, and it was slippery, covered in blood. I tried to find things to say as Saloso continued to pass pieces of the snake to me, then my hand brushed hers as she passed another piece.

"Sorry," I muttered, pulling away.

She cleared her throat. "It is fine."

I nodded awkwardly, taking the piece from her to toss into the bucket. "The bucket is pretty full now, we can probably leave the rest of it, right?"

"I guess you are right, Outsider." She looked at me, and my

heart hammered wildly in my chest. I couldn't get it to stop as our eyes connected, but I wasn't sure I wanted it to. I liked the way Saloso made me feel, it was new and refreshing. The way cold water feels on your skin beneath the hot sun, or the way the gentle smell of vanilla suddenly makes you feel the joy of Christmas, in and out of season. I didn't know what to call what I felt, but it was apparent that Saloso felt it, too.

After packing up, we rode Taki to a better spot for dinner and to camp out for the night. I thought about Saloso the entire time. The way she was different, an outsider within her own family. She always thought our worlds were so different but, unfortunately, they weren't. Being only partially African American made me an outsider at home. Being poor made me an outsider at school. Being from the United States made me an outsider to this tribe. But I'd learned that being an outsider actually made you an insider to God.

We are called to be Holy and set apart as Christians. We aren't supposed to be like everyone else, the difference between a Believer and nonbeliever was supposed to be painfully obvious. However, we conform because we're afraid to be different. We are afraid to have opposing views. We are afraid to be divided but, of course, we're not better than the master, Jesus. And He came to divide. He came to separate the sheep and goats, the wheat from the weeds. Slowly, being in Peru, I'm finally understanding that being a Christian, being different, is okay. My difference means I have a purpose and to fulfill it, I need to be separate from everyone who's the same.

How can anyone lead someone to change if everyone is a follower?

Those words resonated in me as I rode along, reflecting. Reverend Lee told me that before I started college. It was the day I left for Illinois. The entire church came out to the airport to send me off, and after a few teary 'see you soons,' I hugged Reverend. She pulled me tight and she whispered those words to me. Now, as I've been here in Peru, I believe I've come to understand those words. And I plan to live by them.

We arrived at an open field of grass with a few trees. Tying Taki to one, Saloso said to me, "Today, I will make cuyes and potatoes over the fire."

"What exactly are cuyes? What do they look like?" I remembered we'd eaten them before. I thought they were large rats, but Kateri seemed so baffled by it, I figured it must've been something.

"They are furry with many different colors. Some brown, some black and white, they are very cute critters." She pulled the covering off a small cage, and I gasped at the sleeping critters.

"Those are guinea pigs!"

She looked at the cage, and then at me. "Is that what they are called in your tongue?"

"Yes," I snapped, "they're pets."

"A pet? Like the domesticated companion?"

"Yes!"

She blinked at me, and then back at the guinea pigs. "Who would want a critter as a pet?"

I stared at her.

"If you would like one of these as a companion, I will give you one. They are asleep, on heavy medicine. We feed them certain leaves on our travels that will make them sleep, so they will not die of starvation or squeal and scare the prey away." I watched as she struggled with the cage for a second before taking it from her. I couldn't be angry at her, considering this was their way of life. But it did make me feel uneasy.

"I'm sorry I yelled at you," I said, setting the cage in the grass. "I was just surprised."

She knelt and opened the cage. "There are many differences between us, are there not?"

"I don't think so."

"Why not?"

"Well, we're both outsiders." I cringed internally, realizing how corny that sounded. "So we clearly are the same in some sense."

"How can you say that?" She spoke so quietly it was hard to hear her. I stared at her, wondering what was going on in her head. When she noticed my silence, her small hand froze over the guinea pig. "I ... I just meant that," she paused, looking up at me. "Never mind, you could never understand." She closed the cage and stood, but I grabbed her arm before she walked away.

"I'm trying to understand. I want to understand. But I can't if you don't tell me."

Her eyes roved over me before flitting back to mine. Standing so close, I could see her perfect skin and beautiful lashes, a soft, plump lip she chewed before she said, "You are only an outsider here with a home far away. But I am an outsider here with nowhere to go. The only thing I can do is try to be accepted, try to prove that I am worthy of chiefhood, worthy to lead the tribe." She stared at the ground, searching it as if it would respond. Saloso was right. I was foreign in a place that I didn't belong. But the Sand Ribbon was Saloso's home—where she belonged, and yet, she was not wanted here.

When I return home, my mother would welcome me, and classes would begin again. It would be like I'd never left. But Saloso would never get away from here, and she wasn't just trying to prove she should be the next chief, despite what she said. She was trying to prove that she belonged here, that she was part of this tribe as much as anyone else. I ached for her as I watched her shoulders begin to tremble.

"Sunstar," I called. Her head snapped up, dark brows furrowed and lips sunken into a frown. But her eyes were inquiring, bewildered while a mist rolled over them. "Sunstar," I repeated, assuring her she'd heard me correctly. "You belong here. No one can take the chiefhood from you, even if they think you don't deserve it. It's in your blood. You are meant to be chief, no matter what."

A trembling mouth opened to ask, "My name ... where did you get my name from?"

I stood finally, slipping my hand down her arm to take her small hands in mine. "Kateri told me. She said Chief Grey Hawk wanted to take the chiefhood from you because of the choices your mother made. She blamed your mother." I squeezed her hands. "And when your mother left, she blamed you. But she never once blamed her son or even blamed herself. But you're not Saloso, the cry of the wild goose." Her tears had begun to flow and, slowly, I reached out and wiped at one. I took a deep breath, leaned forward, and pressed my head against her forehead. "You are Sunstar de Achille, heir to the chiefhood of the Sand Ribbon Tribe, daughter of Chief Nunca de Achille, and descendant of Grande Chief Zasca. This is your calling, Sunstar, this is who you are. Not Saloso, no matter what anyone tells you."

Weeping loudly, she hiccupped as her hands trembled in mine. "Saloso means the cry of the wild goose." She sniffled. "But Sunstar was given to me by God. I am the one who will be like the sun for this tribe. The sun rises to give light to our people and awaken them each day. But the stars are to be a guide home for the ones who are lost or forgotten. That is the focus of my chiefhood, and that is who I will become."

"No." I shook my head. "That is who you already are. You just didn't know it."

She looked up from the ground, eyes still watery, and I patted my chest twice. Her eyes widened, and she released a small chuckle. "Thank you, Cameron."

I smiled at my name as I let her hands go and took a step back. "You're welcome, Sunstar."

"You have helped me understand my purpose here," she poked me in the chest, "yet you still have not found your own purpose."

"I'm sure I'll figure it out soon. The only clue I've got is a dream I keep having. I'm hoping I can someday make sense of it."

"A dream?" she asked.

"Yeah, a dream about me reaching a well and filling asking hands with water, or something like that. But I'm looking for the *living* water."

She raised a brow and blinked at me for a moment. "You don't know what the living water is?"

"Yeah, kind of."

"The living water is the Holy Spirit."

I nodded. "Okay, but why does God keep showing me a dream where I'm at a well?"

"Because a well represents life, and clearly your job is to give life to others."

"What are you talking about?" I chuckled.

Sunstar folded her arms and said, "God just used you to give me life. I just found purpose again in who I am, it is like you watered a drying part of me."

"You're kidding me," I said, placing a hand on my head. "There's no way this is the right interpretation."

Saloso shrugged. "I'm no healer, but I do know God. If you do not believe me, when we return, take some time to go see Misty or even Kateri. They will help you understand the dream."

I stared blankly at her, wondering if this could be the truth. Something so simple could be what I was overlooking all along.

"Cameron, do not look so shocked. We cannot confirm my interpretation until you have spoken to Misty. For now, we should enjoy our meal."

I swallowed and took a deep breath. "You're right, I shouldn't try to overthink this."

Sunstar grabbed my hand. "Come, Cameron, let us prepare our meal now."

Fifteen
The Way of the Heart

"So, what's going to happen to me when we return?"

I'd finished reading to Sunstar earlier when we first started our return to the tribe. She was pleased with the ending of the story. Turns out, the young woman pretends to be someone else until she can no longer do it. And when she finally accepts herself, that is when she becomes very well-known and produces work that is pleasing to God. It was a big lesson for Sunstar, accepting who she is first, before the tribe can accept her. She was silent for a long time after I finished the story. Her distraught eyes wandered all over while she rode Taki back to the tribe. After a few hours, we were close to home, and we decided we wanted to spend the rest of our time walking beside each other.

"Well," Sunstar said, leaning against me as I held the reins of Taki. His heavy hooves were crushing the ground beside us as he pulled our cart full of supplies. "It is not you who they will punish. It is me."

"Why won't they punish me?"

She didn't respond.

I stopped abruptly. "Sunstar, tell me the truth. What is going on?"

Her eyes avoided mine for a moment before flitting up to see me. "No one can go hunting with the chief, especially not an outsider. Solo hunting is a sign that you are strong enough to provide for the tribe alone."

My heart sank as anger swirled within me. "I never would've gone if I had known," I said, pulling my hand from hers.

"It was not about them!" she shouted behind me. "It was about me. *I* wanted you to go. *I* wanted to walk with you." She paused. "I want to be with you, Cameron, even though I know it is wrong for a chief and an outsider to be together."

I turned. Sunstar was standing perfectly still, avoiding my gaze. She'd struggled so much, and all I'd ever done was bring her more pain, more struggle. "Sunstar," I said. "I'm sorry. I never meant to bring so much pain to you. When we return, I'll keep my distance."

Grabbing Taki's reins, we began walking again, but Sunstar didn't move. I wanted to turn back, but I knew I shouldn't.

"You are just like them." Her words were the coldest I'd ever heard. Sunstar was normally bouncy and warm, but her voice was jarring and empty now. "You do not listen to me. You do not care about the way I feel. I guess I was wrong about you." She chuckled and then sniffled. "I guess 'outsider' is not a fitting name for someone who is so similar to the people here.

You were right, Cameron." I heard her footsteps approaching before she walked by. "Our worlds are exactly alike."

Without notice, I grabbed Sunstar's arm, surprising myself and her, but I didn't let it show. I stared down at the dry ground, and I heard her murmur, "Get off of me, Cameron." But I didn't let go. I held her a little longer, letting her struggle in my grip before she shrieked, "Let go of me!"

"No!" I snapped. My eyes lifted to hers and I said it again, quieter this time, "No ... I will not let you go. I don't want to. But I have to if I want to protect you." I released her wrist, and she stumbled, never taking her eyes off me. The sweltering sun continued to beat down on us in our silence.

"Cameron," she said softly. "I don't want to be protected. I am strong enough to protect myself. I want to be—"

Suddenly a loud explosion went off somewhere nearby.

"What was that?" Sunstar turned away from me.

"I have no idea," I said, stepping beside her. She slipped her hand into mine, but the feelings didn't register before another explosion happened, and black smoke rose from the trees.

"That ... that is our home." Sunstar stepped forward without thinking, but I pulled her back.

"Listen to me, that can be anywhere. That smoke may not be from—"

"Anyone who comes out this far is a visitor. We are the only ones who live in this area." She ripped her hand from mine and took off in a sprint.

"Sunstar! Sunstar!" But she didn't slow down. I yanked on

Taki, pulling him along to move faster. We weren't far from the camp, and I knew I'd never make it pulling the donkey. His cart was too heavy to run with, and he'd need to walk to make sure everything arrived safely. But if I didn't go help, there might not be much to arrive back to.

"Sorry, Taki, we'll come back for you," I said as I pulled him over to a shaded tree. I dragged hay and a pail of water from the cart as quickly as I could before tying him down and taking off towards the tribe.

When I arrived, Sunstar was standing in awe of the scene before her. Someone had invaded the tribe, and the whole place was on fire. The huts were crumbling into dust as fire ate away at them, and the sky had suddenly darkened from all the smoke. The women grabbed children, the men fled to the hunting tent. There was one man lying down, grabbing at his leg. It was bleeding and I realized he must've gotten caught up in the explosion.

A popping noise went off and there were crippling cries rustling through the crowd. Sunstar jumped from the noise and took a step back like she wanted to run.

"We've got to move, Sunstar! Come on!" I shouted, grabbing her arm. But she didn't budge. Her wide eyes stared ahead as rivers threatened to fall from her eyes.

"What was that?" she whispered, but before I could answer, three more loud popping noises went off, and then an explosion erupted.

I froze as the world hummed before me, and the popping noises finally registered... They were gunshots. Sunstar said they were the only people in this area, and that was true. I didn't know how far away civilization was from here, but I knew it was far. The only people who would be here were tourists, however ... this land wasn't on any tourist map in the world because, technically speaking, it didn't exist.

No one knew there was a tribe here, and the only people who might've found out would be anyone who came looking for something ... or someone ...

Someone had finally found me.

Shaking my head, I grabbed Sunstar's hand. "Come on! We've got to get to safety!" I didn't wait for her reply before I ran off. I pulled her along by the hand until she got her feet under her and pumped her legs beside me.

No, I thought. *Not now. Not like this.*

Why had they come for me? Maybe they hadn't. Maybe this was an honest attack. But in all these years no one had attacked these people, so why now? *God ... please. Spare them, spare me. Jesus...*

Despite how much I'd been wanting to go home, now that I had an opportunity to return, I didn't know if I wanted it. There were still so many mysteries I needed to solve, and Sunstar, I didn't want to leave her. I wasn't ready to leave her.

I couldn't focus as I ran through the burning camp when another small explosion happened right in front of Sunstar and I, sending us hurling to the ground. I held my head as I sat up, dazed and a ringing in my ears. Everything blurred, and I could see figures moving forward. Without a second thought, I grabbed a drowsy Sunstar by the arm and nearly dragged her through the tribe. Stumbling, I tripped as my vision cleared, and I made it to Kateri's healing tent. Falling inside, Saloso hit the ground, and I dropped to my hands and knees beside her.

"We have to do something," she said, shaking her head. "We have to find the chief before they get to her, and we have to fight back." She looked over at me and the fear from before began to melt away as she tried to regain her nerves. Shakily, she moved to peek outside the tent. She was a little disheveled from the explosion, and a little nervous, however, I could see her returning to her normal self again. She almost looked like the fearless woman I'd just hunted with.

Another shot went off, and we both jumped at the loud sound. There were cries lingering through the tribe as everyone rushed away.

"Sunstar," I said weakly.

She was peeking out the tent. "There are people here. Outsiders I've never seen before. Dressed in all black with all kinds of things hooked to them."

"Sunstar," I said again, even weaker than before, but she still didn't hear me.

"I need to find a weapon. Anything—"

"Sunstar!" I snapped.

She jumped. Blue eyes stretched all the way open as she looked me over. I dropped my head, and tears rolled down my cheeks, slipping off my nose onto the ground. "They've come for me."

She was silent.

"Sunstar, they've come for me. I have to return home."

"Attention!" boomed a loud voice outside the tent. Whoever was speaking was using a megaphone. "We are looking for Cameron Frierson! Bring him out right now or we will burn this place to the—" a wheezing noise erupted from the megaphone. My eyes darted around the ground as I listened. Thundering steps seemed to make the ground tremble as a horde of Sand Ribbon men called cadence and ran at the intruders.

"We will not let you burn our home!" The voice belonged to Catskill.

I scrambled to peek out the tent's pelt door. There was a group of men standing in all black, aiming guns at the thundering tribal men running towards them.

"We don't want to hurt you! Please!" one of the armed men called, but the Sand Ribbon warriors fearlessly approached.

There was a man lying down in front of the group of intruders with a spear sticking out his chest. Someone sat beside him, pressing their fingers into his neck, and looking fearfully at the moving tribe. Another man in the frontline held a trembling gun, pleading with Catskill's group not to come any closer. But as reckless as Catskill had always been, he charged anyway. It was only a fraction of a second, but a tall man dressed in the same uniform as the others with gadgets and ammo on his vest stepped forward and fired a shot at the Sand Ribbon warriors.

Saloso screamed beside me, covering her mouth and dropping to her knees. It wasn't Catskill who'd been shot, but a heavy man dropped beside the leader. Everyone froze, staring at the man with a bullet lodged in his head.

"Ignorance at its finest," the taller man complained.
"They've never even seen a gun before. But they charged anyway."

That's not ignorance, I ground my teeth together. Outraged. *It's bravery.*

Everyone crowded around the dead man, staring at his head.

"We don't want to hurt anyone," the man with the trembling gun finally spoke up. "We just want to take Cameron home."

I backed away from the pelt and shook my head.

"What is wrong?" Saloso whispered.

"I have to leave."

"You can't leave!" she argued.

"Sunstar, I have to."

"Take authority, will you? These savages know nothing," the pesky voice of the tall man who'd tried to kill Catskill spoke. In another breath, he yelled, "Get on the ground!"

I could hear people shuffling around outside as I knelt and took Sunstar's hands in mine.

"We're looking for Cameron Frierson!" the man yelled again. "We know you've been holding him hostage! Give him to us and we'll leave peacefully."

"Saloso, they've got guns." I squeezed her hands. Tears swelled in her eyes, and I could hardly take it. But I wanted to keep Saloso safe, even if that meant leaving. I knew this day would come, I had just begun to hope it wouldn't be so soon, or so brutal.

"I've got to go out there or they'll kill everyone."

"No!" Saloso shook her head, tears spilling. "Don't go out there! Catskill and the others—"

"Have primitive weapons, Saloso! If I don't go out there, they'll kill everyone and you, too. I can't lose you." I cupped her face. The words erupted from me faster than expected, leaving only the taste of nervousness behind in my mouth.

Sunstar's eyes widened. "Please," she whispered. "I want you to stay."

I pulled her into my chest as the shouting continued outside. I heard Catskill scream bitterly, "You killed my brother! My kin! My family!" The words were full of so much hurt, I knew if I stayed any longer, he'd begin a war he could not win.

"Listen to me," I said, pulling Sunstar off me. I clutched her shoulders with extended arms to stare at her once more. "I'm sorry I brought all this trouble to your tribe. I never meant to do that. And I'm sorry I have to return. I wish I didn't, but I do now. And they're going to want a story, Saloso. They're going to want to make it look like you guys kept me here against my will. But I will do everything I can to paint a better picture of you—"

"You think I care about that!" Saloso cried.

"Get down or I will shoot you where you stand!" the man screamed over Catskill's voice. I glanced over my shoulder to see Catskill through an opening in the pelt door. He was raising his bow and taking aim. Nerves jittered up my spine and I thought my eyes fell out their sockets.

"I don't care," Saloso whimpered, and I looked back at her, nervous and ready to panic.

Please God, I cried in my heart, *help me.*

"Sunstar, I have to go, but please," I paused, "don't forget about me."

I pulled her into my chest once more, feeling her gentle embrace. I longed to stay there with her in my arms, but I was so afraid that Catskill would engage in an all-out shootout, despite how unequipped and outnumbered the tribe was.

"Cameron," she whispered. "I ... I will never forget you."

The pain of never seeing her again hit me hard. Her words made things so final, so permanent, and I didn't want things to end but I had no choice. I leaned down and kissed her.

When one of the men hollered another order, giving Catskill a final warning, I yanked away from Saloso and left the tent without looking back.

I threw my hands in the air and screamed, "Please stop! Wait!"

The men holding guns all froze as I walked through Catskill's men who'd taken aim with him. They were all holding spears while further back, out of view of the gunmen, women archers took aim. Everyone else from the tribe was hidden somewhere or lying flat on the ground with their faces in the dirt.

As I pushed my way forward, I glanced over and saw Kateri peeking out of a tent with Misty. I was certain Grey Hawk was safe at the sight of them. Kateri gave me a weak smile, and

Misty nodded. I made it to the front where Catskill was aiming a bow at the front gunman.

"Are you Cameron Frierson?"

"Yes," I said. "Can you lower your weapons? These people are not hostile, and you have guns verses their arrows! Please," I begged.

The man in front eyed me for a moment before lowering his gun. I exhaled heavily, passing a look to Catskill. He blinked at me, still frowning.

"Just lower the bow." As I looked closer at him, I realized tears were streaming down Catskill's face. I glanced over at the man on the ground beside him, a bullet stuffed in the center of his head. "Catskill," I said, "please. These people will kill everyone in this tribe, truly erasing you from history."

"I do not care to be remembered. I care to avenge my brethren."

"You'll never get the chance, because before you can release that arrow, an ounce of pressure will send a bullet into your head."

"But they will die with me."

"You will never see it." I was almost pleading now, but those words seemed to penetrate the hurting man. With trembling hands, and a tightly locked jaw, he lowered his bow, and the rest of the men followed.

"Cameron," I looked back at the group of men, the weak leader was standing there with a ski mask on. "We are here to rescue you. We need you to come with us now."

"Who sent you? How did you find me?" I asked.

154

"Taylor Security Services was able to find your last location, and Garrith Washington gave us vital information about your trip. All other details of our findings can be relayed later, for now, we need you to come with us. If you refuse, we are ordered to burn the entire camp down." Gasps ensued, and Grey Hawk shouted from somewhere behind me, "You cannot do such a thing!"

I whirled around to find her, but Catskill and the others were standing in my way. Begrudgingly, I turned back to the men from my father's company.

"We will burn this place, making it nothing but a shadow and memory of life here, if Cameron doesn't come with us. We are to *utterly* wipe you out, so that not even the soil remembers you," the tall man was speaking now and the boiling anger I'd been trying to hold in was nearly spilling out.

"Alright," I said hotly, "that's enough." I stared at the man, feeling helpless and angry. My father sent people here to rescue me, but I knew it was all a publicity stunt. *He's using me, and he's given me no choice but to accept his help.*

"Make your choice, Cameron," the man said to me.

"I'll go. I have nothing with me, so I'm free to go like this. But only if you promise to never set foot on this land again. Not you, or any associates of my father. This tribe stays forgotten," I demanded.

The man looked around through his ski mask and then back at me. "You have my word."

I nodded. I've never had a single conversation with my father, and now I was being rescued by him.

155

"It's time to go," the man in front said. "Let's head out." He pressed his finger to his ear and said, "Target retrieved. We are coming home."

I glanced over my shoulder as I followed the man out of the tribe. Kateri was crying and waving, Misty was standing there, strong-willed and grateful.

I stumbled forward, tripping over a rock as I searched the crowd of onlookers.

"Keep your eyes forward or you'll fall," a man called beside me.

"Right," I said. But I couldn't.

I looked back once more, desperately searching … and there she was. Sunstar was standing in front of Catskill with tears streaming down her cheeks. Fire ate away at the huts and tents, casting an orange hue around her. She sniffled as she watched me leave.

In my heart, I whispered solemnly, *Goodbye, Sunstar.*

Part II

Sixteen
I AM LOST

Garrith and I started seeing each other again. It was Garrith and my mother who started filing police reports when I'd gone missing. Garrith told me she figured I'd gone on the trip to Peru alone to clear my head—not that I was actually breaking up with her—and she waited for me to return. But I never did. She noticed I wasn't answering my door and got suspicious after a few days. When she couldn't take it any longer, she went to my job, but they hadn't seen me, either. That was when she called Momma, and Momma called the police.

Initially, the police weren't too invested. My mother told me they didn't want to file a missing person's report because college kids ran off all the time and then reappeared when they felt like it. Garrith wasn't taking 'No' for an answer. She went to the chairman of the school and told them it wasn't just me who was missing, the entire group had dropped off the radar. Fourteen American students from a prestigious university going missing on a Christian missionary trip in Peru was suspicious enough to make the chairman sweat.

The hotel had only contacted the school once, telling them our group hadn't checked out and that they hadn't seen us since day two. The university decided to hold off on calling the police right away because they'd been trying to get in contact with Lydia. UOW didn't want to bear the shame of losing so many students, so they tried their hardest to do things quietly until the police got involved. But the police weren't moving fast enough for Momma and Garrith.

Left with no other choice, my mother reached out to the only man who could pull together a group of military-trained, private investigators.

"John Taylor." My father extended his badly tanned hand to me.

I frowned and looked up at his green eyes. They were just like mine, and I hated that.

"Okay," he said, slowly retracting his hand. "I see this is going to be harder than I thought."

I didn't respond because I didn't even know why I was here. Momma and Garrith were suddenly friends—they'd ganged up on me and made me go to a stupid meeting with my jerk of a father.

"Listen, Cam—"

"Cameron," I corrected.

He exhaled and said flatly, "Cameron, listen, I know we got off on a bad foot—"

"When? Because, as far as I can remember, we never really had a foot to start on."

"You've got your mother's sass." He shook his head.

"I've gotten everything from my mother since she was the only one around."

Standing behind his desk, John leaned over and splayed his hands on the polished wood. His finely pressed blue suit wrinkled in the shoulders as he bunched them and said, "You have no idea what you're talking about."

"You sure? Because—news flash, John—you were never there! How could I not know what I'm talking about? You never had to struggle or watch my mother work herself to the bone just for pay that barely kept food on the table." I glanced down at the pictures on his desk. "While you enjoyed a very polished life."

My eyes lingered on a photo of my father and his family. A blonde woman holding a blonde-haired baby boy with a daughter who had sandy blonde hair and blue eyes like her mother. There was a golden retriever with a red collar sitting beside the family, holding its leash in its mouth. They looked perfect as they stood in front of a grand stairwell, undoubtedly in their own house.

"What a beautiful family," I mumbled, still staring at the picture. I glanced over to another one on his desk. It was of his son a little older, holding a bat; and there was another picture of him and his wife at a Christmas party, smiling widely. As I looked around, I realized my father loved his family. In another frame on a file cabinet behind him was a picture of him holding his daughter in the air above his head while the picture beside that featured him kissing his wife's pregnant

160

belly. There were notes from his children lying all around his office.

Christmas, birthdays, New Year's, all kinds of celebrations that I didn't get. Most of my Christmases I was just happy we had food. My birthdays were just as bland; Momma would come home so late, I'd be too tired to celebrate. She'd bring home a cupcake or some kind of sweet she could find. But my father's children, they wanted for nothing. They played sports, they wasted cakes on birthdays—smashing them into their own faces or giving slices to the dumb dog. Their smiles were real and free of worry. Like they'd grown up in a fairy tale. Meanwhile, I—John's very first son—was completely forgotten. I had been erased, as if I were a mistake.

My father reached forward and pushed the frames face-down onto his desk. "I don't know what you want me to say," he said. "I mean, I spent money rescuing you."

"I'm sorry you had to spend a little money to rescue your own son." I chuckled mirthlessly. "That's what families do. That's what fathers do; they rescue their children." I paused and glanced at the pictures behind him. "Well, they rescue the children they care about."

"Oh, cut it out, Cameron. I'm tired of this sob story. What do you want me to do?"

"I'd like you to apologize and stop treating me like a charity project! Why am I even here?"

"Because I wanted to see you."

I stared at his perfect face. Dusty blonde hair was neatly trimmed, his jaw was free of hair, with perfectly manicured brows. He was a stunning man; I see why Momma liked him. But despite his looks, he was worth nothing internally.

"Your kindness is never free," I muttered. "Why did you agree to help my mother without taking something from her?"

"I have never taken anything from your mother."

"Just her life! And maybe I should applaud you because you've never *given* her anything, either!"

John snatched the red stress ball from his desk and squeezed it hard. "Are you done with the theatrics?"

I pulled my bag onto my shoulder and stood to leave. "Sorry to waste your time, Mr. Taylor."

"Where do you think you're going?" he asked, abruptly standing.

"I'm going home."

"Wait, Cameron," John called as I crossed his lush blue and white carpeted floor.

"What?"

I heard his soft steps behind me and turned to face him, shocked to find that he was a little taller than me. This was the first time I'd ever really seen my father up close. When I'd first returned from Peru, he wasn't there to welcome me home. He'd only come to introduce himself once at my apartment. Momma had let him in against my wishes. Since then, he's been asking me to meet him every day.

"I want to offer you a job here," he said.

"No." I turned to open the door, but he belted, "Wait! Just wait!"

My shoulders dropped as I sighed and turned to him again.

"When your mother asked me to help look for you, it was the first time I'd heard from her since she was pregnant with you. I knew it was serious because, well," he looked away. "Anyways, I agreed. And I got to take a look at your school records, just trying to see what kind of person you are." He nodded. "You're a smart kid. You know your stuff. Breaking down the computer for the laparoscope, and changing the movement of the arms, while increasing the scope visibility, that's pretty good."

"You looked over my prototype?" I asked, frowning. It was something I'd started working on as my final project for my masters. Before I left for school, Momma had needed a hysterectomy, and the robotic surgery didn't go exactly right. So, I'd been researching ways to upgrade the laparoscope used in robotic hysterectomies to help improve the functionality of the machine.

"I had to take a look. And you are exactly what our company needs. A breath of fresh air, new ideas." He slipped a hand into his pocket. "Your design is golden. Do you know how fast I could sell that?"

"I don't care. Mom and I have never lived off you, and we're not starting today. Thanks, but I'm good. Anything else, John?"

Eyes narrowing, he nodded and said, "Just think about it, and if you change your mind, you know where to find me."

"Funny how easy it is to find you now when you need me." I opened the door and left his office.

That conversation was two years ago, only a few months after I returned from Peru. In case you were wondering, I ended up taking that job my father offered. It wasn't for the money—I did it because my mother insisted. Even though I didn't mind pleasing her, I decided I wasn't taking the job without stipulations.

My name had to be on the patent, and I wanted to pick the team I worked with. My father gave me full control of everything, even had a small lab built on the Taylor Robotics grounds. I finished my masters, and even got a little fame for being the sole survivor of the bus crash in Peru. For the last few years, I've been appearing on talk shows, I started an organization for finding lost students, and I even got a public apology from the police chief for not taking my missing person's case seriously.

I was assigned personal security and an agent, and with my new job, I was basically given access to every research lab Taylor Robotics has ties with. I became important to the world, even to Garrith. But I never told a single soul how I survived in Peru, and my father's security detail who rescued me were sworn to secrecy. It was part of the contract I'd signed when I began working for Taylor Robotics. It was my very first condition before I began working.

I still think of Saloso every day. I miss her, Kateri, Misty, even grumpy Chief Grey Hawk. I want to go back there. I want to see Saloso again, but it's better if I'm here. I'd brought too much pain to their small tribe, and I wanted to forget them.

But I couldn't. They really had become like family, and Saloso
… I think I'd fallen for her.

"Cameron?" Garrith called, making me lose my train of
thought.

"In here," I called back.

She rounded the corner of my penthouse. I enjoyed the
place I'd stayed at while attending UOW, but this place was
even better. Keeping the staircase in the middle, and big
windows all around, my new place made my old one look like
a dollhouse. There was a pool just outside my window with a
terrace that offered the best panorama view of the city. The
gourmet chef's kitchen had an incredible number of topnotch
appliances, and my chef worked every day from sunrise to
sunset—on-call for every little craving at almost every hour. I
had a cleaning crew that came in once a week to do a deep
clean and sanitation, while someone from the three-man crew
was at my place daily to take care of small messes.

I was living a cushiony life to say the least, and it helped
crowd out the screaming thoughts of Saloso every day.

"Cammy, are you getting ready?"

"Yeah," I nodded as I sat on a leather ottoman in my
dressing room. Garrith was always over now. At my old place,
she only came over every now and then, but here, she visited
every day after work. Most evenings, we have dinner, watch a
movie, and then she goes home. She's even been going to
church with me. And while it's definitely exciting, I still can't
get Saloso out of my head. The way she smelled of flowers and
honey, her stunning blue eyes, I couldn't forget Saloso as much

as I wanted to.

Garrith had only become a distraction, I wasn't interested in her anymore. But I was too afraid to let her go because that meant my evenings after work would be filled with drowning thoughts of Saloso, and I didn't want that. It was better to leave the Sand Ribbon people as a lost memory. They didn't need an outsider ruining things. I had caused so much trouble for Saloso, I could never return to her no matter how much I wanted to.

"You seem distant today, you alright?" Garrith placed her hands on my shoulders. She massaged them as she stood behind me, trying to help me relax.

"I'm alright," I said. "I'm just tired."

"We don't have to go. It's just a fancy dinner."

"Please." I turned on the ottoman and pulled her close. "I wouldn't miss your award for the world." She smiled and leaned down to press her lips against mine.

She enjoyed the kiss more than I did, but I'd been faking it this long, it didn't matter. I kissed her until she was breathless, trying to emphasize my lie about not wanting to miss her award. Garrith was being honored tonight for her work on a new project her lab had been developing. Garrith's expertise allowed her research to get the FDA's approval of their drug, which meant human test trials could begin.

"Cameron," Garrith said, pulling away.

I raised a brow and smirked at her, but her face looked serious, and I knew what was coming. "I—I love you." Her words, the stuttering, the long pause, it was almost like she was trying to mimic Saloso's last words to me.

"Cameron?"

I blinked, pulling myself from my thoughts. I smiled as genuinely as I could and told her a lie that made me hate myself. "I love you too, Garrith." The words slipped from me with such ease, I was embarrassed for her. But she didn't seem to notice.

Giddily, she threw her arms around me and held me tight.

Seventeen
I AM BROKEN

Garrith accepted her award two hours ago. Since then, she left me to mingle through the crowd. I've been wandering around aimlessly, having random chats about nothing with women in beautiful gowns and men in fancy suits. The hall was stunning, silver drapes covered long windows, while black tiles shimmered every time someone took a step. I watched the crowd, murmuring and talking as a big band played in the background on an elevated stage.

"Cameron Taylor, man of the hour," the wide hand of a hefty man slapped my back hard, and I spilled the cocktail I'd been holding for the past hour. Garrith gave it to me, despite my Christian protests, she said it would make me look more approachable. I didn't think so, but I guess she was right. All the suits and ties floating around looked stiff without something in their hand. They didn't speak, or even make eye contact. But those clutching drinks looked like they were ready to talk, like they were happy enough to tell things they shouldn't. Nonetheless, I didn't *want* to be holding a cocktail, but I'd given in … and now I regretted it.

Grabbing a white napkin, I dabbed my crimson velvet suit. It was finely pressed with matching loafers I'd had covered in dazzling gems that made everyone gasp. Except this fat drunken man.

I glanced down at the wet spot on my jacket before dragging my eyes back up to the hefty man before me. He was smiling widely and holding a mostly empty glass—there was no doubt in my mind that it wasn't his first drink of the night. His cheeks were flushed red and his eyes were glazed over; with the way he swayed on his feet, I'd bet a gentle breeze could knock him off his stout legs.

"It's Cameron Frierson," I corrected, tossing my napkin onto the tray of a passing waiter.

The big man squinted. "I could've sworn Garrith said you were the son of John Taylor."

I sighed. "Who are you again?"

A waitress came by holding a fresh tray of drinks. She stopped and smiled at me before saying, "Would you like another?"

"No thanks," I said before the big man could take one. I set my drink on the waitress's tray, relieved to finally get rid of it.

"So, you're with little miss Garrith, huh?" The man smirked. "She a wild cat or what?"

"Excuse me?"

He held his hands up defensively. "I don't mean anything

by it. She just looks a little frisky, if you know what I mean."
He leaned forward and licked his already wet lips. The alcohol
was talking for him, at least that's what I settled on as I ran a
hand through my hair. "Man, you're one pretty kid. You're
definitely John's boy."

"You seem to know a lot about John Taylor."

He chuckled. "He was a real piece of work, that guy.
Always bitter and unhappy, though he tried to be happy." He
lifted a hand to his head, a silver ring with a big square diamond
glittered in the white light. "John never got the woman he
wanted. Said he'd do everything he could to be with her, but
things were too complicated back then. He's been living in
regret ever since. And poor Betty, she's just as miserable as
John. Got to hand it to her, though; she's stuck it out."

I didn't appreciate the alcohol initially, but now I was
waving over the waitress from before, forgetting my Christian
protests as guilt twisted in my belly. I took a drink and passed
it to the big man to keep him talking. His smile returned and
he said, "Not gonna get one for yourself?"

"I want to be sober for tonight," I said quietly. "In case
Garrith wants to finish the night alone."

He gave me a foxy wink and slapped my back again. "Man,
it must be nice. Between your father and I, we never got the
women we wanted. Chelsea Brooks, she was the woman of my
dreams. But she couldn't wait for me and ended up marrying
young to some rich guy. And Savannah Lee," he paused,
staring at nothing, and I hoped he didn't see me stiffen at the
sound of my mother's name. "She was everything to your

father. But he made some bad decisions and he's been regretting his life ever since. Never knew her last name, he only ever called her Savannah Lee."

"What kind of decisions?" I asked.

A small frown etched its way onto his face, and he said, "The crazy—"

"Cammy! There you are! I've been looking for you everywhere!" Garrith draped her arms around me, and the smell of alcohol on her was horrendous.

The big man grinned at me and winked again, mouthing the words, *wild cat,* to me. When Garrith turned to see him, he said, "Tell your father to give me a call some time. I'd like to catch up. The name is Henry Bik."

"I'll let John know," I said.

"Cammy, come on!" Garrith whined drunkenly.

I grabbed her by the hand and pulled her along, muttering, "Let's go."

Garrith stumbled through the crowd behind me as we moved toward the exit. But just before we made it, she stopped abruptly and shouted, "Wait! I gotta … I gotta…"

A small circle of people began to gather, asking if something was wrong. I pressed my lips together, mind racing as I tried to think of a way to get Garrith to leave quietly. This was why I hated alcohol—beliefs aside. I'd seen Garrith drunk before, but this was ridiculous. She was just standing in the middle of the crowd, swaying and smiling and laughing loudly.

"Garrith, please," I complained, "let's go."

She snapped her head in my direction and burped loudly,

followed by a flood of fluids draining from her mouth. The crowd gasped altogether, stepping back in total sync. Garrith let out a giggle, and then belched again.

"Someone get her a towel!"

"Are you alright, sweetheart?"

"She's certainly had too much to drink."

"Who cares? It's a special day for her!"

"She should have more poise than this."

"One small award, and everything else is out the window!"

I pushed through the crowd, ignoring the mix of comments, and grabbed Garrith so we could finally leave. Outside, Garrith vomited twice on the sidewalk. I gave Grace a call while she wiped her mouth and sobbed incoherently—he was one of my bodyguards and my driver.

"Hello? Mr. Frierson? Are you ready?"

"Please hurry up and get here. We're going to my mother's house," I said.

"Of course, sir. I am heading to the car as we speak."

Once we arrived at my mother's house, I had Grace stay in the car and Carter, my other bodyguard, carried Garrith inside.

"What happened?" Momma said as she tied her nightrobe closed. She was holding open the door for us as we climbed the large steps to her house. She had finally moved out of the dinky apartment in Alabama, since Dad built this house for her, per my contract.

"She passed out," I said, following Carter inside.

"Where would you like her?" Carter asked.

Momma pointed down the hall. "We can go to the second guestroom. I'll tuck her in, you just leave her in there."

"Understood," Carter said as Momma followed behind him. They disappeared into the hallway, and I crossed the foyer and found my way into the kitchen. Draping my jacket over the counter, I searched the cabinets for something to eat. The place was fully stocked, but the only thing I found ready to eat was cereal.

Carter appeared as I pulled a bowl from the cabinet. "She's in bed now, I'll wait in the car."

I nodded as he left the room. The ceramic white bowl clinked against the counter as I set it down and poured myself some sugary cereal and milk from the fridge.

"I put her in the bed," Momma said. She moved closer to where I sat at the counter and sighed down at me. "You know, there was a time when things like this didn't bother you."

I crunched my cereal. "Well, that was when it didn't matter. Things are different now. As a Christian and as a public figure, it matters if my girlfriend gets dead drunk at events."

Mother harrumphed and left me to pour herself a glass of orange juice. "Two years ago, you would've made an excuse for her."

"Two years ago, you wouldn't have."

"I'm forced to, since you're no longer happy."

My appetite was gone suddenly, and I dropped my spoon into the milk. "Momma, I am happy, alright? I'm just busy more often now."

Her face didn't look tired like it used to. Her vibrant dark chocolate skin had regained some youthfulness since I'd been able to take better care of her. I sent my mother to the best spas, and salons weekly to keep her stress-free and youthful. She has a personal trainer come to her house a few times a week, and a personal chef from morning to late evening.

"People change, Cameron and sometimes we don't like their changes, even if it's everything we used to want them to be. Sometimes we change, too, we mature, and we don't even know it. But," she paused, "circumstances change people. They make a person grow and mature."

I nodded, staring at my soggy cereal.

"Garrith has changed a lot. She loves you—she even started going to church with you."

"She still got drunk—"

"One mistake shouldn't make you this upset," she said over me.

"Momma, it was a big mistake."

"Where has your forgiveness gone so suddenly? You would've given anything to forgive Garrith before—"

"Two years ago, yes," I cut her off. "But things are different—"

Momma shook her head. "You don't love her anymore."

I stared at her in silence.

"I didn't ask earlier out of respect for your privacy," my mother said. "But I think it's about time you start being honest about Peru."

I took a deep breath and exhaled all the sudden thoughts

174

of Saloso.   "I've told you the truth."

"You've told me the bare minimum. When did you start grouping me in with everyone else, Cameron? When did you stop being able to talk to me?" Momma was looking right at me now. A sincere sadness had taken over her face; she always looked that way when I disappointed her or hurt her feelings. It wasn't often Momma and I had disagreements, but when we did, it was hard to recover from them.

Loosening the silk black tie around my neck, I sighed heavily. "Momma, the things that happened in Peru, you wouldn't believe me if I told you."

She quietly sipped her orange juice. "Try me."

Momma was always ready for a story. She loved a good one, and often read books when she was working. But she particularly loved old tales, the kind that were most likely fish stories passed down from generation to generation.

I adjusted on the stool, because I knew I wasn't leaving that thing until she'd heard the entire story. "There was a crash," I started, "and I was rescued by a small tribe hidden in the desert. The tribe of the Sand Ribbon."

Momma nodded, taking another small sip of orange juice.

"I was out for some time, and when I came to, I met some people. They were all pretty nice and welcoming. Except for the leader of the tribe, she hated me. But her granddaughters loved me."

"Did these Sand Ribbon people know English?"

I nodded. "It was one of the languages they learned in the markets and from their travels."

"The markets?"

"Yeah, the Sand Ribbon tribe wouldn't be known for surviving the desert lands if anyone ever found out about them. They're called the 'Sand Ribbon' people because they found sources of water, like a 'ribbon' in the sand."

"I see, and they go to the market to sell their water?"

"No." I chuckled. "They go to sell other things, and to trade for supplies they can't get in the desert."

Momma nodded, silently urging me to continue.

"They made good food, made me clothes, even gave me a job."

"They must have really put you to work; you came back with raw strength, and muscles. Not scrawny and weak like I thought you would." Momma laughed.

I joined her light chuckles as I remembered chopping wood and raking the fields.

"Cameron?"

I looked up at my mother.

"What really happened out there?"

Somehow, she just knew there was more, and there was no escaping her clutches. I didn't want to admit it. I didn't want to talk about Peru. I didn't want those thoughts to surface again.

Swallowing hard, my eyes drifted from Mom's to the quartz countertop. "I think I…" I paused, trying not to say too much.

Momma said, "You fell in love."

I snapped my head up to find her smiling down at me.

"Cameron, it was written all over your face the moment I

176

saw you. But I knew it was better to let you deal with your own heart than to have me poking around with it."

I shook my head, returning my gaze to the countertop. I didn't want to admit, because I didn't want it to be true but, somehow, I'd fallen in love with Saloso.

"She was the most beautiful woman I'd ever seen," I told Momma. "Flowing hair, like finely woven silk had been placed on her head instead of hair follicles. And her skin…" I paused as thoughts of Saloso swarmed my mind, making my heart pound incredibly. "Her skin glowed like the harvest moon. She looked like a field of wheat with the richness of the morning sun just pouring over her. But her skin wasn't the only thing that glowed, Momma; her eyes did, too. They were a color blue I've never seen before—but it wasn't just her looks that got me. It was her heart. Who she was inside."

"She sounds absolutely lovely."

"She was amazing. Kind and gentle. She even believed like us. She was a Christian."

"Ain't that 'bout something?" Momma said with a smile.

I nodded. "And she was a leader, even though she was still figuring herself out. I loved her without even knowing it. But I … I couldn't have stayed in Peru, anyway. Things were getting out of hand and her grandmother was so vicious. All I did was bring her problems."

"I'm certain the young woman didn't feel that way."

I shrugged. "It doesn't matter. She's better off without me."

"Are you sure?"

"How could I not be?"

Momma chuckled and drank down the rest of her juice. "Men aren't very good at understanding the hearts of women. Even if staying would've caused trouble, I'm sure this young lady would have felt the trouble was worth it. It was something she could have fought and conquered because you were with her. Women depend on their male counterpart just as much as men depend on the woman."

"Is that what happened with John? He misunderstood you?"

She froze momentarily, and then turned to take her empty glass and my bowl to the sink. "Your father didn't understand a lot of things, and that ultimately drove a wedge between us. But," she tapped the faucet, staring down at the rushing water as she went on, "we're talking about you, Cam. Not John."

She dried her hands on a towel and turned to face me. There was a half-smile on her face, the same one she used to wear when I asked questions about my father as a child.

I didn't press the issue; it was clearly something she didn't want to talk about. "Well," I muttered, glancing away from her, "there's not much else to say."

"At least give me her name," she pried.

I felt hesitant to say it. I hadn't said Saloso's name in so long, it seemed taboo now. "Her name was Sunstar." I paused. It suddenly felt like the mere mention of her name had brought back her sweet smell—honey and flowers. "Sunstar de Achille. But everyone called her Saloso."

"Why did they call her Saloso? Is that a nickname of some

sort?"

"No," I muttered. "It was a name given to her to shame her."

Momma blinked in confusion, but as I'd let her situation with dad go, she decided to do the same for me.

"I will talk to Garrith in the morning," she told me, moving from the sink to my side again. "I'll tell her to give you some space. But you have to make a decision in that time, Cameron. You have to be straight with Garrith. What are you so afraid of?"

I didn't have an answer. I couldn't explain why I didn't want to leave Garrith, just that I felt like I couldn't. I was scared that I'd be miserable if someone didn't distract me from the thoughts of Saloso. I was in the height of my career, taking a trip to Peru was just out of the question.

"Cam, I'll talk to your father in the morning."

"For what?" I asked, frowning at her.

"To make arrangements for you to go to Peru. You need closure, not an abrupt ending. Go to back to the Sand Ribbon people, find out if that girl still loves you. If she doesn't, then come back. But if she does, stay a while and work something out with her."

I shook my head. "Momma, I can't go—"

"You can, and you will, Cameron Frierson."

Eighteen
Fatherhood

I sat in my father's office for the first time in two years. I didn't even sign my onboarding papers with him, I signed them via email and sent them back to his secretary so we didn't have to see each other.

Nothing has changed.

There were still pictures of his family all over his office—and still no pictures of Mom and me.

I sat in the comfy chair, looking at the faces of my father's children, looking at Betty. Henry Bik, the big man from the party, told me she'd done her best staying by my father's side. Surely it was for the money at this point, but maybe she really did love him. I wondered briefly if Momma still loved him.

My leg bounced wildly as I waited for my father. His secretary, Cassidy, told me he was in a meeting that should be wrapping up soon, but she rang him anyway. I stared out the large window behind my father's desk, trying to swallow the nerves I couldn't shake since Momma told me to return to

Peru. I was excited to see Saloso again, but I couldn't help but wonder if things had changed.

What if she married Catskill? What if she ran away because of all the pressure? What would I even say to her? I had a million things I wanted to tell Saloso, a million things I wanted her to tell me.

I took a deep breath and draped my head over the back of my chair. In the silence, I could hear the bustling office outside my father's door. Then his booming voice came, "Morning everyone."

"How'd the meeting go, Mr. Taylor?" Cassidy asked.

"It went great. I think we're moving along well."

"Excellent to hear, sir." There was a pause and then in a lower voice, Cassidy said, "He's been waiting for about ten minutes."

I rolled my eyes and lifted my head before my father entered the room and said, "Good morning, son."

"It's Cameron, John, and I need a favor."

"You are straight to the point." He sat behind his desk, wearing black pants and a white button down with a simple black tie and silver cuff links. "What's this favor? Your mother called me this morning."

"Then you know what I want," I said.

"Don't you want to chat for a bit?" He smiled widely, but I said curtly, "No."

He shot his brows up quickly before rolling his eyes. "I don't see why you still hate me. I've given you everything you've asked for."

"As if you don't at least owe me that." I chuckled. "Come on, John, you've been in my life for two years. And when I say, 'in my life,'" I used air quotes, "I mean you gave me a job because you wanted my design. You saw an opportunity for growth and decided to take it."

"That's absolutely not true," John argued, sitting back in his chair. He was amazed, as if he had no idea where this was coming from.

I took the liberty to explain. "It's absolutely true. Why else would you help your son after twenty-three years—now twenty-five? Because a good sob story always makes the headlines. Father and lost son reunited." I rolled my eyes. "Not to mention your son happens to be pretty good at what he does, so hiring him just took a quality asset off the market for your competitors."

"Alright, I get it," John said. "Your mother says you need time off."

"I need three months."

"No."

"And I'll need that tactical team you used to rescue me."

"There's no 'and,' Cameron. No means no."

"And I'll probably need a few other things for this trip. I don't want to—"

"No!" he shouted.

I stared at him, silently wondering how often he told his other kids no. "Three months is a lot of time. Even for my own son."

"John, I *need* three months."

"I can't do that."

"I only ask for things I need, and I need this time off."

"Cameron, cut it out!" he ordered sharply. "You're a young man with responsibilities to uphold, and I will hold you to them and treat you like the young man you are."

"Because you can't treat me like a son."

"Because you won't let me!" He slowly rose to his feet and leaned across the table. "Even if you hate my guts, I am still your father. I am still your boss. So, either way, my word is final."

"Alright," I muttered, standing too. His green eyes mirrored mine as I looked him over once more. "I'll figure this out on my own. I always have. Thanks for your time, Mr. Taylor." I faltered for a moment, holding in the anger that burned in my chest before I took a deep breath and turned away, trying not to feel hopeless.

When I reached the door, I stopped and said, "Henry Bik said to give him a call," then I opened the door and left.

My father's words bounced around in my head as I stood just outside his office door. Maybe he was right. Maybe I needed to stop clutching to my 'absent father' sob story. Maybe I should try to let John be my father...

I shook my head, taking off down the hall, but I heard John's door open behind me. "I can give you two months, Cameron," he called. "But that's it. My tactical team is yours. I'll send over the documents from my secretary. Send her a list of things you'll need, and she'll have it ready for you."

I stopped walking and turned to face him. He wasn't

smiling, but he didn't look angry, either. "You'd better return, son. And while you're gone, your team better not fall behind."

"Understood, Mr. Taylor." I couldn't get myself to say thank you, but I nodded at him as he turned on his heels and went back into his office. Everyone in their cubicles glanced over at me before returning to work.

"Mr. Cameron," a thin woman with skin like mine said from behind her large desk. "Let me assist you."

I crammed a hand into my pocket and walked over to her. "Thanks, Cassidy."

She nodded, clicking away on her computer. Her bright skin reminded me of Saloso's, and I supposed if Saloso was simply a secretary, she would look like Cassidy. Well-kept coils of hair, large blue glasses, and red-painted lips.

"Alright, your father said tactical team documents, right?"

"Correct."

"I'm sending those over to you now. They say the tactical team is still part of Taylor Securities under the guise of Cameron Frierson-Taylor."

"Thanks," I said.

"Oh, no problem. I'll put it in the schedule that you're on a company vacation and will send a memo to your team. Anything else?" She looked up from her computer for the first time, smiling.

"A plane. I'll need arrangements to get to Peru. And books. Literature, textbooks, leisure books, Bibles, anything." She was nodding as she jotted down what I said. "And I'll be in a very remote location; how can I get some internet connection out there?"

"You'll probably need to leave the area every so often, just so that the connection device I'll have sent over to you will be able to ping a tower."

I nodded. "Good, good. I also want to meet with the leader of the tactical team, can you set something up for me?"

She clicked around for a moment. "One o'clock at the café down the street sound good?"

"Perfect."

She gave me a firm nod. "Also, I can get you a private jet in three days."

"That fast?"

"You know the company is always ready for anything."

"I'll take it. Send the café location to Grace, he'll be driving me to the meeting."

"Absolutely. Anything else?"

I waved her off as I turned and left the office.

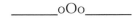

I entered the café, Carter and Grace walked in front of me as we made our way through the empty place. *Cassidy must've rented the hour out for us to talk in private,* I thought as we walked through empty booths and tables.

Red and white tiles decorated the wall, and a white floor stretched across the entire building. We rounded a corner to find a small lounge where bands often played. There was a tall man sitting on a comfy looking couch in front of a coffee table with his back to us, sipping from a mug.

As we approached, I said, "Afternoon, Fred." I extended a hand to him. Dull brown eyes met mine, and the sunburned man nodded and shook it.

"Afternoon, Cameron. You bring the boys everywhere?" He raised a brow at Carter and Grace.

"My guards? Yeah, why?"

"Seems a little much, don't you think?"

"That's more of my style," I said. That was a lie—Carter and Grace had kind of become friends to me, and I liked having them around.

"Fair enough." Fred motioned to the chair across from him, I waved off Carter and Grace to find corners to stand in, then sat down.

"How did you find me in Peru?" I asked.

A single brow on Fred's face lifted. "Well, I knew it was suspicious that you wanted to meet, but I thought it was because Taylor had a job for me."

I sat back in the cushiony red chair, lazily draping my arms over the rests. I tried to seem relaxed, but I was eager to know, and didn't care for the small talk. "I need to get back to that place."

"For what? Did you realize two years later that you left something there?"

"Can you just answer the question?"

He chuckled and reached for his coffee. "We went to the location of the bus crash and sent out drones in every direction, except the one we came from."

I nodded; it was a genius idea.

"Why didn't we see the drones?"

Fred frowned over his mug. "Do you need to know all my secrets?"

"I pay you for those secrets."

"Your father pays me," he corrected.

"And my father has given your tactical team—and its secrets—to me." I leaned forward in the chair. "So *I* pay you."

Fred dropped his gaze to the table where I slid a piece of paper to him. I didn't take my eyes off him as he took it and read it quickly.

"Now," I said, sitting back again and resting my ankle on my knee, "tell me why we didn't see your drones."

"It's called the shadow effect," he admitted, staring at his coffee. "We put a cloak over the drone to lower its humming. Plus, the design of the drone is small. Like a little black camera floating atop the tree line. It can zoom in twice the distance of a spotting scope in a fraction of the time it takes to zoom in on your phone. Taylor designed it himself."

"You used it at night?"

He nodded. "It can travel a long distance, so once we picked up heat signatures, we swapped focus and used facial recognition to find you."

"And when you came looking for me, the drone had obviously etched out the best path to take, right?"

Another nod. "It laid out a path that brought us right to the little village."

"Good. I'll need the path you took, and a drone sent over

to me in two days."

He scoffed. "I'm not sending my equipment with you on some wild goose chase."

The words made my heart flutter, and I took a deep breath to stable myself. "Didn't you say my *father* built the drones you used?"

He swallowed, and then sniffled dryly. "Yeah."

I nodded. "Send me a drone and the path to that village in forty-eight hours." I stood to my feet and waved over my guards. "Carter, Grace—let's go."

Nineteen
I AM FREE

Taking Momma's advice about going back to Peru was liberating. For two years, I'd been secretly hoping I could return, but I didn't know I was looking for permission. It seemed like it was finally okay for me to go back to Peru after Momma boldly told me to go. With all my responsibilities in Illinois, I never thought I could actually go back. There were too many loose ends, and too many other factors that I couldn't just walk away from with no plan to return. But things were different now. I wasn't being dragged into someone's home to be saved. I wasn't miraculously walking away from a bus accident. I wasn't stumbling into love. I was charging right at it. But I could only charge for two months. I was limited to sixty days in Peru to recapture the heart of the woman I loved. But even if I captured it, then what? Another teary goodbye, and years apart?

When I decided to return to Peru, I gave myself three months, which was shortened to two, to change Sunstar's mind about staying with her tribe. However, my chances at winning her love were nonexistent, and I knew I couldn't change her mind. So, I settled with just getting closure. I would travel to Peru and spend time with Sunstar, be upfront and tell her I was only there to give her a proper goodbye, and when it was time to go ... it would be for good.

Returning would be harder this time because I now knew there was no going back. But I also knew when I returned home, Garrith wouldn't be there.

Today, I had to tell her goodbye for good.

Garrith's prissy hands were painted lavender, it was a dull color for her smooth, pale skin. Pulling the silk strap from her gown back onto her shoulder, she sipped her water nervously. We hadn't seen each other since she'd gotten disgustingly drunk a few days ago. She'd been calling my cell, but I had all her notifications silenced.

I watched her pout over her straw as she drank. For two years I'd kissed those pouty lips, and I'd never felt my heart race the way it did with Saloso. For two years, I'd sat beside Garrith late at night and never made a move on her. For two years we'd been in this odd limbo, where Garrith was desperately trying to get me to feel something, desperately trying to get me to love and acknowledge her, while I did nothing but sulk selfishly.

I've hurt Garrith. I knew that. So, today, I would make things right with her. I'd put an end to the pain and desperation I've made her feel and I'd hope she would be relieved instead of heartbroken.

Stirring the straw around the ice water, Garrith didn't make eye contact with me. She watched the moving scene around us. Waiters and waitresses dressed in black pants, black vests and white shirts with bow ties carried large trays of steaming food. Couples laughed and chatted while some people sat alone, tapping along the table to the tunes of the live performance. The performer was a woman playing the piano. She played some slow songs, and some faster paced songs, but the melodic tunes were calming background noise. Garrith had been watching the woman for a while. Sometimes smiling as her head bobbed along or tapping a single finger on the table.

We'd decided to wait to order. Trying to simply enjoy each other's company. It was my idea. I'd been procrastinating all night because I was nervous. I didn't know how to tell her the truth, but I knew I needed to do this.

Sighing heavily, I finally called to her, "Garrith."

She looked up at me, green eyes blinking through dark square frames. They didn't make me blush the way they used to. I stared at her wide eyes because I hadn't really looked at Garrith in a long time. There was pain written all over her face that no amount of makeup could hide or distort. I felt horrible, but I could only imagine how she was feeling within.

"Listen, Garrith, I don't want to drag this on. So, I'll make this quick—"

"Let's go someplace quieter, alright? I don't think I'd like the food here."

I glanced down at the menu and back up at her. "But you love pasta."

She shrugged. "I'm not feeling it tonight."

"Alright. I'll call Grace and tell him—"

"No!" she blurted, and her eyes suddenly watered.

My chest tightened a little, and then I understood. *She's seen this coming for a long time.* All the church services she didn't want to attend. All the drinks she didn't get to have. All the time she spent at my place instead of out doing other things she considered fun; it was all for me. But, despite her efforts, she knew we weren't the same as before, and there was a growing emptiness that neither of us could continue to ignore.

The thoughts of Garrith's troubling two years with me made me feel guilty. An innocent woman was hurt, all because I was too broken to heal. Too immature to ask for space. Too lonely to let go. It wasn't very fair to end things now, but it wouldn't be fair to keep going, either.

"Let's walk," she said as she stood to her feet. Her long black evening gown dusted the floor as the silk straps on the bustier tightened over her shoulders and her arms. Garrith always overdressed. Givenchy just for an evening with pasta and her boyfriend. Presumably the last evening with her boyfriend, and so maybe tonight, she'd dressed to say goodbye.

I threw a tip onto the table, despite the only things sitting on it were two sweating waters. Placing a hand on Garrith's back, I led her down the stairs and onto the sidewalk. The night was warm, and the sky was free of clouds. Just the darkness pierced by stars and streetlamps, and the quiet of the night disrupted by humming engines and croaking bugs in the distance. Silver Prada slingbacks clicked against the pavement as Garrith walked beside me. We were holding hands, aimlessly going nowhere, just walking together like we did sometimes before Peru.

Back then, there had been times when Garrith would call me on a school night at one in the morning and ask me to come walk with her. I always did it, even in the dead of winter. I'd get up and walk with her until she wanted to go home. Sometimes it was hours, and a few times it turned into hiking trips, or even spontaneous road trips. We'd find a place to rent a car and buy food and clothes and go wherever we wanted for a few days before we were reported missing. The memories made a fleeting smile stretch across my face. Fleeting, not because this was the end of the road for us, but because I realized Garrith and I hadn't truly smiled for two years.

But here I was, smiling genuinely as I prepared to say goodbye to a woman I once believed I loved.

"Why do things change, Cameron?" Garrith asked. Her voice interrupted my walk down memory lane and pulled me back to reality's quiet evening walk with her.

"We're supposed to," I responded.

"Why? Why are we supposed to change? Why can't things ever stay the way they are?"

"No one would ever mature. No one would ever fall in love if things never changed."

"But they wouldn't fall out of love if they didn't change."

Silence.

"Garrith…"

"Cameron," she cut me off, pulling our pace to a halt. Tears were streaming down her burning red cheeks. "Why did it have to happen to us? Why did we have to fall out of love?"

Slowly, I lifted my hands to her face, letting my thumbs rest on her wet cheeks while the rest of my fingers relaxed at the base of her neck. I watched her shed tears for me, for us, and I thought I would, too. Swallowing the hard lump in my throat, I said, "Garrith, stop blaming yourself. You've loved me more than I deserved."

She hiccupped. "Why wasn't it enough? Why couldn't you just love me back?"

I chewed my lip as she began to weep. Tears drenched my hands as I couldn't pull them from her face. There was no amount of preparation that could've readied me for breaking her heart like this. Somehow, I'd been hoping that she'd be relieved about this. I'd been hoping she would welcome her freedom, be happy that she didn't have to keep faking for me.

Surely, I'd hurt her because I rejected her attempts at making things work for us. But I didn't know that Garrith was *truly* in love with me despite the emptiness that'd been growing between us.

Is it possible that I'm the only one who felt empty? Maybe Garrith felt it but wanted to actually do something about it. I'm ... so sorry Garrith.

I chewed the thoughts a little longer before I finally said to her, "I never meant to hurt you, Gary. Things just weren't the same when I returned. We tried, but I didn't try hard enough for you. And I'm sorry."

She shook her head. "You did good, Cam. For two years

194

you pretended to love me. Gave me what I wanted. I should be thankful, shouldn't I?"

"No," I said sternly. "No, you shouldn't. You should be furious with me."

She pulled away and dropped her head from my hands as her shoulders trembled. "I want to be," she whispered. "I want to be angry at you. I desperately wish to hate you. But I can't stop my heart from loving you. I can't make my heart stop aching."

I watched as she began to cry again. "Garrith," I said, raising her chin. Her eyes were so full of tears, I didn't know if she could even see me through them. "I will always love you, no matter what."

She clenched her jaw for a moment, before exhaling heavily. "Goodbye, Cameron."

Suddenly, I felt my chest heave greatly. My heart began to beat to a new rhythm with the release of Garrith's hold on it. Embarrassed by my freedom, I tried to hide it in the warmest kiss I could produce for her. "Goodbye, Garrith."

Twenty
Things Have Changed

When my father's business went international, it was one of the highlights of his career, or so I've heard from Cassidy. John Taylor went international to broaden his business' scope, but he ended up broadening his own scope and started a second business. Having his own business meant my father travelled a lot, so he had his own custom jet built with precision German engineering. The plane was cool and all, but John Taylor was a man who liked to get things done on his own. He didn't enjoy depending on others.

Five years ago, my father bought the German company that'd built his jet and relocated its main base to California. He created jobs for thousands of people, but there was still an outcry from the public. People complained that he was taking away opportunities from the original German engineers, but my father has always been a schemer. All his factories remained in Germany, so he got the precision he'd always wanted—now with the American stamp of approval—but the labor and design were done cheaply overseas.

It was all a publicity stunt to boost his international appeal … and it worked. Two years after he made all the major moves, Japan, Italy, and a horde of other countries were offering their factories and designs to John. Now he owns more than jets— his businesses include planes, airbuses, even business Boeings. But the best part was that whenever I needed one, it was one phone call away.

I relaxed in the leather chair, feeling the heated seat warm my back. I liked the jet. It was grand, and the interior design was one my dad created himself. It was built to look like a yacht inside, with light brown seats trimmed in white and blue backings that ran into a neatly carpeted floor. There was an optical illusion in the carpet which allowed it to look like a wooden floor. There was a mini bar, completely stocked, and a dining room trimmed in a casual blue and white. Blue was my father's favorite color, as if that wasn't obvious, and he was also a nerd for windows, which was why he'd had skylights built into the jet. The lights had shades which could be operated with the flick of a button or an app via cellular device.

As I drifted off to sleep, I remembered the first time I traveled to Peru. I was alone and had to take several flights to get there. Now, I was flying on a custom jet with a small team and would be there in seven hours. I felt so small in all this, but I spoke with Reverend Lee before leaving, and she told me I still had a purpose in Peru. There was still work that needed to be done, a well I needed to reach, life which needed to be given. Her words were parallel to what Sunstar had told me on our hunting trip. I decided after greeting Sunstar, I would go see Misty to ask her to give me more clarity.

As I excused myself to head for my room, Fred called, "Cameron, wait a second."

I turned to see him coming from the bar with a bag in his hand. "What's up," I said, glancing down at the bag.

He raised it. "We'll be there soon; I'm giving you a little parting gift."

I rolled my eyes. "Thanks."

"Let me explain it to you first." Fred waved me over to a table and we sat as he pulled two small devices from the black bag. They were matte black cubes which he twisted and pried open slowly to reveal a silver button inside with a glowing red ring around it.

"What are these?"

"They're panic buttons. All you have to do is press them and they will ping me. I'll get your location and will be there to rescue you in twenty-four hours, as long as you stay in an area with internet and cellular service. Even if you don't, I'll have equipment with me to scout you."

I raised a brow as I stared at the buttons. "So, I press one and you'll come rushing back?"

He nodded.

"And they're activated now?"

He shook his head and dug through his pocket to fish out a white slip of paper. "Read this aloud, starting with the word, 'code.'"

"Code: X-five-zero-four-six-one-S-fourteen-three-two-one-eight-seven-nine-six."

The light flickered from red to bright blue, my father's signature color.

"Now they're activated," Fred said. "If you blow your hand off, you can scream, 'Code X5,' and it'll ping me." He shrugged. "Your father insisted on voice recognition."

I rolled my eyes and closed the devices. "Thanks. I'll put them in the tech bag you gave me."

The landing in Peru was smooth. Our pilot, Captain Belle, was hired by my father two years ago. She normally only flew my father around, but she made an exception for me. She landed us in a remote location in Lima, and when I stepped off the plane, I was greeted with the warm air I'd never truly forgotten. The heat was always a bit stickier here since there was sometimes fog in the air. Pulling my small duffle bag over my shoulder, I waved goodbye to Fred, the tactical team, and Captain Belle. It would be two months before I saw them again. I was a little excited about that.

Making my way through the bustling city, I picked up the vehicle Cassidy had arranged for me. I would only be able to drive so far before I'd have to leave the car. Fred had connections with one of the tour guides in Peru; they would meet me this evening where the bus accident happened and take the car back nearly seven hours to its drop-off location. From there, I'd have to walk.

"Hi, my name's Cameron Frie—" I paused. The big,

copper-skinned man was looking up from his tablet at me as he sat perched on a stool that was too small for him. "Cameron Taylor," I cleared my throat, ignoring the churning in my stomach. I hated dropping my mother's maiden name for my father's 'when it counts.' That's what Fred told me before I got off the jet. He said I could use my mother's last name, but when it counts or when it's something important, I should use Taylor because it held more weight. I didn't like it, but not just because I had a disliking for my father that was still rather strong, I hated it because I knew it was true.

The man on the stool smiled and nodded, returning his eyes to his tablet. "Yes, Taylor, we got a reservation for you a few days ago. Ringo will bring around the car; he'll be your driver."

I nodded and muttered, "Thanks."

Adjusting the bag on my shoulders, I glanced around the shop. It was a small tourist shack with post cards, maps, and tour guide information. There was a single freezer in the back filled with drinks and a few candy bars in nearly empty cartons in the rack in front of the checkout register. I'm not sure how Cassidy or Fred got me a car from a place like this, but I decided not to ask any questions as I stepped outside to wait on Ringo.

He pulled up in a small blue Honda that was rusting severely on several spots, specifically on one of the hubcaps. I clutched my chest as the distinct popping noises of the bus's tires rang through my head as I stared at the rusted hubcap.

"Aye! Let's go! I got to get you up there and back before

dark. That's fourteen hours in the car for me." A slender man with copper-toned skin like the stool guy stepped out of the creaking blue Honda. He waved his arms as he came around the back of the car. "Hello? Are you listening to me?"

I shook my head, trying to push away the single memory of the accident. I still had no recollection of what'd happened. I remembered the tire popping and Lydia going to check it out. But another tire popped and when the bus rattled, it knocked Lydia to the floor. The last thing I remember was screaming for her to wake up. The next thing after that was...

"Give me this." He pulled the duffle bag from my hand and threw it in the trunk. I swallowed thickly and moved to the car, gasping at the ragged seats inside. I wasn't 'too good' for torn up seats, but I definitely didn't want to sit on them. But then I remembered I was about to spend weeks in the Peruvian desert, dirtier and filthier on most days than these seats, the thought made me chuckle and I hunkered down inside.

The seven-hour ride was brutal. Ringo talked periodically. We would ride in silence for an hour, but then for the next two he was talking nonstop. He talked the most about his pregnant girlfriend, how he didn't think the baby was his but, somehow, whenever he felt her pregnant belly, he knew the baby couldn't be anyone else's. He tried to tell me about some ancient rubbing technique his mother taught him that would tell him if the baby was his or not. I stopped listening after a while and stared out the window. The dark trees gave us shade which was a blessing since the air conditioning only blew out of one vent on my side.

I thought about Sunstar, how she would react when she saw me. If she'd be happy or angry. Angry because I took too long to come back, and she ended up marrying Catskill. Angry that I returned because she'd moved on from a single summer two years ago.

It didn't matter since I was only returning to say goodbye. I knew Sunstar couldn't leave her people, and I didn't think I could even ask her to do that. *I'll just make my feelings clear, and then I'll leave. I'll leave early if I have to and return home. When I return, I'll be free of thoughts of Sunstar and Garrith.*

"Alright, we're here," Ringo said as he slowed the car. He leaned forward over the steering wheel, taking a closer look at the tree in front of us. "Must've been where that tourist accident happened a few years back. The bus crashed so hard, man, it took the bark off the tree."

I opened the door and got out, snatching my duffle bag from the back seat.

"Aye! What's wrong with you? Why are you mad?"

"Thanks for the ride, Ringo." I dug two-hundred dollars out of my pocket and passed it to him. He took it with a nod. "Thanks, man. I really appreciate this."

Adjusting my backpack of electronics, I waved at him and started my way up the dirt road. The headlights of the car burned behind me as Ringo backed away, giving me two horn beeps before turning around and heading back to his shack.

I followed the map Fred sent to my phone. If I got lost, I could always stop and turn on the drone which'd been programmed with the route. It would fly above me, and I'd wear goggles synced to the drone to follow the path it took. The map didn't have many twists or turns. It would lead me through some dark, forested areas once I reached the end of the road where the bus accident happened. The thoughts made me jumpy and agitated.

I was frustrated that I couldn't remember any more than the few moments before the whole thing went down. I hardly even remember the trip. The things I remember most are Garrith and I before the trip, arguing at dinner, and I also remember the headlines of multiple articles written about my return.

When I first returned, the articles all reported the same thing, 'Cameron Frierson, Sole Survivor of the UOW Christian Group, Found in Remote Location in Peru.' There were dozens of headlines all over for weeks. No one could believe I'd survived. The mystery? I always told them it was God, which was true. I just never wanted to say that God sent me into a village where I fell in love with the future leader and was hated by the current one.

I stopped walking as the thoughts of the current leader, Chief Grey Hawk, were summoned. I wondered how she would take to my return.

I shook my head and kept walking.

Darkness had begun to settle, but I still had a few miles to go before I was close enough to set up camp. I was keeping a good pace, considering I'd done a lot of fitness training when I'd returned. I never told Momma that I'd lost my first fight. Instead, I took up kickboxing and got a personal trainer. I'm certain now that even if Catskill tried to catch me off guard, I could take him.

A crackling noise sounded through the dark night. I stopped walking immediately. Sweat began to form on my forehead. Turning in a circle, I swung my flashlight around, looking for what could be lurking through the trees. Another crackle came, and I clutched my flashlight a little tighter as I turned in the direction of the noise. Silence rang out.

Without any more delay, I turned and began walking briskly away. I kept my head down and pumped my legs as I marched along the path. But the sound of my footsteps doubled, and panic began to form in my heart.

Should I call Fred? No! I haven't even seen Sunstar... But I'm being followed!

I threw the thoughts away as the footsteps picked up behind me, and I took off in a desperate sprint through the forest. My flashlight was barely any help. I couldn't hold on to it and run fiercely, so I tripped through the forest blindly, rushing away from whoever was following me.

I came to a clearing and stopped. Panting hard, I turned around, but the darkness was everywhere. I finally raised my flashlight to find no one. But before I could turn around, someone came up behind me and covered my mouth. I screamed and flailed, but the person fought me and wrapped a blindfold over my eyes and hauled me away.

I tried to fight as I was dragged through the forest, but my assailant suddenly stopped and slung me into a tree. I scrambled, but the blindfold was suddenly snatched off and I was dazed for a moment.

"Outsider?"

Immediately, I glanced up. Brown eyes and a chiseled jaw, the perfect brute with a betraying gentle voice stared back at me.

"Catskill?"

He squinted. "What are you doing here?"

"What are *you* doing here?"

"Catskill? Who's there?" The voice was womanly. I was instantly eager to see who it belonged to.

A woman the color of copper stepped out. She was stunning, only wearing her tunic dress, no shawl. Her hair was neatly shaved, which made her big eyes look charming instead of doll-like. But for some reason, it seemed like I'd seen this woman before. *Maybe she had longer hair?*

The fire flickered in the wind, making the shadows dance on and off her. Catskill suddenly looked nervous, as his gaze drifted from hers back to mine.

"It's Cameron, the outsider." She paused for a second, looking me over, before coming a little closer. Up close, she favored Sunstar, like she could be her sister...

"Kateri?!"

She smiled. "Outsider? What are you doing here!" She closed the gap between us and hugged me tightly. The sweet scent of Kateri had changed, she smelled no longer of fruit, but just of sweetness. I squeezed her tightly, nearly succumbing to tears of joy. "I have longed for this day, Outsider," she whispered into my ear.

"I have, too."

She held me a moment longer before retracting from my embrace. "You have changed so much, dear Outsider. You look stronger than Catskill now." She laughed, and her youthful giggle seemed to be the only thing that remained of the young girl I once knew. Silently, I wondered if Sunstar changed. If she changed as much as her sister had then, surely, I'd never leave Peru again.

"Kateri." I clutched her hands. I had no idea what I would say when I was reunited with the tribe, but the words flowed naturally as I gazed at her. "You've changed quite a lot yourself. You are absolutely beautiful."

She blushed and dropped her gaze. "Oh, goodness, Outsider. You are making my heart flutter. I cannot imagine what Saloso will think when she…" her eyes shot to mine, and joy spilled from them. "We have to go see Saloso right now!" she shouted as she pulled me to my feet.

"Hold on a second," Catskill said, rising quickly. He glanced between Kateri and me, the flames highlighting his perfect face. "Chief Grey is in no position to be dealing with the return of this outsider."

"You are right, kitten, grandmother would not fare well with this news."

"Kitten?" I glanced between the two and then it hit me. Catskill and Kateri were out here together … Alone.

Are they running away? Why is Kateri with Catskill? And why is he being so nice?

Kateri raised a brow at me and then shrugged. "It is what I

call him."

I took a step back. "What's going on with you two?"

"A lot has changed since you left, Outsider—" Kateri said.

"I can see that." I nodded at Catskill. "How could you run away with him and leave Saloso behind?"

Kateri's saddened eyes perked into rays of sunshine before she (and Catskill) burst into laughter. "Run away? Oh no, Outsider! We are not running away."

"We are here because we have found a spot that is safe to talk about what needs to be done in the tribe."

Kateri's mouth was still open as she stared at the side of Catskill's face. The warrior never looked at her, he simply moved from the shadows and stepped closer to the both of us.

"What do you mean 'what needs to be done?'" I asked.

Kateri only chewed the inside of her lip before crossing her arms while Catskill answered, "Our tribe is not in the best shape. We need to do something before all of our water goes bad, and all of our crops die."

I blinked at them. This wasn't what I was expecting to return to. I thought I would come back to the tribe and pick up where I'd left off. But things had changed. I had changed. Everyone had changed. Which ultimately meant Sunstar had probably changed, too. How could she not? It wasn't fair to just pick up where we left off like two years hadn't passed. It wouldn't be fair to be disappointed in all the changes that'd occurred with the tribe while I'd been gone—as if I was the only one moving forward while they remained on pause until I was ready to come back. Besides, things needed to change. I was only a gust of air passing through, hoping that everyone would feel my presence while I was there. And remember me when I'd gone.

"What's going on?" I asked.

"Well, a major water source for us has been polluted," Catskill explained. "And some of our other waters have been getting more mineral pieces in them, making it hard to drink or use."

"The pollution is new," Kateri chimed in. "But the minerals are not. The only new thing about all the rock pieces being in our water, is that there is a lot more of them now."

"I think I remember Misty talking about something like that before," I said.

Kateri agreed. "She did. And now, if we do not do something soon, we will be in big trouble."

"What kind of trouble?"

"Like having to move the entire tribe. Find new land. We're a few years off from that course, though." Catskill sighed.

"How many years off?"

"Three at most. We've still got a lot of puquois, but there is only so much time before they get filled with rocks and either stop flowing or get polluted."

Silence hung over us as I thought it all over. Then I asked, "Why is your water getting rocks in it all of a sudden?"

Kateri shifted her weight. "The wind. It has been windier than usual, bringing more drought across the region, but it is also causing sandstorms."

"I see. And the storms are carrying sand into your water

resources?"

They both nodded in unison.

"You don't have a way to cover your wells or something?"

"Our puquois bring water to the wells. They cannot be covered because we use the wind to push along the water into our fields, wells—or wherever we need water."

I'd never heard of this kind of watering technique. But it sounded like an ancient hydraulic system where the wind acted as a modern-day pump. Someone had mentioned before that the watering system of the Sand Ribbon was modelled after the Nazca.

"So, what have you two come up with so far?"

They looked at each other nervously before Catskill said, "Really, it is getting quite late. We should get some rest soon. I will go guard the perimeter; Kateri, get him something to eat."

She nodded as the warrior took his leave, then she waved me over to the single log at the fire. "Sit, I will fix you some of the stew."

I wanted to ask why they were suddenly acting weird, but it wasn't my business to bud in after disappearing for two years. "So, why did Catskill say Chief Grey Hawk couldn't deal with me?"

Kateri pulled the top off the stew and steam twisted into the air, rejoicing at its freedom. A smell so warming filled my nostrils and a sudden hunger struck me. I didn't notice until then that I hadn't eaten much since the plane ride over.

"Grandmother is very ill from the polluted water," she said as she ladled stew from the pot.

My eyes widened at the nearly joyous news.

"It keeps her in bed some days, but she is still active enough to be our chief. She will hold on to the position as long as she possibly can, I suppose." Kateri extended the bowl to me, and I took it, bobbing my head as I inhaled the fragrance.

"Is she going to be alright?" I asked as I began to blow over the stew. It was a dark, thick goop in my bowl. It almost resembled slop, but it smelled more delicious than any southern kitchen—except for Momma's kitchen, of course.

From the smell alone, I couldn't tell what was in it. I assumed with the nearly solid consistency, and the lack of utensils, this was one of their hands-on meals. I'd had a few while I was here before, they've always been my favorite.

A dark jelly liquid with some kind of meat and corn and rice. It always was so tasty; I was excited to be served one of my favorite meals on my first day back.

"Grandmother will be alright," Kateri said as she poked at the fire with a jagged twig.

"And you? Are you going to be alright?"

She sighed and nodded slowly. "Grandmother has been all but kind mostly, but I do not wish death upon her."

"I understand." I stuck a finger into the bowl. The hot gel stuck to my finger, and I pulled it out, shaking away the heat.

"Careful, Outsider." Kateri laughed. "You will lose your finger."

I chuckled. It was what she told me the very first time I'd had a hands-on meal. The crickets chirped their racket as we sat in silence while my food tried to cool in the heat of the night. So much had happened while I was gone, and I was beginning to wonder if I'd made a mistake by coming here, or by waiting two years to return.

With a sigh, I called, "Kateri?"

Kateri giggled. She and I had spent much more time together than myself and Saloso. She knew me well enough to know my question before I could even ask it. "Saloso is a very beautiful woman," she told me. "She has changed a lot since you left, Outsider. She is the strongest I have ever seen her. You have nothing to worry about. She will be very pleased to see you."

Twenty-One
Helpful Conversations

The next morning, Catskill woke me early and we took a walk down the way while Kateri rested.

"What did you return for, Outsider?" Catskill asked as we walked along a dirt path. It looked like the path was beaten from foot travel, not carved out like other paths.

Brushing a hanging leaf away, I tried to think of the best way to explain my sudden presence. *How do I tell him I'm here to say goodbye to the woman he's supposed to marry?*

The thought summoned another, and I asked him, "What are you really doing in the forest with Kateri?"

He didn't flinch. His broad shoulders moved rhythmically as he led me deeper into the forest. "When Valley was killed, I finally realized something had to be done. He was like a brother to me. And those people," he looked over at me, "*your* people, killed him. They took him from me, and I was willing to do anything to avenge his life. But Kateri..." He stopped walking and stared at the ground. "She told me that healers do not only

212

specialize in physical treatments, but they also specialize in matters of the heart and the mind."

"Why can't you just use a healer's tent for these sessions?"

He chuckled, baring pristine white teeth instead of his usual fangs. "She caught me a few times trying to run away. I'd always told her I needed fresh air, so she started coming along with me. We leave at night some days and return in the early mornings before Grey awakens."

We were walking again, making our way back to Kateri as I listened to him. I remembered when the tactical team showed up. They lost a member; I learned it was a man named Richard. But the team ended up replacing Richard with a guy named Samuel, and the report came back saying the body could not be retrieved. Richard didn't get a burial; he got a memorial service. But that was the price that came with the payment for working on a private security detail. No one remembered you when you died, but everyone would remember Valley.

Valley was family. I'd met him on a few occasions. He was as much of a brute as Catskill, and he believed in Grey Hawk's ideals just like the rest of the warriors. Catskill and Valley had been inseparable. They weren't *actually* brothers, but you'd think they were with how similar they looked. Catskill had dark hair, Valley had light hair, but they shared the same skin color, eyes, nose, and even the same ungodly muscles. They were a strong team. I imagined losing Valley must've been hard on Catskill—especially since he'd softened and turned to Kateri in the aftermath.

"Using a healer's tent would be fine, but I still work for

Grey. I am still—"

"Under her thumb? Her henchman."

He raised his brow at the last comparison but simply nodded with a sigh. "Yes. I cannot escape her, and none of the warriors understand. They did not love Valley as a brother. They loved him as a warrior."

"So you sneak away to talk about your feelings?"

He rolled his eyes. "I go out to clear my head sometimes and Kateri comes along. We just recently started talking about plans for the tribe. Something must be done."

The concern in his voice forced me to feel sorry for him. Catskill seemed unbreakable but losing his close friend and spending time with Kateri, it was obvious he was learning kindness. Apparently, he was also learning that the tribe was in trouble. If Grey continued in her terrible leadership—running a dictatorship and letting everyone die because she'd chosen to do nothing—then the tribe would crumble in three years or less.

"You really want to save this place?" I asked, trying to steer him clear of his initial question to me.

"Yes, it is my home."

Kateri came into view, her slumbering body lay beneath a blanket as she breathed deeply. Catskill was smiling as he looked her over. "I will go wake her." He left my side, crossing the grass to the sleeping woman and gently knelt beside her to shake her shoulder.

Glittering brown eyes opened and Kateri immediately smiled up at Catskill. They leaned in close and whispered to

214

each other. Something felt off. The way Kateri's eyes were bright and full of joy, and the way Catskill seemed to melt when she reached for his hand. Watching from afar, the two looked like they were in love—not discussing Catskill's bottled anger from two years ago. Grieving did take time, but that didn't look like grief at all.

"Kateri," I called.

She searched for me and when her eyes found me standing by a tree, they widened. "Good morning, Outsider! I had nearly forgotten you returned. Did you walk with Catskill this morning?"

Catskill stood and began to fold Kateri's blanket for her.

"Yeah, I did. And he told me you two come out here to talk about Valley."

She nodded before she pulled a brown shawl over her head. "Yes, that is true."

Forget what I said about minding my business and not being around for two years. Something was going on with these two, and I needed to know what.

"And Saloso? Does she know about these meetings?"

Both froze, and then Kateri cleared her throat.

"Saloso doesn't know, does she? How could you, Kateri?"

"What is there to know? I am a healer. I am responsible for tending to the needs of others."

"And Misty? Does she know all about these new responsibilities?"

"Misty does not always need to know," Catskill cut in. "She would never believe I was struggling with Valley's death."

"Because you aren't."

"What is wrong with you, *Outsider?*"

That was the first time Kateri had ever referred to me as an 'outsider.' A *real* outsider. That wasn't the nickname she used to call me because I wasn't from the tribe, the way she'd said it now held malice behind it. Like she wanted me to remember there was a distinction between us, but I wanted to remind her that there wasn't. As long as Grey Hawk was chief, Kateri would be considered an outsider, too. She was an outsider because she was only partially Sand Ribbon. Half of the blood pumping through her body belonged to the Mohawk tribe.

"You're right," I said, swallowing the sudden urge to point out how much of an outsider she was, too. "I'm just an outsider."

Her eyes began to water. "I didn't mean it that way, Cameron. Please."

I held up a hand as she took a step toward me. "It's alright, Kateri. I understand."

Silence loomed over us as I gathered my things.

Our trip was quiet. Catskill led the way while Kateri followed, and I walked behind her. Our plan from the previous night was to return early; I'd go to the maize fields and work there until evening. When evening came, Kateri would bring Saloso to see me, but I changed my mind. I wanted to go see Priest Misty, so I'd let them drop me off in the fields and go find her. I just had to stay out of Grey's sight. As long as she didn't know I was there, everything would be fine.

They took me along a secret entrance to the maize fields

where I stayed for a while. The sweet smell of their corn would always be one of my favorite memories. I knew there would be things I'd forget during my time in Peru, but I hoped I wouldn't forget anything—not even the smell of the cornfields. I walked through the tall stalks, unable to ignore the fact that the field was not as plentiful as it once was. There were burned stalks, weeping stalks, stalks that never produced. The grounds were dry, and some of the stalks were feeble. It was odd to see such a beautiful land swept up by the wings of heat and drought. Pressing my hand into the dirt, I wondered how much longer this place truly had.

After a while, I left the corn maze and found my way to the forested area where Misty stayed. I remembered it was there at Misty's place where I had my first encounter with God. Technically, it was my second encounter since my first was the vision He showed me when I was eight years old. I had never come face to face with God before; I remember feeling jittery for a while once I woke up afterward. The experience I had, feeling the raw power of God, it was something I would never forget.

Standing before the grand wooden cabin, I knocked on the front door.

"Who knocks?" Misty's voice hadn't changed.

"It's me, Great Mist of the Sea. Cameron."

The door creaked open, and Misty stood in a blood red tunic that fell to the floor. Her long sleeves with wide cuffs flopped over her hands as she held open the door. "Dearest Cameron," she smiled, "you have returned." She stepped outside and leaned forward to hug me tightly.

I'd missed Misty more than I thought. Relief flooded me as I squeezed her. When she stepped back, she patted my shoulders and eyed me closely, then her eyes fluttered shut and she stood perfectly still, as if she was listening for something.

When she opened her eyes, she said, "You have come seeking wisdom, have you not?"

I wanted to be amazed, but as the Great Mist of the Sea, I'd expected nothing less. A tightlipped smile spread over my face. "I have."

She nodded. "What is troubling you?"

"The truth. And some other things."

"The truth makes us free, Cameron, of all burdens, doubt, and guilt. It is the truth that will remove shackles from you."

"What if I can't tell the truth?"

"Then you must return home until you can," Misty said.

Dropping my head, I stared at my toes, wondering if I'd made a mistake.

"I see that you are worried about Saloso. All will be well, just be honest."

I raked a hand over my hair and nodded. It was no secret that I had feelings for Saloso, I just didn't think Misty would've notice, even though she had impeccable discernment from God.

Raising my head, I was greeted by her warm skin and welcoming eyes. "Do you know where she is?"

"She is in the chief hut."

I lifted a brow. "Why?"

"Worry not. Chief Grey Hawk will be gone for some time. Her illness worsened recently, so she went up to our kindred in the mountains for better aid. They have access to a special herb which God requested we give her. The journey there to retrieve the herb and return would be far too long for Chief Grey alone. She was escorted this morning."

"Hold on, Chief Grey left just last night?"

She nodded, her long brown hair lazily shifted with the movement. "Over the past few days, her condition worsened. Saloso made the decision last night to send Grey Hawk up the mountain instead of waiting for someone to return with the herb."

"I see." I glanced away.

Misty didn't seem worried at all, perhaps she'd already known the outcome of Grey Hawk's mountain trip. Whether or not it was bleak was hard to tell since Misty had great control over her expressions. However, Grey Hawk's sickness was not concerning, it was Saloso's decision making. If she was making decisions, that meant she was now the acting chief, and I had absolutely no chance of asking her to return.

"You seem sad," Misty remarked.

I forced a smile. "No, I just…" I paused, picking my words wisely. I was too afraid to lie to her so I swallowed and said, "I think telling Saloso the truth may be a little harder than I thought."

I left Misty's place, dragging my bag through the forested area. I was exhausted, but since Grey wasn't at the tribe, I could tromp loudly through the forest and ignore the turning heads as I appeared from the bushes. Children had grown, pregnant women had birthed, marriages had been performed. The tribe had changed. Even the tents looked different, considering many of them had been scorched. The memory of the tribe on fire forced me to keep my head down and move swiftly to the chief hut. I didn't think anyone had expected me to return or be happy that I *had* returned when it was because of me that the tribe was nearly set to ash two years earlier.

Without hesitation, I lifted the flap over the hut entrance and rushed inside, escaping the scrutinizing glares and stifling silence. Glancing around, I found no one inside. I was secretly relieved. It was better for her to find me than for me to find her, in my opinion. I looked around a little, finding the three huts—one large hut set between two smaller ones—were separated by different animal skins. The big open room was spacious with different types of pelts along the floor, and animal trophies along the walls. On one of the walls was a black panther.

Dropping my duffle bag to the floor, I removed my backpack and tossed it to the side. I reached out to touch the panther. Its golden eyes peered at me as if she were ready to lunge. Her skin was stretched across the wall of the hut, sprawled on display. She was a trophy. I placed my hand on her soft nose and closed my eyes. I felt a little relaxed as I exhaled, then something moved beside me. Taking a quick look over my shoulder, my heart nearly stopped.

Twenty-Two
I AM COMPLETE

"Cameron?"

I stared at the figure. She was the most regal-looking woman I'd ever seen. Her skin looked velvety, like someone had ground peaches into flesh. The sweet smell of honey and flowers filled the air, and chocolate tresses flowed over her shoulders. A single-strap dress made of animal hides with a blue accent along the trim hugged her womanly figure.

Fringes hung across her chest at a diagonal angle, and there was a rope of some sort tied around her waist, making her hips more pronounced. The dress barely reached her knees, where splits up the side allowed the bottom of her dress to fall like a loin cloth instead of the regular tunic dress. Long legs and strong arms were free of covering allowing me to take in the beautiful woman. Along her right arm was a tribal marking, it looked like a winding river between two sandy brown bangles. Around her neck, where once only one fang hung, there were now two tied together so the points touched at the bottom, making something of a circle on her chest.

My eyes skirted up her entire frame, flitting finally to the eyes that could freeze my heart or make it melt. They could stop its beating or make it erratic. Royal blue eyes drowned me in an intense stare. Dark lashes moved quickly as she searched me like she was trying to remember me, or maybe she was trying to see if I was real or not.

Standing before me was not the shy woman I once knew two years ago, standing before me was the chief of the Sand Ribbon tribe. As far east as the winds would take you and as far north as the mountains could guide you.

Chief Sunstar de Achille.

"Cameron," Sunstar whispered, "is it really you?"

"Sunstar." I paused, almost lost for words. "I'm back."

She rushed into my arms. Holding her made me feel like I had everything I needed. Nothing in these past two years has made me feel the way Saloso did. I loved her, but I wished I hadn't returned. I wished I would've stayed away, to never feel this wholeness again. Now I didn't know if I could live without this feeling. Or, at least, I didn't want to.

"Cameron," she cried, taking a handful of my shirt in her hand. "I cannot believe you have returned. You are here right now. I am not imagining this?"

"No. I'm here … but," I paused, holding her close. I didn't want to tell her the truth. But I didn't want to hide it from her either. It was a lot easier when I'd gone through the scenario in my head on the jet.

Taking Misty's advice, I said, "Sunstar, I didn't return for

223

the reasons you think."

She pulled away from me, slowly stepping back. Her piercing eyes demanded the truth, and it spilled out at her silent command.

"I only have two months before I have to return. I didn't come to stay."

She jerked back, taking a wider step away from me. I reached for her, but she smacked my hand away. "Why? Why would you return just to leave again?"

"Sunstar, I want to be with you more than anything. I spent these last two years unhappy and thinking only of you."

Her tears would not stop, despite her fiercely wiping them away. "I do not understand," she whispered.

"I ... I wanted to do things properly. To properly say goodbye this time."

She was mid wipe when she dropped her hand to her side, scowling deeply. "You came back to tell me goodbye?" she yelled. "How dare you return for such a reason!"

"Sunstar, please calm down—"

"No!" she shouted, and she shoved me back hard. I stumbled, tripping over my bags and landing on the floor. She was on me before I could recover. "You have returned to make a fool of me! You are an evil man who toyed with my heart." Tears rolled down her cheeks, fleeing from her chin to drip onto my face. "You do not love me, Cameron. You do not love me at all!"

"That's not true, Sunstar," I whispered as I sat up onto my elbows.

She forced me back down, flopping onto me as she wept into my chest. "I have loved you and waited for you to return. I could not forget you, Cameron. So why? Why have you returned only to tell me to forget you?"

Staring up at the ceiling, I slowly wrapped my arms around Sunstar as she leaned over my chest, crying. I hadn't realized she'd been waiting for me, too. I had always hoped she would, but listening now, realizing Sunstar had longed for my return with no clear sign of when I would, the thoughts crushed me. I held her a little tighter.

"I'm so sorry, Sunstar," I whispered. "I didn't know you were waiting for me. I came back because I wanted to ask you to return with me. To come into my world but," I paused, noticing her tears were quieter now. "I know this tribe is your home, and I can't ask you to leave them."

"Ask me," she whispered abruptly. The chattering locusts and busy bugs chirped around us in the silence. "Ask me."

"I won't ask you to choose. I won't—"

"Ask me!" she shouted into my chest, a strained cry ripped from her, and she beat my chest softly. "Ask me to leave with you. To run away from this place. These people who are cold, and only have love for Grey. They have rejected me, despite the blood of Grande Chief Zasca pumping through me."

All this time, I'd thought Sunstar wouldn't want to come with me because this was her home. But it was the opposite.

"I cannot run away from my problems, can I?" She raised her head finally. Tear-stained cheeks were red and matched her misty eyes.

"No." Slowly, I sat up, so she knelt right beside me. "You've changed."

Her eyes flicked back to mine. "I am glad you noticed." I smiled softly at her and slowly, she reached out to stroke my cheek. Her soft hand against my face nearly made me melt, and the sweltering heat would've boiled the puddle I'd melted into. "I will make things right," she said, "and then, will you ask me?"

I nodded. "I will."

For the first time since I saw her, she smiled. Her tender pink lips caught my attention, and slowly, I lifted my gaze to meet hers. Her hand slipped down my neck and rested on my shoulder.

"I missed you, Sunstar," I said.

She whispered, "I missed you too, Cameron."

I placed a hand on her back and pulled her a little closer. Her lips found mine, and suddenly my heart was pounding in my ears. It was not as I imagined it ... our first kiss. I always thought it'd be romantic, but I was sitting on the floor of her hut, kissing her in a way I'd never even kissed Garrith.

Slowly, she pulled away with bright red cheeks. "I have not kissed anyone before."

"That doesn't matter to me."

She laughed lightly, and it was the sweetest sound I'd heard in a while. I wished the moment could've lasted forever, but the animal skin flapped open and the moment was gone when Catskill and Kateri walked in. Their worried looks turned to relief when they saw me.

Kateri marched across the room and punched me in the shoulder. "Why did you leave the fields?"

"You knew he returned and had not told me, sister?" Sunstar asked as she got to her feet.

"Well, yes, but it is complicated."

"How?"

"The fault is on me." Catskill stepped forward.

Sunstar's eyes darted between the two of them. "Where were you two in the early hours? We needed you to escort Grandmother."

Kateri scowled. "Escort Grandmother? Where … where is she? We were coming to see her."

I blinked. "For what?"

"We think another hole is filling. The watering spot for the animals has shrank even more. It is diminishing more rapidly than we anticipated," Kateri said.

Sunstar shook her head. "We must do something."

"What can be done if the chief is not here?" Catskill asked as he crossed his arms over his chest.

I watched Sunstar, she stood still, staring at nothing. The swirling thoughts had taken her away briefly before she looked up from the floor and said, "With things getting worse, more rapidly than we expected, I will take the seat."

"Hold on—" Catskill opposed, but Sunstar lifted a hand and hushed him quickly.

"It is my right, and I will take it. All I ask is that you all support me."

"I am with you, sister. It is your right," Kateri said.

Sunstar nodded but Catskill shook his head. "This is dangerous. You know they will require a trophy."

"I know the guides. I was there when they were rewritten and refreshed," Sunstar snapped. Her piercing eyes made Catskill cower, and he turned and left the hut.

"Do not worry about him." Kateri shrugged. "He will support you."

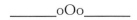

"I brought these for you," I said as I unpacked my backpack. It held all my technology and a few books and learning materials I'd packed for Sunstar and the tribe. The ocean in her eyes had never seemed so vast until they lit up as I laid the bundle of books on the floor of her hut.

"Goodness," she whispered, extending a shaky hand. She hovered over the books and materials, unsure of which to pick.

"Now we can continue our lessons," I said.

"And mine!" Kateri interrupted, shooting her hand into the air.

I nodded at her. "And yours."

Catskill sat in the corner, glancing over his shoulder at the books in front of the girls. Sunstar hadn't muttered another word about Kateri and Catskill's disappearance, and neither did they. They left the mystery to hang in the air, but it was eating away at him. He absently stirred his porridge with a thick wooden spoon, not joining the conversation. I wondered if there was actually something going on that he and Kateri were hiding. Was the tribe in imminent trouble?

"Cameron? Did you hear me?"

I shook my head, looking away from the quiet warrior sitting in the corner. "Sorry, Sunstar, can you repeat that?"

She sighed and placed her bowl beside her. "Why are you so absent all of a sudden?"

"I'm not." I gave her a weak smile, but she saw right through it. "I'm just wondering about Grey and the tribe. Everything is so different now."

"Well, it is true that much has changed. Just as we had begun to rebuild after," she paused, unsure of how to say my rescuers nearly burned the whole place down. "Our tribe is falling apart now, but we must save it."

"What do you mean the tribe is falling apart?"

"The heat has been incredibly strong, and there has been countless droughts and sandstorms. Our waterways are getting filled with sand and stone. Two of them have already been clogged completely shut while a dozen more are halfway there. It is only a matter of time before the rest of our puquois are completely filled with sand and stone."

"And do not leave out the burning of our fields," Kateri added, as if we hadn't had this conversation. *Was she always this good of an actress?*

"Yes," Sunstar nodded. "The fields have burned, and we have lost many crops. The heat has forced us to shave our animals, but that leaves very little wool for our own use or to sell."

"We would not sell it anyway," Catskill muttered. We all

glanced over at him, and he noticed our onlooking eyes immediately. "With the heat, no one would buy our wool. We barely have enough crops to trade, and when we run out of that, then what?"

"We have to think of something soon," Kateri said, her eyes were ladened with sadness. "We will starve and thirst if we do nothing."

"I will come up with something," Sunstar said. "For now, I have to focus on what to say in the meeting I will call."

"Are you really going to take the seat?" I asked.

Sunstar nodded, her eyes never reaching mine. "It is the only way changes can be made."

"And us?" I asked. "Where does that leave us?" I didn't mean to ask her in front of everyone, but I'd somehow hoped that Sunstar really could make things right and leave with me. Unfortunately, I think I was asking for too much.

"I have not forgotten," Sunstar replied. "I am going to return with you." She patted her chest twice, and Kateri gasped.

"What do you mean, sister? How can you be chief and leave?"

"I am not sure yet, but there is certainly a way to do it."

I took a deep breath and lifted my bowl of porridge. My hopes were broken, and I was ready to return home. I shouldn't have hoped so easily, but when you desperately want something, it's hard not to.

"Is there anything you can do, Outsider?" Catskill asked in the silence.

"What do you mean?"

He said, "If Saloso goes with you and returns with a solution to our problem, that will prove our worlds need each other. She will be needed in your world while she is still our chief."

"That seems kind of complicated," I said with a shrug.

"No, Catskill is a genius! I can prove to the council that Cameron's world and our world need each other. They will have to let me be with him and be here."

"How though?" Kateri asked, stirring her soup.

It wasn't a bad idea; it just required frequent flying and for their tribe to get some kind of technology. Doing that would bring attention to the tribe, attention they wouldn't like. They'd become a tourist spot, or at least a reservation, and people would want to know them. They'd lose all their privacy.

"I am not sure," Sunstar said, a gentle smile capturing her lips. "But I will make this work."

They didn't know how much work (and how much money) it would take to revive the tribe, or how much privacy they would lose, but I decided I'd mention it later.

Catskill suggested, "You still have your six months, I think now is a better time than any to use them."

"I agree." Kateri wiped crumbs from her skirt and set her bowl beside her.

"Well, I guess it is more complicated," Sunstar said. "Who will lead in my stead if I am away?"

"Misty," I said. Everyone glanced over at me. "If you leave, you can have Misty be in charge. She's the high priest here, and she's more than qualified. It'll only be six months."

"I think the outsider is correct," Catskill said. "Misty would know what to do, and she is aware of the situation. She has been monitoring it and taking it to prayer daily."

"This seems like a good plan." Sunstar was looking at the floor, the cogs turning in her head as she thought of a way to present this to the council.

The silence in the tent was thick with an uneasy feeling of joy. We wanted to rejoice but, secretly, everyone had their doubts, their uncertainties of this plan. We wanted it to work, but in reality, there was a lot more to consider—like whether Sunstar would even be able to return in six months with a solution to the tribe's problem.

What if Sunstar didn't want to return? What if she didn't want to stay? What if she hates the world I live in?

Twenty-Three
The Black Panther

Before dinner finished, Sunstar called a meeting of the council for the following day. I'd been in Peru for forty-eight hours and I had already second guessed my return more times than I liked. Each second guess was reasonable, however, since Sunstar would return with me. It would only be for six months; I had a lot to consider. The lingering thoughts of Sunstar hating where I'm from wouldn't leave as I tried to eat my breakfast. It was grits with strips of pork in it. They were extremely lumpy, but I'd grown to like them since the last time I was here.

"Good morning, Cameron." The priest's voice rolled like a mist over my shoulders.

"Good morning, Misty," I answered as she sat on the log beside me.

Other tribe members sat on logs, passing me nasty glances, and muttering quietly. Initially, I was sorely confused, but then I remembered my father's little rescue mission almost erased this place from the earth, and I sat as far away from the rest of

233

the camp as possible.

"Where is Sunstar and Kateri? They are not with you?"

Misty stirred her grits a moment before lifting a spoonful to her lips.

"No. Kateri is helping Sunstar get ready for the council meeting today."

"Ah, that is today. Our young leader seems to be stirring with a plan, is she not?"

"She is," I chuckled.

Misty nodded with a smile and watched the rest of the tribe walk around passing bowls of food to one another. "I am certain that whatever you two are planning will be just fine for our people."

"Yeah," I sighed, "for your people."

"You seem bothered. What is pressing you?"

"You mean you don't already know?" She looked up from her bowl, and her eyes smiled before her lips curled into one. Releasing a girlish laugh, Misty waved a hand and said, "Surely, you cannot believe I know everything?"

"You took one look at me after you hadn't seen me in two years and knew what was bothering me."

She glanced up and nodded. "That is true, but it is the Spirit who reveals to me. I do not know everything; only what God allows me to know."

I looked down at the ground. "Why didn't He tell you about this?"

"Sometimes, it is better to come and talk. That way, God can reveal to you where the root of your problem lies. If I always have an answer, you will never look for one. That is why God does not always answer us."

"What do you mean?"

"If God answered every time we asked Him something, we would never need to believe. If He always gave the solution, problems would never arise. That would mean Jesus did not tell the truth when He said, 'Trouble will come,' which would make the Word invalid."

I searched the dirt, watching my bare toes dig through the warmth into a coolness when Misty said, "Jesus warned us about trouble. If His warning were not true, He would not have said it. But through our problems, we can learn to trust God— to have faith in Him."

"Because faith pleases God, right?"

She smiled warmly at me as I looked up from the dirt. "Exactly, Cameron."

"Well then, I don't understand my dilemma. How can I trust God in this situation?"

"Which one? There seems to be much warring within you." Misty set her bowl down and touched my shoulder. "Confusion, regret, even uncertainty and betrayal. What truly is the problem, Cameron?"

I looked away, turning the spoon in my bowl around. "I want Saloso to return home with me. But I can't keep her away from her tribe."

"What else?"

I paused, wondering how much more I felt comfortable telling her, but I had nothing to lose. "This dream about a well and helping people—and the living water. It's all so confusing. On top of trying to figure out what's going on with Catskill and Kateri. I just … I just feel like I shouldn't have returned."

"God's plan for you has only just begun. You are right where God needs you to be."

"In confusion?"

"Come with me," Misty stood and left without waiting for me.

Setting my bowl beside hers, I stepped over the log and followed her into the forest.

"Have you ever heard of Queen Esther?" she asked.

"Yeah?"

"Did you know that God placed her on the throne to rescue His people?"

"Well yeah, everyone does." I stepped over a big vine before stopping just short of Misty. She was standing still in the middle of shrubs and trees. Her white dress seemed to glow in the dark forest as she stood there facing away from me.

"Everyone knows that God placed her on the throne, but many have forgotten that God will do the same for any one of us. He will place us in a throne-like position because there is a purpose there. We can only serve our purpose when we trust God."

"How does any of this relate to my problems?"

"Because you must stop seeing them as problems and look for God's Hand in the midst. You must realize you are in a position for something bigger than yourself." She stepped forward, touching a thick leaf hanging over us. "If I perish, I perish," Misty whispered.

"Esther said that," I replied.

"She did. She said those words because she trusted God, and she trusted that her purpose to go before the king was the will of God."

"How can you be so sure?"

"Because she went to the throne room, did she not?"

I chuckled, slipping my hands into my pockets. "Yeah."

"So, when you begin to trust God, you will see things differently. You will understand life differently. And you will be able to serve your purpose."

"How do I know if I am trusting God?"

"When there is no more worry in your heart. When you stop trying to force things to work in your favor, but for the glory of God. And when you can walk into a situation and believe that if you perish, it is for the will of God. Then you will know that you trust God."

A strong wind came, and the bushes began to rustle, kicking up leaves and dirt. I squeezed my eyes shut and covered my ears, kneeling to resist getting blown away. When the wind calmed, I opened my eyes and realized Priest Misty was gone.

I took the trail back to the tribe to find the council room. The council room was a hut far off in the distance of the tribe. I didn't mind the walk as I thought over everything the high priest told me. She said I was exactly where God needed me to be, but I felt so unsure; I was having a hard time believing it. However, I figured she was right. My disbelief was because I didn't trust God. I was worried about Saloso's decisions, and I was worried about the tribe.

I was worried about everything.

But fully trusting God meant not knowing the future, and still believing him to make things all right. It was a tough pill to swallow, but I was willing to try it to make sense of everything.

My thoughts continued to swirl as I reached the council hut. There was a stunningly elaborate design across the wooden frame. Tribal carvings, telling the story of Grande Chief Zasca, and every other chief since. Chief Nunca's carving was left unfinished, and only Sunstar's name had been carved into the wood. I stared at her name, wondering how to trust God in this situation. I was confused because I didn't even know what I wanted. I wanted Sunstar to love my place, and to be part of my world. But I also wanted her to stay here because this was her home.

What do I do, God?

I sighed, letting my eyes trace over the hut. Looking over the carvings, I allowed myself to be consumed by the drawings so I could forget the lingering, confusing thoughts.

Each chief had done something impactful for the tribe. Grande Chief Zasca's carving was the story of how she prayed for direction and lightning struck the earth, guiding the tribe home. Chief Nebuya was the next chief right after Zasca. Her depiction was of a woman befriending a man, and he showed her how to build the puquois. Apparently, the aqueducts here were only a replica of the aqueducts originally built by the Nazca tribe.

238

Each story was unforgettable, and I loved making out the carvings. They were the length of the hut but only about three inches high. They were each in a row with Zasca at the bottom on the back of the hut, and Sunstar's name on a different side. I waited and let everyone else file in before me. Hobbling old people, a few young people, along with Kateri, Catskill, and a few warriors entered the wide hut and waited for their leader to arrive. I stepped inside and found it looked nothing like anything in the rest of the tribe. Wool covered the floors and seat cushions around a long flat table. Hollowed out rocks held water, and bowls of fruit were set down the center of the table.

There were thirteen spots in all, each one taken except the seat on an elevated throne where Sunstar would sit. There was a chair seated on the wooden platform made of stone with the word 'Chief' etched into them and a black cushion on it.

There were sheer dark drapes hanging from the ceiling, covering the entire throne while inky ones covered the backwall. It looked like someone had placed a palanquin right there in the room.

I could feel everyone's eyes on me as I stood in the corner. I wore tribal clothes today. Sunstar was able to get me something that was more appropriate than my joggers and shirt. I tried not to let the stares bother me, and I kept my head down with my hands behind my back. There was muttering and whispers; I told myself they weren't whispering about me to keep from bursting with nerves. I knew I wasn't one of them, but it couldn't have been more obvious as I waited in the corner and not in a seat amongst them.

239

I heard the shifting of the curtains, and the murmuring and fussing stop completely. Lifting my head, I almost lost my breath.

Sunstar walked in through the black wall of drapes, and everyone stood to greet her. She wore a large straw hat with a sheer drapery hanging from it, covering down to her nose. There was black tribal paint over her eyes that reached the bridge of her nose, and dark lines that looked like whiskers on her cheeks. There were other markings on her neck and on part of her exposed chest. The sleeves of the sleek gown, made of white hides, clung below her shoulders and rested on her arms. A dark cloak made of an animal's black fur was draped over her where the front paws of the beast rested on each shoulder. When she turned to enter her palanquin, you could see the back paws and the tail of the animal dragging behind her as a train. But it wasn't until I recognized the dark head of the beast grimacing down her back with a missing fang that I realized this was Sunstar's first prize.

It was a black panther... *she* was the black panther.

Twenty-Four
The Council

Sunstar explained to me once that every chief's first trophy determined how they would lead. Those who killed wild beasts were deemed to be strong and forward. The ones who killed small animals were destined to do very little for the tribe.

But even the small should not be forgotten.

There were women whose first kill was a majestic beast, like the black panther. A rare beauty that was hard to come by, and even harder to kill alone, would speak to them being extremely impactful and graceful in their leadership. They would rule with God's mercy and wisdom, proving to be some of the greatest leaders in their tribal history.

The women who killed panthers were always the ones who encompassed the rarity of the beast, the beauty of the beast, the grace of it. They changed the tribe the most. When such a role was bestowed on the shoulders of a young child caught in the feud of her parents, no one believed that child could lead the tribe. Thus, Grey Hawk rose in her stead.

Everyone inclined their heads to Sunstar as she entered the room. Bending at the waist and bowing before her. She took her seat on the stone chair. "Rise," Sunstar spoke in a voice that I'd never heard.

I watched as a man opened the dark drapes and pinned them around the pillars beside her chair. Sunstar lifted her head, ready to address the council when she saw me standing in the back. Her piercing eyes nearly made my knees buckle at how stunning and intimidating she looked.

"Cameron," she called. I gulped and stood stiff as a board. "Come and sit."

With no choice, I followed her command, but a hoarse voice stopped me in my tracks. "Excuse me, Lord Chief, you cannot let an outsider sit on the throne beside you. It is an offense to the ones who have walked before you." The bald wrinkled man had hunched forward, speaking forcefully to the chief.

Sunstar only smiled. It was incredibly frightening. "The ones who have walked before me have finished their journey and are no longer walking. If it is punishment you fear on my behalf, fear not. Let our ancestors pour their rage on me as I extend my rage to you. Settle. My word stands." She looked up from the old man and nodded at me.

I gripped my pants to dry my sweating hands and walked tensely to the front. She extended a gloved hand to me before casting it to the side. I followed her orders and sat on her right side before the council. Kateri sat beside Misty with Catskill across from a group of warriors. Everyone looked mortified, except Misty, Kateri, and Catskill. Kateri and Misty looked amused, while Catskill looked bored.

"Let us start now with a word from the scrolls."

Misty stood at Sunstar's words and moved to the front of the room. A man walked out with a scroll and passed it to Misty. She unrolled it and said, "The scroll of Proverbs. Chapter eleven, verse fourteen."

I took a quick look around the room, everyone's head was bowed. I dropped mine as well. Misty read about people with no guidance falling, but the help of counselors kept them safe. It was an insightful message, reminding each of them that these meetings were about what was best for the tribe, what would keep the tribe from falling, and what would keep it alive and safe.

Misty rolled up the scroll as she finished. "Let us pray. Dear God, we have come together for knowledge and wisdom. Bring us peace and unity as we harmonize beneath You for the progression of our tribe. In Jesus' name, amen."

"Amen," everyone said.

"Thank you, Priest Misty. Let us begin," Sunstar said.

Misty nodded at the young chief and returned the scroll to the man who backed away with his head bowed. Once Misty was seated, Sunstar began.

"There are urgent matters at hand, two of which I must address today. The first is Chief Grey Hawk. As acting chief, I have decided to usurp the chiefhood from her."

Gasps echoed, and everyone glanced around at each other. A bald woman who wore a purple robe seated in the front raised her hand. Sunstar nodded at her.

"I agree," the woman said, and everyone was as shocked as I was. "As an elder on this council, it is only correct that the chiefhood is passed to Saloso now. With Chief Grey Hawk's health in the unstable condition it has been in, we cannot be certain of her survival. It is time we offer Saloso the seat."

"Absolutely not!" a heavyset, shirtless man interrupted. He had a single thick brow stretching from one end of his head to the other, and his voice shook the earth as he spoke. "She is not ready! She holds no regard to the traditions of this great land. We cannot pass her the chiefhood."

"Then who do you believe we should pass it to?" Misty chimed in. Her chocolate skin stood out amongst the copper and golden people, but it didn't bother her. She spoke like she was one of them—not of the mountain tribe. "If we do not pass the throne to the rightful one, then it will be jostled around until it eventually comes back to her."

"That is true," the woman in purple spoke. "Even if someone else sat on the throne, it would be brief, as her time as a chief is only one birthday away now."

"It matters not how close her time is for chiefhood, Elder Atik," a short woman with a snarky voice spoke. "Saloso is not to be on that throne until the set time."

The room began to reach a boiling point when the thick man spoke up again. "Lady Falls is correct. And if it is not for the sake of breaking tradition, then certainly she is not ready until she learns to respect us. Lord Hakan simply stated an *outsider*, not to mention one who brought fire and danger to our tribe, cannot sit beside her. Yet she gave him a belligerent response."

"Hardly." Priest Misty threw her hand up. "I think you just dislike this outsider, and we all know what happened was not his fault, Commander Kumya."

"The situation you speak of, Commander, is no longer relevant. I do not wish to hear any further of that event," Sunstar said coldly.

"My Lord Chief," Commander snapped, "it needs to be addressed now that he is here!"

"Settle," was all she said in reply.

The room stirred in a suffocating silence when a man seated beside Commander Kumya said, "Acting Chief Saloso has taken many valuable actions to keep our tribe on its feet while Chief Grey Hawk has been sick."

"Inti, you do not believe her actions are worthy of question? As an elder, I believe every single action of Saloso has been questionable since she took the seat as the Black Panther of the tribe."

"Coya," Elder Atik said, nodding at the tall woman who'd just spoken. "From elder to elder, we have advised Nunca, Grey, and now Saloso. Can you not see that her intentions are greater than those of the previous?" Elder Coya's nose wrinkled, and she shook her head.

"I see nothing but a stubborn girl planting roots of terror in this tribe."

"Agreed," Lady Falls said.

"Is it fair to say that?" Kateri murmured. That was the first time she'd spoken up. Her eyes met mine immediately. "What has Saloso done that is grounds to believe her roots lie elsewhere than in purity?"

Kateri had always supported Sunstar. From the very first time we met, it was like she wanted to convince me that Sunstar was good before I was met with all the negativity surrounding her.

"Her roots lie in tearing this land apart!" Lady Falls barked. "She wants this tribe to depend on the means of the world beyond our own. For years we have survived. There is no need to turn our backs on the way of the ribbon lying in the sand."

"But," Kateri slid her eyes from mine to Lady Falls, "our lands are burning, our water sources are drying. You do not see the damage, but I have seen it with my own eyes. Reaching the outside world surely will help and not hurt."

"You are but a child," Commander Kumya said. "You are tainted with the same blood as Saloso. If it weren't for Misty, you would not be here, and you would not be trusted."

"Careful, Commander." Catskill leaned forward. "That is High Priest Misty, the one who is the Great Mist of the Sea. She is due respect when you speak of her, as is the young healer at her side." Catskill was not as thick as Commander Kumya, but he was just as headstrong, just as intimidating.

The commander looked stunned. He turned his attention to the warrior and said, "Are you speaking boldly to the one who raised you and placed a spear in your hand?"

"Was it not I who picked up the spear in the first place? And I who trained countless days and nights?" Catskill replied sharply, thumbing his mighty chest. The black strips that were printed onto his arm seemed to stretch the ink around his muscles.

Commander slammed a fist on the table, making everyone jump, except for Sunstar. She stayed put in her stone chair, only watching the madness unfold.

It was starting to become clear why Sunstar always had problems with this council. No one thought she was ready because she didn't rule with an iron fist, and she wasn't stuck on tradition. Sunstar wanted solutions to the problems beating down the door, even if it meant breaking tradition and invading the beauty of their forgotten tribe. Which was why she asked me to sit beside her; it was a resemblance of my world and hers working together. She was on the throne, still in charge. But I was at her side, ready to aid. I raised my chest, thinking of the symbolism, but it quickly deflated when the commander began to shout,

"I raised you! I trained you!"

Elder Coya raised a hand at the young warrior, stopping him from replying as she said, "Let us not make this an argument about yourselves, Commander Ri Kumya, and Warrior Catskill Ve Paquari. There are still matters at hand."

"What can we do then?" I recognized the younger man sitting further away. It was Killa, the one who was great at making pelts, using venom, and was in love with a woman named Elainnis, despite her being married to a warrior named Lee.

"Let us take a vote," Lord Hakan said.

A booming noise echoed beside me, and I jumped at the startling sound. Sunstar was holding a stick in her hand, it was thick and rigid. I wondered if that was the piece of wood she'd chosen for her Chief Rod, like what Grey walked around with. It was customary to have the chief before you carve a stick for you, but since Grey was sick (and didn't like Sunstar), and Nunca was gone, Sunstar kept the rod bare and rigid— symbolic of the life she'd had so far.

"We are not voting. The matter is closed. As acting chief, I am taking the chiefhood from Grey Hawk. It is of my blood and my birthright to rule as the head of the Sand Ribbon tribe."

"A usurp demands a challenge or a trophy!" Lady Falls yelled. "You cannot challenge her if she is not here."

"I cannot challenge her because she is past challenging age," Sunstar replied. The room fell quiet. "Because she is past the set sixty-five years that is considered appropriate for any acting chief or challenges, she can be deemed as incapable of handling the chiefhood. Therefore, it is passed to the next chief. In this case, me."

"Then a trophy!" Lady Falls demanded.

"That is of no problem for Saloso," Misty chuckled. "She is the best hunter of the tribe, yes?"

"I refute!" Elder Coya stood, her purple robe rippled and straightened. Grey waves fell over her shoulders and anger shrouded her face.

"As reigning chief, I am removing you from this council." Sunstar turned to the man sitting on her left. "Strip her of the elder robes and send her out."

"You cannot do this! I have been an elder for thirty years! I know what is best for this tribe!"

Sunstar didn't answer, she sat patiently, as her assistant tried to untie *former* elder Coya's garment. I knew what Sunstar was doing—she was making an example of Coya. Setting the bar for nonsense low, and the bar for respect high.

The young man couldn't get Coya out of her robes. Two warriors rose and escorted the screaming woman out.

When things settled, Sunstar spoke into the silence. "The second order of business." She looked over at her little sister. "After I am seated as Chief, I will take my six months to find a solution to our drying grounds."

"Objection!" Lord Hakan raised his hand.

Sunstar nodded at him.

"Once a chief is seated, she cannot stand. It is not possible."

"Unless there is a need for her absence," Misty replied. "Our tribe will perish if we do nothing. Sending our leader out on our behalf is necessary."

"Should not someone else go on our behalf?" Elder Atik asked. "I do believe that searching for a solution is what needs to be done, but should we send our *leader?*"

"I am, for once, agreeing with Elder Atik." The commander shrugged. "We cannot afford to lose our leader."

"Then which of you will go in my stead?"

The room was silent.

"None of us can go in her stead since we are all the council. Once inducted, council members give up their expedition time to be here to lead when the chief is away," Catskill explained.

"Six months, who will sit for you?" Lady Falls asked.

Sunstar looked over at Misty. "O Great Mist of the Sea, she is to be honored at my coronation. She will be added to our hut as a serving chief and will serve for me while I am gone." Sunstar paused and glanced around slowly. "If there are no objections, the matters have been settled, and this meeting can end."

Twenty-Five
The Taming of the Flame

"Cameron? Are you ready?" Sunstar was sitting in the cart, extending a hand to me.

I'd chosen not to question her about how intimidating she was in the council room. I didn't really have a chance. Everything after that was a blur to prepare for this expedition. Sunstar insisted that Catskill, Kateri, Killa, and I join her on this hunting trip as her travel team. Catskill was her guard, Kateri her aid, Killa her assistant, and since she did not want to leave me behind, I served as her right side, helping her make decisions.

"Yeah," I said, passing a glance to Kateri who sat beside her in the cart. "But I think I'll ride one of the horses for now."

"Aww," Kateri sighed. "I was hoping to get some lessons done."

"We've got five whole days." I took Sunstar's hand in mine, gave it a peck. "We'll have time later."

Sunstar was blushing now, but Kateri was extending her

hand to me with a smile on her face. "I want my hand kissed, too, by an outsider."

I chuckled, shooting a glance at Sunstar who nodded before I took Kateri's hand and kissed it. "There," I said. "Now you've been kissed by an outsider."

She stared at her hand, then glanced up at me. "There is magic that you practice. My hand is tingling all over."

"You are simply nervous." Sunstar took her hands and examined them.

I slung my small bag full of electronics into the cart, and closed the door, leaving the two women to chat.

Our caravan consisted of two carts. One for Sunstar and Kateri to travel in, and the other was full of supplies, hunting gear, and Misty's special healing herbs—just in case. On this five-day journey, we would travel for two, hunt for a day, and then return to the tribe.

"So," Killa said loudly, "you are riding with the men?" He was a strong man, although his youthful face made him look kinder than his muscular frame. His face wasn't perfect like Catskill's, but it was angular and his dark facial hair against his glowing copper skin made women flock to him. He was more popular than Catskill, but that was only because Catskill was standoffish and had been promised to Sunstar. Killa was the second-best thing after Valley who died two years ago. Killa trained with the warriors, but he was injured some time ago, so he now served as a pelt maker instead.

Grabbing the reins of one of the horses from the bigger cart, I sat beside Catskill. His cart was the one full of our supplies and hunting gear, and it was a bit wider, requiring two horses.

"Nice of you to join us, Outsider," Catskill said. "Now I will not be the only one tortured by the stories of women Killa has experienced."

I snorted. "Is that really what the next five days will consist of?"

Catskill rolled his eyes and chuckled, his wide shoulders dancing as he silently laughed. "I am not even sure why he came along, but yes."

"I am here serving our chief as her loyal leftist. I will be tending to all her needs."

"Where did the other guy go from the council meeting?" I asked.

Killa leaned forward. "Qispi stayed behind at the Panther's request. He'll be helping the High Priest make arrangements for our new chief's coronation."

"And you were the only person available?"

Catskill burst into laughter, but Killa only clicked his tongue, and his horse took off, pulling Sunstar and Kateri.

"Come on before he leaves us behind," Catskill said, clicking his tongue the same way Killa did, and both our horses began to trot.

"So, when are you marrying Kateri?" Killa asked.

Silence fell over us, only the noise of the tromping horses and rattling carts, with occasional outbursts of laughter from Sunstar and Kateri, could be heard. I craned my neck to stare in disbelief.

"What are you—" Catskill began but Killa cut him off. "Come on," he said, his lips stretching into a devious smile. "Everyone has seen the way you two interact. The way you are no longer tense. The way Kateri smiles at you."

"That is enough," Catskill mumbled.

"Or maybe it is simply the fact that you two missed going up the mountain with Grey because you were off again."

"You know about that?" I asked.

Catskill frowned down at me.

Killa said, "Yes. Who would not know? Besides Saloso, because she is so naïve, and Grey because she would never suspect anything."

Catskill sighed, loosening his grip on the reins. "It is true, what I told you, Outsider. Things were not supposed to end up this way. But I made a connection with Kateri. She was like a flame in my hand, burning so fiercely I could not stop her. But the fire did not hurt—it healed, it warmed, it made me feel something I thought I never would."

I watched in silence as the big angry man I once knew suddenly softened before me. He had been changed by love.

"Normally, one is afraid of a flame," Killa said. He was looking straight ahead, bobbing as his horse stomped its hooves into the ground. "But if you are never burned or hurt by such an amazing force of power—it must mean the flame obeys you. It is bound to your command. Fire will only submit to the one who can tame it. Because fire can never truly be tamed or controlled, but it can be nurtured and stoked. Only by choice does the flame flicker and yield."

"That is a way of putting it," I said. "There's a scripture about wives submitting to their husbands. It is very controversial where I'm from. But I think if more people heard what you just said, I think it wouldn't be so dividing."

"Your world sounds like one I would not want to be part of." Killa and Catskill laughed heartily, but I didn't understand. Glancing over at Catskill I asked him why.

He said, "Well, taming a fire might sound like I control it, I yell at it, or I force it to do the things I tell it to. But that is not so. Yelling is sometimes a sign of a lost temper, or a sign of no control, or even a sign of a weak person. A burning flame will not give in to weak hands, it will only allow itself to be handled by those who are capable. Those who do not seek to control but to assist."

"You cannot tame a flame without first recognizing its power. It's scorching heat," Catskill said, a focused look on his face. "You must respect the flame."

"A flame has full range of how submissive it will be." Killa leaned forward. "It must be stoked and coaxed into submission. Really, the flame requires the one who wants to tame it to first submit to it. To serve it and learn everything about it before attempting to groom it. You cannot groom a flame without knowing what will make it grow."

"*And!*" Killa exclaimed. "Every flame is different. A fire fueled by wood burns low and slow. A fire fueled by coal is hotter, wilder." He gave a thoughtful nod. "If you try to tame a flame incorrectly, you will either make it spread like wildfire, or you will put it out. Flames are meant to light the way, to help you, guide you. If you cannot allow it to do those things, you will simply snuff it out. It will lose all purpose."

I nodded as I listened to the tribal men talk.

"And you, Outsider, what do you think?" Catskill asked beside me.

"Uh—well," I stammered for a moment, trying to gather my thoughts. In my country, it was different. Christian men were often taught to just take control. While Christian women were taught to obey without question. And everyone pretended not to know why Christian couples held the highest divorce rate in America.

"Well," I said, "I agree with you both. If a woman is a fire to be tamed, then we have to learn how to be tamers. The only way to learn how to do that is to look at our own instruction and examples. God tells us to love our wives as Christ loves the church."

"Oh, absolutely," Killa nodded. "If you are not willing to put your life on the line for her, then you do not love her the way God intended for her to be loved."

I smiled. "Only way you can get to that point is if you get to know her the way God gets to know us individually. He spends time with us, loving and grooming us, even serving us—as Christ came from heaven as a man and served the church through His sacrifice, His provision, and His kindness. He washed the feet of His disciples, He prepared food for them in their hunger. He comforted them in their pain.

Christ is the head of the church, but His headship is one of *servitude*. And in return, we serve God; we love Him, and we submit to Him. That is our example as men—as future husbands. It is our guidance on how to love a wife," I said.

Killa chuckled and Catskill said, "Seems you have been considering things surrounding a wife."

"What?" I asked nervously.

Killa burst into laughter, reeling backwards. "Catskill, I think he intends to love the chief the way Christ loves the church." He fell back again, laughing.

I gripped the reins so fiercely, my knuckles turned pale. My mouth was suddenly dry, and I felt so embarrassed, I could've jumped from my horse and ran all the way home.

"It is of no matter to me," Catskill said. "If this outsider believes he can love our chief properly, I give him my blessing." His thick hand slapped every nerve out of my body, and I coughed.

"Thanks."

"Of course. Do not give attention to Killa, he is sad the only woman he has ever loved has fallen for a different man."

"Hey!" Killa shouted. "Do not bring up Elainnis!"

"Here we go," Catskill chuckled, bumping me with his elbow. I smiled.

We rode on for a while, listening to Killa complain about his love for Elainnis, and his empty threats to Lee.

"Lord Chief," Killa called as he slowed his horse, "our horses are tired, and we covered very good ground today. Is it all right if we rest here?"

Kateri pushed aside the curtain, I hadn't seen her or Sunstar since we took off in the late morning. "It is fine to stop, Killa. We are tired of sitting back here, we are ready to stretch."

"Of course," Killa said.

"Good, my back was hurting." Catskill threw a leg over his horse and climbed off. We'd only taken a short ten-minute break earlier, since I wasn't used to riding horseback and my legs felt tight. Kateri and Sunstar had fallen asleep and missed the short break. Hopping down from the horse, I sighed as I rubbed my legs.

"You will probably be sore in the morning. Drink plenty of water if you plan to ride with us again tomorrow," Catskill said as he passed by. It sounded like an invite, like Catskill had enjoyed my company today. I held in the smile tugging at my lips and only nodded.

"Cameron, come help Saloso from the cart," Kateri called as she took Catskill's hand and stepped off.

"Coming."

Sunstar stepped into the light, moving from behind the curtain and the evening sun greeted her with pink hues that washed over her radiant skin. I stared at her for a moment, and she suddenly flushed red.

"Why are you looking at me like that?"

"Oh, sorry," I said, her voice breaking me from my trance. "I didn't mean to stare." The golden sun rolled off her shoulders as she reached for my hand. Taking her small one, I helped her down from the cart.

"I wish you would stare at me like that every time you saw me," Kateri said to Catskill.

He grunted and rolled his eyes.

"Someone start a fire before Kateri explodes into one," Killa joked as he lowered the back hatch of the cart to pull out some firewood.

"I will help unload," Catskill muttered, joining Killa at the hatch.

"I better go help, too," I said to Sunstar. She only nodded, and I leaned down to peck her cheek.

"Hold on." Kateri stepped in front of me. "What is this box? I have been trying to open it for hours. I even tried to cut it with Saloso's knife, but it will not open."

I looked over the black box in her hand, there was a gash and scuffs all over it. Taking it from her, I sighed, "Where did you get this?"

"I told her not to go through your things," Sunstar said.

"You both want to know what's in here?"

They nodded quickly, and Kateri stepped closer. I rolled my eyes, twisting the box, and then lifting the top. "It is a button. You press it, and it will send a rescue message to someone I know."

"Can I press it?" Kateri squealed.

I snapped the box closed and she jumped. "No. If you do, a team will come looking for me."

"Like last time?" Sunstar studied me quietly, wondering if she had wrongly defended me in the council meeting. But I turned to her and leaned down to kiss her cheek again. "Nothing like that will ever happen again. I promise. Even if I press this button right now, it won't work. I need to be somewhere more populated to get it to work. So you're safe."

Sunstar's smile reappeared.

Killa yelled, "Hey, Outsider, stop getting all the attention and come help us."

Twenty-Six

Again

We began our ride early the next morning, and only stopped once before finding a cave to rest in. The weather had changed, and the normal high sun had a thick overcast, and the heavy clouds looked like they'd give at any moment. The mud had already alerted us that it had been raining just south of the tribe, and we traveled a little slower because of it. As we arrived at the mouth of the cave, Killa noticed footprints leading in and out of the cave. Getting off his horse, he and Catskill retrieved their weapons and moved to check it out.

I moved to the cart where Sunstar and Kateri were. Pushing the curtain aside, I slipped a finger to my lips, silently telling them to stay quiet. Sunstar lowered her brows and passed a look to Kateri. She shrugged, glancing back at me. The three of us waited in a pressing silence, unsure of what the others would find, passing stressed looks to each other.

Finally, Killa appeared, waving as he came over. "You are not going to believe what we have stumbled across."

"What is it?" Sunstar spoke before I could, leaning out the cart.

Killa sighed. "Grey Hawk is inside the cave. She was too weak to travel, and the rain made it impossible for them to move. They have been here four days."

"What?" Kateri shouted.

"Where are their horses?" I asked.

He shrugged. "One ran off, and the other is inside the cave. We are going to have to keep going, there is no room for us to stay there."

"Our horses are tired, and it's getting late," I said. "This will slow us down."

He nodded. "It will extend our trip; however, we always plan for extra travel. We just did not plan to run into Grey."

"Where is Catskill?" Kateri finally realized how pressing the matter was. Catskill and Kateri were supposed to ride up the mountain with Grey. For him to appear here, escorting Sunstar, our worlds were about to collide … at least that's what we were all thinking when a scream bellowed out.

I snapped my head toward the cave, and Killa looked back at me. Before we could move, Sunstar was out of the cart, racing toward the cave.

"Saloso!" I called, but Kateri also brushed by me and raced into the cave before I could get there.

"Come on," Killa said, taking off.

We ran around the horses to the cave to find Grey Hawk and Catskill arguing loudly. The frail woman looked like she could die any second. Her paling skin sagged more than I'd ever seen it, and her grey hair had turned snow white and was thinner than before. It was taking everything in the old woman just to yell, but she didn't stop until Sunstar stepped into view.

Blinking up at her, slowly, Grey looked back at Catskill. "You... you have traveled with her?"

"I am sorry," Catskill lowered his head.

I stepped forward, sloshing the mud beneath my feet, drawing Grey's cold eyes. She stared, and slowly her mouth fell open. "He has returned, and you have brought him here to me, Catskill..." Grey Hawk shakily stood to her feet and, without warning, she lunged at Catskill. The old woman shoved him weakly to the ground, and Kateri raced forward.

"Stop it! Get off him!" Kateri was pulling on Grey.

Sunstar shouted, "Kateri, no!" But Kateri wouldn't listen, and the entire cave broke out into an uproar. Grey Hawk had a fist of Catskill's hair, yanking on it, and beating him fiercely in the face. He was trying to stop her gently, but the old woman had summoned the bit of strength she had left and wouldn't stop screaming and hitting him. Kateri raced forward, snatching Grey up to her feet, pulling on her arm as she tried to untangle her hand from Catskill's hair.

"You are making it worse, Kateri! Let her go!" Sunstar wrapped her arms around Kateri's waist, trying to stop the wild girl. Suddenly, our horses outside started bucking and kicking, and Killa went to them, trying to keep them from running away while the horse in the cave squealed wildly.

The two men who were traveling with Grey were now up, one tending to the horse, and the other trying to pull everyone apart. Kateri had gotten away from Sunstar and pulled Grey's hand loose from Catskill's hair, but Grey swung and hit Kateri across the face. Kateri, regaining her composure, slapped Grey Hawk back. The old woman stumbled backwards, holding her cheek, panting heavily. It was only a fraction of a second, but in that moment, Grey Hawk had snapped.

I finally moved and snatched Sunstar away from the chaos that was about to unfold.

"Kateri, just leave her!" I called. Before I could say anything else, Grey Hawk lunged at Kateri, but her hand never connected with the young healer. Catskill suddenly moved forward to defend Kateri; his arm lashed out, blocking Grey's attack, but the sudden interruption knocked her off balance. Grey fell to the ground with a cry, but her yelp of shock and pain was silenced as a distinct crack echoed through the cave.

Silence cried out, panting breaths ensued, and the rain began to fall.

"What did you do?" Killa said, standing in the mouth of the cave. He stared at Grey's still body. She hadn't moved since Catskill had knocked her down, and now, there was blood coming from her head.

"I ... I didn't mean to." Catskill's eyes were wide as he backed away from Grey Hawk. "This wasn't my fault!" he screamed.

Kateri shakily moved beside him and peered down at her grandmother.

"I didn't mean to," he repeated, staring down at his trembling hands. "She was going to hit you... I was just," he paused, looking up at Kateri, "I was just trying to help."

"I know…" she whispered. "I know…" her voice cracked the second time.

I stared at Grey's lifeless body, wondering what to do. Sunstar had a hand over her mouth, and all her nerves twisted together on her face. "What do we do?" she whispered. "They will kill him."

"No!" Kateri turned around swiftly, tears in her eyes. "It was an accident!"

"Our grandmother is dead, Kateri! She was a *chief!* The punishment is death!"

"I know what the punishment is! But it was an accident, sister!"

"It matters not! What is done—"

"No," I said. Sunstar blinked at me, as if she'd forgotten I was there. "It was an accident."

"They will never believe that." She glared at me; I'd never seen her so broken. She was angry because she was afraid. She didn't know what to do.

Taking her hands in mine, I said, "It was me."

"What?" Killa stepped forward.

I looked around at everyone. "It was me. I killed Grey Hawk."

"No." Sunstar began to shake her head, but my mind was made up. I was never going to have my happily ever after that I wanted with Sunstar, but if I could do this for her, and save her people from killing their best warrior—from being divided. If I could save Sunstar's relationship with Kateri, I would do

265

it.

"I killed her, that's what you have to tell everyone. And I ran away." I glanced around looking for a weapon. "Put some blood on a weapon, and say you went after me—"

"I will not!" Sunstar squeaked. Tears began to pool, and I pulled her into my chest.

"I would do anything to stay with you," I whispered as she began to sob. "But I would also do anything to protect this tribe because it is your home. And I … I …"

"Do not say it," she whispered. "Do not or my heart will fail me."

I pulled back from her, taking her in once more. This was it. I could never return, even if I wanted to. "Catskill," I called. His frightened eyes slowly drifted to mine. "Take care of them for me." He only stared, there were no words from him, but I didn't need an answer. Catskill would protect this place, Kateri, and Sunstar with his life. He'd done it before when my father's team infiltrated the village.

I nodded at Killa as I pushed past him to grab my things. The rain beat down on my shoulders as I pulled my bag from the cart. A small black box fell from my open bag, the one Kateri could not open. Clutching it, I returned to the cave where Sunstar stood.

"If you ever need anything, just push that button." I passed it to her and shoved my arm through the straps of my bag.

"I will never see you again, will I, Outsider?"

"It's better this way," I said, cupping her face.

"Outsider!" Kateri raced to the cave entrance and dropped

to her knees. "Thank you," she cried.

I leaned down as the rain poured heavily over us and kissed her head. Then I looked up. "Goodbye, Sunstar," I said, holding in the tears. The rain was heavy enough to wash down Sunstar's cheeks, confusing the streams for tears.

"Goodbye, Cameron."

"I thought you needed three months? I gave you two, and you returned in a little over a week. What happened?"

I returned from Peru last week without notifying my father or mother. Unfortunately, my mother had been bringing flowers and checking on my place while I was gone, despite the ex-military guard who'd been by my door, and she found me in my apartment.

"A lot happened," I muttered.

John pushed back in his chair, sighing slowly, and watching me carefully. I'd been trying to forget everything, but the nightmares of Grey's stiffening body, the loud cracking of her head, and the teary goodbye with Sunstar wouldn't stop replaying in my head.

"When Savannah called me," John began, "she said, my son, he's in danger." He chuckled. "It was as if she weren't speaking to your own father, like she was calling a complete stranger who'd be kind enough to help her just this once. But I deserved that." He sighed woefully, lifting a red stress ball from his desk. "I haven't been there like I was supposed to be, and I'm sorry, Cameron."

I squinted. "Why are you apologizing right now?"

The red ball shrank in his hand, pushing air out as he squeezed. "Because if I had a father who could've helped me when I needed it, I would've been a real father to you, and a husband to Savannah."

"Isn't it a little late now?"

He nodded. "It is. But even if you can't tell me what's wrong, if you need something, Cameron, don't be like me. Don't be prideful, don't run away—do something. Ask for help. And if it's a woman, and she's any good like your mother, don't let her go."

"I had to," the words slipped from me, and I couldn't stop them. My chest was suddenly tightening and the tears I'd been suppressing were surfacing. "I couldn't let her lose everything because of an accident."

"What kind of accident?"

"Why should I trust you now?"

John's face became gentler, his brows fell low, and he set the red ball down. "I'm not asking you to trust me. I'm just asking you to give me a chance at being your father. That's all."

I thought I didn't want him in my life, but that wasn't entirely true. I always said that to cover the desire to have a father, the desire to know John. Now, I was letting my pride get in the way of a relationship that could be good for me. It was time for me to stop being angry at John, and acknowledge that these past two years, he has tried to be a father. It wasn't fair to keep being this way towards him. Losing Sunstar, never being able to go back to Peru, no more making up with Garrith, it was time I started fixing things I could, like my relationship with my father.

Swallowing, I took a breath and said, "A leader in the tribe was killed, and I took the blame so they would have a story. So that the council wouldn't kill the man her sister loved, and it would make it look like Sunstar had finally come to her senses about the outside world."

"So, you didn't actually kill anyone, did you?" His voice wasn't condescending, it was calm, almost fatherly.

"No," I said, wiping at the tears. "But they think I did."

"Who?"

I paused, my mother, my tactical team, and I were the only ones who knew about the tribe. Telling John meant that I trusted him. Gripping my pants I muttered, "The Sand Ribbon Tribe."

_____oOo_____

I thought about the conversation with my father all day. For once, he'd treated me like a son, and for once I'd treated him like a father. Thankfully, God revealed to me that the root of my poor relationship with my father stemmed from an old, unforgiving anger. That anger turned into resentment, and when the opportunities arose for me to forgive him, it was pride that reared its ugly head. But today, I was able to forgive him, to let it all go. And I remembered Henry Bik, the big man from the award ceremony for Garrith, I remembered that my father didn't have the happy life I thought he did, and I found that my anger really had no root.

Carrying grocery bags, one in each arm, I saw Annie standing outside of my door as I walked up to my place. She wore her signature jet black bob, tactical pants that tucked into combat boots, and a green shirt that showed off her muscular arms. She leaned against the door as if she was waiting for me to give a command. I wondered if she always stood like that, or just when she heard the elevator ding. She was stationed at my apartment to guard while I was gone, but she still hadn't left, despite me returning.

Walking briskly down the hall in front of Carter and Grace, I called out, "I thought I told you to go home?" I glanced over my shoulder at Carter. "And I thought I told you to get rid of her."

He shrugged. "I didn't want to make it so obvious you'd returned; Annie reported a few visitors coming by while you were gone."

I rolled my eyes. "They wouldn't have known I was gone if there wasn't an ex-soldier standing outside my door twenty-four hours a day."

I heard Grace chuckling beside me as we approached Annie. "Annie, go home. My place is fine."

She glanced over at Carter first, then at Grace who nodded at her. "All right." Her eyes returned to mine. "We're off for the night. Have a good night, Cameron."

"Wait a second," I called as the three of them turned to leave. "Annie, why did you just dismiss them?" They were acting so suspicious suddenly.

"Sorry, Mr. Frierson-Taylor—" Grace said, but I cut him off

"Just go, I've had enough these past two weeks."

"All right, bye." Carter turned to leave.

I held in an intense eye roll at Carter's curt response. Grace and Annie gave me a nod and followed him down the hall, chatting quietly with each other. Carter tossed a heavy arm around Annie's shoulders, and she blushed beside him while Grace merely walked in step with them, scrolling his phone.

"That's why Carter kept her." I shook my head as I jumbled my bags of groceries around to type in the door code.

Inside, the lights came on at the front door and Krytonia, my electronic voice assistant, welcomed me home. "Welcome home, Mr. Frierson. The current time is eleven twenty-two post meridiem."

"Thanks, Krytonia," I called.

"Of course, Mr. Frierson."

As I traveled to the kitchen, an evening light came on, keeping the penthouse dim. I placed my two grocery bags on the counter when a loud crash cried out beside me. The sudden noise nearly made my heart stop. Exhaling deeply, I rested my hands on the black marble countertop and regained my composure.

"What was that?" I asked myself as I stepped back to search the floor. The pristinely cleaned floors glowed as I walked around the counter where my eyes landed on a little matte black box. I blinked.

Shakily, I retrieved it to look it over. Panic began to set in as I turned the box over in my hand. "Someone's been in my house. But how? Annie's been standing there the whole time!"

I left the little device in my bedroom, not on the kitchen counter. Maybe the thief dropped it on the counter on his way out? But my floors are clean, not a single shoe print.

"Krytonia! Roll the camera."

I paused as I turned the box once more in my hands. There was a familiar scratch across it... a deep scratch that nearly cut a hole through the box. I gasped.

"How is this here?"

"You have not finished your command, Mr. Frierson," Krytonia said.

How could this get here? I left it with Sunstar... Don't tell me something happened to her. Where did this come from?

"Krytonia," I whispered, staring at the box. My hand traced over the gash where some of the paint was missing.

"Yes, sir?"

"Do you know when this box got here? Is there anything in your footage that recognizes this box?"

The house hummed for a moment, and then she said, "There is an audio message from Fred. Recorded on August twentieth, two thousand twenty-five at eight forty-one post meridiem."

My jaw clenched, *that's today.* I swallowed nervously. *Maybe she pressed it because she was in danger. Is this all that was left?*

"Would you like me to play it?"

"Yes." I clutched the box, waiting for the bad news.

Fred's voice boomed over my speaker system. "Pretty nice setup you have here, Cameron. You're a bit classier than Mr. Taylor. The way the lights only turn on if you're in that room is definitely signature Taylor. But keeping the traditional light switches is definitely signature Cameron. Always on the cautious side. Anyways, try the switch in the living room, I left you a little surprise in there."

I sighed, looking at the box. "He must've meant the kitchen. He left me this box, but why?" I paused as I stared at it, remembering Sunstar's face when I'd left this for her. Her eyes wet with a mist, and her shoulders slumped. It was yet another tearful goodbye, but it was supposed to be the last tears I shed for her. For us. However, I couldn't hold back the tears as I called out weakly to Krytonia, "Was ... was there anything else?" Silence loomed, and the seconds ticked by, allowing my emotions to unravel. Each tick made my heart ache a little more.

I want to see Sunstar again, this can't be it. Please, God... don't let this be it.

The robotic voice of Krytonia came back and said, "There are no other recordings."

I held the box as tears fell into the gash and trickled onto my hand. Shoving it into my chest, I dropped to my knees and cried loudly, "I said goodbye, but I didn't want to! I didn't want this to happen! I'm so sorry. I never should've left! Please, forgive me, Sunstar."

I was hunched over, my tears soaking the floor when I heard a sniffle. I stared at the floor for a second and wondered if I was hearing things. Wide-eyed, I moved to my feet, scanning the kitchen. Slowly, I walked through my home. The evening lights came on as I crossed from the kitchen to the dining room, and finally into the living room where I thought I heard the sniffle come from. The lights didn't come on when I reached the living room. Squinting into the darkness, I wondered if I had truly lost it.

"What am I doing?" I sighed and wiped at my tears. But I couldn't get my feet to turn back. It was ridiculous to think someone was hiding in my living room, that whoever was hiding might be Sunstar, but I was hoping I wasn't just crazy. I wanted this to be real.

The thick darkness wouldn't surrender to the moonlight, and all the light was gone in my place as the heavy blinds kept out the city lights. I was forced to follow Fred's instructions and turn on the light switch. Methodically, I crossed the wooden floor, and felt along the wall when I heard a sniffle. I turned quickly, staring into the darkness.

"Who's there?" I called frantically. The box I'd been holding against my chest slipped to the ground and tumbled onto the floor of my living room. Without thinking, I dived for it, trying to save the last bit of Sunstar I had left.

Tumbling down the stairs, into the sunken cushioned floor, I felt around for the box. "Where is it?" I said angrily. Tossing pillows aside, I called out, "Krytonia, override the switch. Turn the lights on in the living room with the evening settings."

"Overriding the system. The lights will now turn on."

Suddenly, the evening lights came on in the room, and I

searched the floor in front of me. When I didn't find the box, I turned around...

In the golden hand of a woman, the matte black box was extended to me. Her white and black shawl with fringes draped her taupe tunic that raced to her knees. From the box to her gaze, my eyes fleeted in disbelief.

Cascading chocolate waves didn't drown her, they only magnified her beauty. Her nose and cheeks were a flush red, and tears streamed from her eyes. Eyes that could drown you in emotions you never felt before. They could make you melt despite their icy cold color. Eyes that I loved to look into and watch the tides dance in them. Eyes that were crippling blue and had taken my breath away two years ago... but they hadn't changed much, because today, they'd done the same.

Part III

Twenty-Seven
The Runaway

I opened my eyes and smelled something. It was fragrant with a floral hint. I was not sure whether I liked the smell, but it was new. Everything was new. The beds were not pelts against the ground, there was something called a *'mattress'* and a *'box spring'* that sat atop a frame elevated from the floor. I stared at the ceiling, it was white and smooth, not dried hides.

Slowly, I rolled over, and I could smell him. His scent was so strong, the way the wind carried nostalgia on its wings. I could not name what he smelled like, but I pulled the thick stuffing for resting my head into my chest and inhaled deeply. *Cameron*, I thought, my chest quickly tightened, and I buried my smile into the white stuffing. It was his scent, and I thought I'd never smell him again, hear his voice, see his smile. But when I pushed a button, a team of men arrived two days later and brought me here.

The tribe had fallen into an uproar when we returned. Only half believed Cameron was the one who killed grandmother, the other half was split between Killa and me. Killa had always disapproved of grandmother, and since I was next in line for chiefhood, they assumed my hunting went rogue, and I killed grandmother instead. So I disappeared. I ran as far as I could away from the ones who would not accept me. Somehow, I ended up here without looking back. I miss them, my family, but I am not sure when I will return. *If* I will return.

Releasing the stuffing, I rolled over again to stare out the framework etched into the wall. Misty had something like this in her grand hut. I believe she has called them *windows* before. Regardless, I stared out of it, watching the sun reach into the room as it touched the blue sky. There was not a single cloud in sight, but a few black birds whipped by.

I liked it here thus far. I had only been here three days before Fred escorted me to Cameron's home. It was quite nice; so many things I had never seen before, never even knew existed.

There was a knock on the door. "Sunstar? Are you awake?"

"I am," I answered.

"May I come in?"

"You may enter."

The door opened, and he stepped inside. Green eyes greeted mine shyly, and the tall man with the boyish grin came around to greet me. "Good morning," he said, smiling down at me. My eyes slowly traced his figure, broad shoulders and strong muscles, Cameron looked nothing like the warriors or tribal men I was so used to seeing. His skin was only a little darker than mine, and the curls atop his head were almost golden. Most men of the tribe had dark long hair with small waves or none at all. I had never seen such a peculiar man before, not even in the market.

"Good morning, Cameron."

He smiled, and my heart began to race. He had such a kind smile, I wanted to make it last forever. I wanted to give him a reason to always smile, so that maybe we would never be apart again.

"There's breakfast in the kitchen, and I brought you a few things I thought you might need." He held up a bag. "I didn't buy you any clothes, but I will as soon as we go outside. These are my clothes, just something for you to wear for now."

Sitting up, I extended my hands to retrieve the bag from him. I recognized some of the things inside.

Cameron sat beside me and reached into the bag. "This is a toothbrush, and this is toothpaste. You just squeeze this onto the—"

"Toothbrush," I finished.

He nodded slowly. "You learn quick."

"Your mother taught me."

He frowned in confusion. "My mother?"

I nodded. "It is where I stayed before Fred brought me here. It is where Killa, Catskill, and Kateri are staying."

"Hold on," he shot to his feet, "how long have you been here?"

"Today is day four."

"You've been here for three days and didn't tell me? And Killa, Catskill, and Kateri are here?"

"I was not sure I was ready to face you, Cameron."

"What are you talking about?" Cameron's voice softened. "Sunstar, why are you here?"

"I ran away."

"What?"

"They did not believe our story. They wanted to kill me and Killa."

He was quiet for a moment, resting his elbows on his knees.

"Misty did not believe our story, but she did not want to know what happened. She tried to get the council to drop the issue, but they would not listen. So I ran away."

"Misty knows everything, that's why she didn't believe you."

"That is true." I patted my chest twice.

"How did Catskill, Killa, and Kateri all make it here?"

"Kateri followed me, and Catskill followed her, bringing Killa along to get him away from the tribe. Kateri brought that box and reminded me that we could actually run away and not get caught."

"Wait," he paused, "you don't plan to stay here, do you?"

"They do not need me, Cameron, it is better that I stay away."

He shook his head and stood.   "Sunstar, you have to go back and clear your name. You can't be thought of as a murderer."

"I do not care," I said, finally lifting my gaze to his. "They have never loved me. I thought you would be happy."

"I am more than that." He patted his chest twice. "But they

need you, Sunstar. They will die if they don't get help. Could you really live with that?"

His words burned me because the death of my grandmother did not. I had never felt so relieved or free than when I saw her lying still in that cave. I had never wished ill on my grandmother, but I was relieved by her death. That frightened me. If I could live with the death of my own grandmother, I feared I might be able to live with the death of all my people too.

But… they are my tribe. I still have a duty to them.

"I do not know what to do, Cameron. I am torn," I admitted, "because I do not wish for them to die. But I also do not want to be apart from you again." I was too afraid to say what I really meant, but I do not think Cameron noticed.

He moved, and knelt in front of me, blinking his green orbs. "I want you to stay by my side forever. But," he took my hands and kissed them, "we can't let your people die, either. I promise I'm going to do everything I can to figure something out."

Pulling one hand from his, I caressed his cheek and whispered, "Thank you, Cameron."

I emerged from the bathroom in Cameron's baggy clothes and tiptoed through his house. The floor was cool; I'd never seen anything like it before—little stone squares shoved into the surface. It was similar to the floors in his mother's home. Even the walls were different from the ones in the chief hut. They were better, with colors and windows bigger than any I'd ever seen. Other walls were lined with things within a frame. Flowers, colors, shapes, animals, the things in the frames were fascinating.

I slowed as I crossed the floor in front of a frame on the wall. This one was of a person, one I knew. He was walking, except he wasn't. Somehow, time had stopped around him as he walked along the ocean shore, leaving his footprints in the sand. A long white robe rippled and crinkled from the wind, and his long covering flowed behind him. Dark hair was blown from his face, and there was a smile capturing his lips.

I have only seen him in my head, I have never seen Jesus in the flesh.

"Do you like it?"

I jolted, turning abruptly to find Cameron standing behind me. Clutching my chest, I said, "It is majestic and beautiful." I turned back to look once more as Cameron stepped beside me.

"Do you know what they call this?"

"No."

"It is a painting." He glanced over at me, smirking kindly. Cameron enjoyed teaching me new things as much as I enjoyed learning them.

"A painting?"

"Yes. It's a type of artwork where a moment is captured and made to express what the artist felt at the time."

I considered his words for a moment. I understood why time had frozen Jesus on the oceanside. I flitted my eyes back to Cameron and said, "Like the way God made grass green instead of red?"

He chuckled. "That's exactly right."

He took a step forward, and instinctively, I took one back. He smiled and reached for me. But it was not my hand he grabbed—it was my waist. He slipped his hand to my back and closed the space between us. His touch sent a shudder of warmth up my spine that resonated in my lips, cheeks, and chest. It was the same feeling I got when we'd kissed for the first time. My lips tingled and were not satisfied until his had touched mine. I knew this warmth would turn to tingling. I had hoped it would.

Cameron leaned forward, his eyes studying mine before dropping to my lips. I wanted to shy away, but when his eyes met my gaze again, there was a raging in my chest that wouldn't stop unless he stopped it … and he did.

My heart settled as his lips pressed over mine, tenderly. Slowly, I placed my hand against his cheek, and he pulled away. His cheeks were redder than the first time we kissed, and there was a timid look on his face.

"We should have breakfast now."

"We should," I agreed.

He took my hand and led me through his house to eat.

Twenty-Eight
The Distance Makes a Difference

"Grace." A man with light brown skin extended a hand to me. I took it and shook it slowly.

"He's my driver, and my guard," Cameron said as he walked into the garage with another tall man. He looked similar to Grace, almost brotherly, but there were small differences between them. Their eye colors, the texture of their hair; both shared the same light brown skin, and round nose, but Grace's jaw wasn't as hard as this man's.

"And this is Carter, my other guard."

He nodded with a smirk. There was something coy about him, and I asserted myself to be mindful of the slick man.

"Annie isn't here now, but she will be your guard, Sunstar."

"Mine?"

"Yeah, she'll look after you the way the warriors did in the tribe."

"Aren't you glad I didn't fire Annie?" Carter said, leaning forward to open the door for Cameron.

He laughed as he ducked his head, "*You're* glad you didn't fire Annie."

"Your door," Grace said over my shoulder.

"Sorry," I muttered as he opened it for me. The inside was like no other carriage I have ever seen. I rode in a car three times in my entire life. Each ride made my stomach turn, but not worse than the plane ride. I could not settle, and my stomach would not let me rest. Slowly, I sat in the car, and Grace closed the door for me. A monstrous growl erupted all around us when the car started, and I squealed.

"What was that?"

Cameron laughed and patted my leg. I noticed Carter's shoulders were bouncing; he, too, laughed at me.

"It's the engine," Cameron explained.

I nodded. I had only heard an engine roar three other times, and none sounded as thunderous as this one. I could feel Cameron's eyes on me, but I would not look at him. I was embarrassed. I did not know much about this world. I had not realized how foolish I was.

As we pulled out of the garage, I watched out the window. Cameron and I did not speak, but I was not bothered by the silence. I was able to think about Cameron, how he was not incredibly stupid the way I was. He arrived at our tribe, unable to chop wood, but he did not arrive in ignorance. He knew what an axe was, he knew what ointment was. But I knew nothing. I did not even know there was a tool for cleaning my teeth. I did not know the world I lived in was so different from the rest. Cameron had always told me our worlds were similar,

285

but they are not.

I watched people and other cars move by us at an incredible speed. There were no horses, no carriages, no donkeys. Only cars. Some big and long, some wide, and others small—each carrying people inside. Our worlds were nothing alike, and I realized that I was always going to be an outsider, no matter where I went.

We arrived at Cameron's mother's house. It was more beautiful than Misty's. It was the first place I went to when I arrived with the others. Cameron's mother was a kind woman, sweet and gentle. She was incredibly smart and patient, teaching us things, showing us things. I understood why Cameron was so good at teaching. She was a graceful woman with dark skin and tight coils. Her skin glowed differently from the way ours did, but it was beautiful. It looked like the night sky had been kind to her and loved her so much that it could not depart from her. So the sky wrapped around her, letting the stars glow from within.

The door to the car opened and I stepped out. Cameron waited for me as Grace walked me around the car. He forced a smile, and I forced one back. We were caught in an awkward state suddenly. Embarrassed, I tried not to let the pitiful thoughts of how ignorant I was overtake me as Cameron took my hand. We started up the pavement to the house on a hill. It was wide and high, quite large for one person. Rolls of the greenest grass I have seen stretched out like a field before the house as we made our way to the front door. Cameron did not knock, he pulled out a key from his pocket and unlocked the door.

"Mom," he called as he stepped in.

"In here," I heard Savannah calling.

Cameron closed the door behind me, and we walked through her house. She was seated on the couch with Kateri. Killa sat on a chair, Catskill leaned against the wall. Everyone looked odd in their clothes, not like my people.

"Outsider!" Kateri chirped as she jumped from the couch.

"Outsider?" Cameron said as he hugged her. "Am I still an outsider in my own place?"

Kateri laughed as she stepped back and leaned over to squeeze me. Her clothes may have been different, but her warmth was still the same, and it grounded me, making me feel less awkward and out of place. Kateri wore her ignorance on her sleeve. She did not care much to know things for the reasons of not being unlearned. Kateri wanted to know things because they were interesting, and I longed for that in that moment.

"Sister," she said, calling me to focus, "are you alright?"

"Yes." I forced a smile. "The cars always give my stomach a knot."

She giggled and crossed the room to the couch. "Mine as well."

"I can't believe you're all here." Cameron made his way to his mother. He kissed her forehead, and I could see their similarities and their differences. Cameron looked similar to his mother, but he also looked like someone else, possibly his father. My thoughts froze for a moment. Cameron had never mentioned a father. I wondered briefly if he knew him.

"Cameron." Catskill stepped forward from the wall. "Thank you," he said.

Cameron shook his head. "I was only protecting Saloso. I was being selfish."

Catskill shrugged and offered him his hand. "I still need to thank you."

Cameron lifted his hand and Catskill gripped his forearm, offering one solid shake.

Killa said over their shoulders, "Saluting by the forearm is a sign of strength and trust. We are brothers now." He stood and greeted Cameron the same way. "You are one of us now."

"Thank you." Cameron's eyes glimmered with joy as he glanced between Killa and Catskill.

"Cameron, I raised you better than that. Welcome these young men into our family, too," his mother ordered.

Cameron rolled his eyes and offered Catskill a hand. Catskill took it and was quickly pulled into Cameron's embrace. "That is how we greet family or brothers," Cameron explained as he and Killa performed the action again.

"I want to be family!" Kateri whined.

"You already hugged me." Cameron laughed. "We've been family, Kateri." He patted his chest twice, and my sister smiled greatly.

"There's one more, Cameron. She's been awfully quiet." Savannah was looking at me now, and I felt my nerves unhinge. My eyes slid to Cameron's as he locked his with mine while he crossed the room to me.

"When you fall in love," he said boldly, and my heart began to rush like it had somewhere to be, "you greet the one you love with a kiss."

I couldn't process his words before he lifted my chin and kissed me.

His confession was abrupt and left my heart hammering. *I am the one he has fallen in love with*, I thought as my hands rested in the soapy water. After Cameron kissed me, the entire room erupted in laughter and joy. When things finally settled, Cameron went to work and we all made ourselves useful around Savannah's house.

"How are those dishes coming along?" Savannah asked as she entered the kitchen.

"They are well," I said, shaking away the thoughts of Cameron. I grabbed the rag and began twisting it about in the glass. Fred had brought me one on the plane ride when my stomach would not settle. He told me it was drinkware, something to get liquid into my body. I had only ever drank from our waterskins, however, I presumed it was no different than finishing the broth like we often did from our bowls.

"You have been distant today, you alright?" Savannah asked as she picked up a bowl I'd cleaned and began drying it.

"My thoughts seem to be very forward today."

"You have a lot on your mind?"

"Very much so."

"Like what?"

I paused, twisting the rag in the cup. Small bubbles melted back into the soapy water. "I realized I am an outsider no matter where I am. Completely unlearned of everything, knowing nothing, not even the man who loves me."

"Do you love the man who loves you?" She picked up another bowl.

"Very much." I pulled a soapy hand from the water and pressed it into my chest. "Here is where it hurt when he was gone. And it is here that feels so complete when he is by my side. But I am confused and uncertain if I should love this man. I do not know if we can remain this way."

"You don't want your heart broken," she said.

"Yes, I want it to stay whole."

Savannah set the bowl down and threw the towel over her shoulder. "Sunstar de Achille."

I looked up from the dishes to find her smiling. She was peering out the window in front of us, watching the rustling trees bend and wave to God.

"How do you know my name?"

"My son. He said it like it was the only words he knew. He's been in love with this girl for two years, thinks the world of her, really. He has never loved anyone the way he does Sunstar; it's special to see. Watching my son fall in love."

I looked out the window, wondering what it was about her words that made my heart race even more.

"He had the same look in his eyes as his father did the day he left for Peru. Cameron was so adamant about bringing home the woman he loved, but he was so cross because it was better to give it all up than to force her to return with him. He loved her enough to let her go." She chuckled and dropped her head. "He is more similar to his father than he thinks or wants to admit."

Her words were crippling my heart, but the mention of Cameron's father snapped my attention to her. "His father?"

She nodded. "John Taylor. I loved him more than anything. If I'm honest with myself, I still do. But he's married now, and he's made his choice."

"You are not the one he is married to?"

"No." She shook her head. "That's Betty, world class model. She was a stunning woman, now all that surgery makes her look a little," she paused to look at me, "fake."

"Surgery?"

"I'll explain it another time." Savannah patted my shoulder. "Keep cleaning those dishes before the water gets cold."

I grabbed the rag again. "I am sorry."

"Don't be. When John and I were seeing each other, I never thought things would end the way they did. Broke, jobless, and pregnant while he was making his way to the top of the world." She placed a dark hand on her hip. "But we don't know the future, if we did, what need would we have to trust God?"

"You trusted God because of John Taylor, Cameron's father?"

"I didn't know God at first, but I had no choice but to get to know Him and trust Him," she corrected. "I can't blame

291

John; we came from two different worlds. I was a Black woman from the button shop, he was a white man making a good penny."

"Black and white?" I paused. "Cameron told me once that these colors did not get along. He said there was a man of peace who rose but was later killed."

"Reverend Doctor Martin Luther King Junior." She smiled again. "What Cameron told you is almost correct. It would be a lot easier if we saw black and white as nothing but colors from a crayon box, but we are imperfect people. Some of us see our color as our worth."

"You have different worth because of your color?"

She nodded, and I set my rag down again. "But why? Everyone has been gifted a color from God. How is the worth measured?"

"I don't know," she answered. "But there are terrible people in this world who believe you must look a certain way to be of any value."

"But that is not fair. That is like saying I am better than Kateri because I am pale, and she is brown. But we are sisters. We are of the same tribe. A family."

"If people looked at the world the way you do, everyone would be a lot better off." She grabbed a glass to dry. "Even John and I would've had simpler times, but we didn't. I remember that day at the button shop. Two men caught me with John and tore us apart. Threatened to even kill me if they ever saw me around John's neighborhood again." She shrugged like it meant nothing, but I could see the pain on her face. "It wasn't the first or second or even the third time John and I had been caught. But each time things were worse. Then one day, John stopped showing up, and I was out of a job because of all the drama I brought to the shop. I was able to get in contact with him the day I had Cameron, an old friend from the button shop took me to the hospital and called John for me. His only words that day were to never call him again."

I clutched my chest, blinking at Savannah.

"I stayed true to that. Never speaking to John. I knew it'd be a hefty price to pay if I did. So, Cameron and I struggled. But God worked things out. We never had much, some nights we didn't even have food to eat. Now look at us." She looked up at me, not even a tear in her eyes. She was smiling, like she'd told some glorious story that she should be proud of.

"God kept us, took care of us, and things worked out."

"And John," I asked carefully. "What happened to him?"

She smirked. "Funny story. I called him two years ago to find Cameron. A friend a few years back had gotten his office number, and I gave him a call."

I nodded, remembering how Fred had explained the button I pressed called him back to find us. "Were you afraid?"

"I was terrified that I'd lose Cameron more than I was of making a phone call." She began to laugh. "I knew John would either say yes or no, and that's what scared me. The possibility of him saying no. But I thank God he said yes, and we were able to bring Cameron home."

"So you and John are together, then?"

She waved her hand. "Oh no, John is married, remember?

We have no hatred between us, I see no need for that. We deal with each other when we have to, but there's not much of a need for communication, so we don't see each other."

"It must hurt." I turned back to the dishes. "Falling in love and being apart, even when you are so close. It is what I felt earlier when I found that Cameron and I were so distant. I did not know if the distance could be closed, but—"

"He loves you," Savannah said. "He loves you very much, Sunstar. As John believed it was best to leave me alone, Cameron thought the same for you. He thought he'd give you a proper goodbye but found he couldn't live without you. And you discovered that, too, didn't you?"

I clenched my jaw shut, trying not to let the tears surface. "Yes," I whispered. "I do not wish to be apart from him, despite the distance and differences."

"Then don't be apart." Savannah touched my shoulder. "You two must figure out a way to stay together. Two is better than one, believe me. God will make a way. He always has, and He always will. As long as you trust Him."

Twenty-Nine
The One Who Guides the Lost is Lost

When we ate dinner in the tribe, it was never around a table. We all ate at the same time within the designated common area. There were many of us so we could not all sit at one table, however, it seemed so familial to sit beside Cameron and across from Kateri and Catskill. Killa sat at one end of the table while Savannah sat at the other, sharing stories and smiles, like our tribe did not exist, like this was where we belonged. Did we belong here? Was this really a better place to be than where we came from?

"Saloso."

I looked up at my name.

Cameron said, "I'm going to take off work tomorrow to take you guys shopping instead. You'll need better clothes than mine."

I nodded, not even sure what I was agreeing to. My thoughts were always swirling, always so forceful now. Granted, I now had more to think about than whether I could prove myself at the next council meeting. Now, I was wondering if I should even return, and if I stay, would Kateri and the others stay? What would come of the tribe? What if my mother returned to the tribe and I was not there? That was an old thought, one I believed I had buried.

I never wanted to leave the tribe when I was a child because I was afraid I'd miss my mother's return. As I got older, despite how apparent it was that she would never return, I desperately waited for her. But that was my weakness, and if I wanted to be the next chief, I could have no weaknesses. So I forced myself to give up on the hopes that my mother would return, and forced myself to love the outside world. To embrace it. But I never expected to actually reach it, and I never expected to fall for someone who was part of it. I just wanted to give myself something else to think about. It allowed me to learn about God in a different way, and to feel something other than desperation. Now I was in the world I forced myself into loving. What was I to do?

"Only the skin and the coats are used from animals," Cameron said as he munched on the slender green food. It was a bean of some sort, that was what Savannah said when dinner was served. Green beans, rice, scalloped potatoes, and roasted turkey.

I have had rice before, although it was never white, and I have had potatoes, just never scalloped. The food was delicious, but my appetite was fading the more I receded into my thoughts. I did not want to disappear into them, but I could not clear my head of them.

"At what hour shall we rise tomorrow?" Kateri said as she lifted her glass. She looked like one of them, like she belonged in this world, and not like she was a woman of the tribe, a healer with great spiritual aptitude. Catskill, seated beside her, still looked like the brute he has always been, but somehow, he looked like Cameron in his clothes. He and Kateri fit well here. Killa stood out, his long ponytail and baggy clothes, he looked like he was not from this world. And then I wondered, do I look more like Killa or more like Catskill and Kateri? Which did I *want* to look more like?

"I hope you guys don't mind staying at my mother's place," Cameron said apologetically.

"Savannah is great," Killa said with a wide smile.

Savannah returned one to him. "I don't mind having you all here at all, but what are your plans? Are you looking to stay here or are you planning to return soon?"

The laughter and chatter disappeared.

Cameron spoke up beside me. "I think it's a little too early to tell right now."

Savannah nodded. "I didn't mean to pry."

"No," Killa said. "We are indebted to you. You should at least know how long we plan to stay. Although, I am certain Cameron is right. We are not sure of an answer to that question."

"We did not have a plan," Catskill said. He had been mostly quiet ever since his incident with Grey Hawk. He has smiled when necessary, laughed when it seemed appropriate, but it was clear Catskill was aching inside.

Kateri had been the only one to get him to smile warmly, genuinely, like he used to. I had not noticed it before the death of grandmother, possibly because my own heart was in quite a bind but, somehow, Catskill and Kateri had fallen in love. Her ability to soothe him did not happen overnight. It became apparent in the glances they shared and the things they did not say. The way it always seemed like they didn't want to discuss things because it was a private matter, or rather, it was a matter that had already been discussed in private.

"We simply ran away, and it is all my fault." Catskill's voice trailed off, and Kateri reached for his hand.

"Whatever happened, it doesn't matter in my house," Savannah said. "Sometimes running away clears your head, and gives the other people involved space to think about their decisions. You, Catskill, are not the only one at fault." He looked over at her, a hardened jaw twisted closed as he tried not to breakdown. "While you're here," Savannah continued, "I don't want you thinking about what happened back there. None of you." She glanced around the table. "Understood?"

We agreed and Savannah sighed. "I've gone and ruined dinner. But, where I'm from, there's no meal that can't be rescued. Ain't that right, Cameron?"

He laughed. "Momma is the long-time victor of the Back Porch Cookout in Alabama. She's planning on going back at the end of August, so she's been practicing what she's going to cook. You guys want to taste it?"

"I do," Killa said, pushing his plate aside.

"We do as well." Kateri gripped Catskill's hand a little

tighter. I watched his hand as it slowly closed around hers. My eyes drifted to Cameron's hand. One was wrapped around a glass, and the other was resting on the table.

"Saloso?"

"Yes?" I dragged my eyes from his hand to his eyes. He squinted, his eyes shooting to his own hand before looking back at me.

"You want to try it?"

"Yes, of course."

His eyes lingered on mine a little longer before he nodded and turned away. I do not believe we were thinking of trying the same things.

"Alright," Savannah said. "I'll go get the food heated up."

"You want some help?" Cameron asked. She refused him.

The table was quiet again. Awkward shifting, and the unspoken thoughts fighting not to pour from us. We held our composure for a while as Savannah clanged dishes around in the kitchen.

"What are we going to do?" Catskill broke the silence.

"I think Cameron is right, it is too early to know what we should do."

"I want to stay," Kateri said boldly. Everyone eyed her, but she was used to people looking at her. She shrugged. "I am enjoying this new life. I do not think it will be difficult to adjust here. Besides, no one wants us back home. They want us dead."

"No," Killa said. "They want me and Saloso dead. You and Catskill are fine. You can return and get a tongue lashing."

"You think I want to return?" Catskill snapped. It was the most emotion he had shown in a while. I was almost excited to see him come alive again. "I could hardly breathe there. I am not going back. I have no reason to."

"Fine," Killa said. "Maybe you do not, but Kateri is a healer! One of the best in our tribe. She must return."

"I have no obligation to a people who have never accepted me!" Kateri yelled. "I became a healer and worked hard because God, Saloso, and Misty were the only ones who would talk to me. The only ones who did not cast me aside because I am a mistake."

Killa shifted but did not answer.

"Kateri and I shared the same tragedy because of our father," I spoke. "I do not think it is of importance for Kateri to return. For any of you to return. Catskill's guilt will not let him. Kateri's unhappiness will keep her here. And Killa's suspicion will return if he does, if nothing else, it may get him killed."

"And you?" Cameron asked.

"I have a duty to save my people. I must return."

"But you don't have to stay," Cameron replied.

"Who will lead my people?"

"They are no longer your people." Cameron moved closer. "You gave that up when you left. Do you really think they'll accept you back?"

"You do not know what you speak of," I said darkly.

"I do," he spat. "You've shared the same fate as your sister! To be dishonored and disliked by the people there. They don't want you to return. To them, you're no better than Nunca."

I gasped and shot to my feet. "How dare you!"

"What are you trying to prove?" Cameron snapped. He was standing now as silence bombarded us again.

I had no answer, I had no words. There was no answer to his question because I did not know all along, that is what I have been asking myself. What was I trying to prove when I waited for my mother? What was I trying to prove in accepting the outside world? What am I trying to prove now… or maybe the better question was, why? Why was I trying to prove myself in every aspect of my life when there were people who loved me?

I looked up at Cameron's blazing eyes, *he loves me*. Glancing around, I told myself, *they all love me*.

"Everyone," Kateri said, standing slowly, "we need to calm down. We have not been here even a week. There is no reason to find an answer."

"The longer we wait, the more comfortable we get while our kindred die," Killa answered. "When did we become selfish?"

"When we had to grow up and take care of ourselves," Kateri hurled at him. Her words were heavier than any I'd ever heard. Musky and foul, her words would have smelled ungodly if they were a scent. But it was because of the brokenness and anger that stirred inside her.

Killa did not grow up without love, therefore he would never understand how Kateri and I felt.

Cameron shoved his chair in and turned away.

"Where are you going?" I called.

"Home," he answered quickly. He disappeared before I could say anything else.

"I need to rest." I pushed in my chair. "Goodnight."

I lay in bed watching the clouds move slowly across the night sky. I did not taste Savannah's food, but I heard Killa exclaiming it was frightfully good. I sighed, rolling over to stare at the wall. I felt so uncertain of everything, but Cameron's words were truth. They might have been cruel, but he was right; the tribe would never accept me, even if I returned with a way to help my people, they would likely not accept it. They think I am like my mother, the one whose sins I bear. I guess, in a way, I am just like her, and the tribe was right about me. I would follow in my mother's footsteps and leave the tribe.

A sudden breeze pushed through the window, and it was like God was trying to force the drowning thoughts away.

A knock came, and Kateri's voice followed. "Sister? May I come in?"

"You may." I sat up in bed.

Kateri entered, wearing a long gown that met the floor. She climbed into the bed and hugged me tightly. "It is frightening to never return," she said. "But I think we belong here."

"Only because you are free do you believe that," I replied while still holding her.

"Is it wrong to be enlightened?"

"I … I do not know."

"We have never been loved in our tribe, sister, but we are loved here. We can start over; we do not ever have to return."

"Then we have sentenced them to death."

"Then let it swallow them whole."

"Kateri—"

"We have given them everything. It is time for us to give ourselves something now."

"I cannot sentence them to death," I said flatly.

Releasing me, she dropped her hands in her lap and said, "I knew you would never leave them, sister." She looked outside, blinking at the shining moonlight. "Sunstar, the one who guides the lost home."

Kateri never used my real name. She only called me Saloso out of respect to grandmother. It was strange hearing my name from her, but I had grown quite fond of it on Cameron's lips.

"You were never able to be her."

Weakly, I answered, "I still want to be her."

"I know."

The wind howled and I listened intently as the blaring silence tried to muffle it. I could always be honest with Kateri since we were in the same boat, and I knew she would understand.

Taking a deep breath, I said finally, "Kateri, if I do not return, I will be what they always believed me to be. I will be the cry of the wild goose."

"Is that who you are?" She was looking at me now, brown eyes against her copper skin glowed in the light.

"I do not know who I am," I answered.

"When Jesus was brought before the council of pharisees, they asked him who He was. They asked if He was the Son of God. His reply was, '*You say that I am.*' It was neither yes nor no because Jesus knew who He was. He did not need it confirmed by the pharisees. How can you guide someone if you do not know who you are?"

"You act as if I do not already know this," I grumbled.

"I am telling you this because there is something keeping you from knowing exactly who you are." She took my hand. "Before the pharisees asked Jesus if He was the Son of God, He told them, '*If I tell you, you will not believe, and if I ask you, you will not answer.*'"

"I am not sure I understand."

She nodded. "What He meant was this: it matters not what I tell you, your mind is already made up. You have already determined that I am guilty of a crime worth death, you have a predisposition." She shook her head. "It does not matter if you save the tribe, it does not matter if you bridge the gap between our world and this one. The minds of the tribesmen are already made up, so it matters not if you return. To them you will never be Sunstar de Achille, you will always be the cry of the wild goose."

"I cannot change who I am, can I?"

"You do not need to." She squeezed my hands tighter, and I almost felt relief at her words. Like there was a burden that wanted to lift from my shoulders, but that would mean I did not have to prove myself.

All my life, I had clung to that. Believing that someday I would prove to the tribe that I was more than the cry of the wild goose. But I have been more than that for a very long time, I just did not know it.

I exhaled deeply, releasing the burden from my shoulders. "I can let it all go now, can I not, Kateri?"

She pulled me into her chest. "You can let it all go, sister. You do not have to *prove* that you are the one who guides the lost home. You are Sunstar de Achille, and you will always be her."

Thirty

An Encounter

The next morning, I found my way through the maze of Savannah's house to the kitchen. The only one seated at the table was Cameron. He was a tall man with a broad chest, strong arms that made you feel safe, tan skin that looked like the coast, and green eyes that always reminded me he was an outsider. Like me. My blue eyes set me apart from everyone else in the tribe, and the same was for Cameron's green eyes. But his most charming attribute, the one I longed to cling to, was his smile. Surely Cameron had a wonderful personality, and a welcoming demeanor, but it was his contagious smile that could make my heart stir.

As he sat at the table, he did not smile. Saddened eyes avoided mine, clasped hands bore pale skin at the knuckles, and his bouncing knee made him bobble. Slowly, I approached the table, unsure of what to make of his sadness. I was not certain of where it lied, whether in the previous night's conversation or elsewhere. But it did not take him long to point me in the right direction.

"I'm sorry, Sunstar," he said as I sat down. He was seated at the head of the table, and I sat beside him.

"For what?"

"For saying what I said yesterday. It was out of line."

"I am also sorry, Cameron. For so very long, you have tried to get me to see my worth, but I was afraid to do so."

"That didn't give me the right to snap at you." He leaned across the table and opened his hand to me. "Sunstar, I will have you no matter the cost. I am willing to do anything to keep you by my side. Even if that means returning to the tribe with you."

My hand stopped just short of his, and I traced my gaze from his arm to his eyes. "You would leave your home for me?"

"I want your heart to be my home, so that wherever you are, I am too."

"I … I do not know what to say, but I do not think my heart can take much more. It will burst if you are always kind." He exhaled and it was there finally—his smile. Charming me the way it always had.

"I would do anything for you, Sunstar. I mean that." His eyes held such intensity in them.

I took his hand, and I squeezed it. "I do not wish to return, but I must."

He nodded.

"But I have thought it over, Cameron, and I will not be staying. I will return to properly give the seat to Misty, and then

I will come back to you."

"I'm going with you," he said quickly.

"No, it is all right."

He shook his head, insistent on returning with me. "I want to go with you. And when you go, I think I'll have a possible solution for your tribe. Something to carve into the council hut for your story."

I clutched my chest, truly afraid my heart would burst from excitement. *My story*, I thought as I took a deep breath to slow my hammering heart, *it will not be left unfinished*. I was relieved and grateful to Cameron.

"Thank you. You have done so much for me."

He lifted my hand and kissed it. "Thank you, Sunstar, for allowing me to do what I can for you."

"I am not going to chaperone a bunch of adults. How old are all of you?" Carter snapped at us, but we were not listening.

We walked slowly, staring at the clothes hanging on silver racks. Nothing looked like our tribal clothes, although, I had not expected it to since we made our clothes ourselves. There were so many options, so many things to choose from. Cameron told us each to get what we wanted, but to make sure we got something fancy for the Sunday services he wanted to take us to.

"There are too many options!" Kateri whined as she pulled a shirt from the rack. There was an oddly shaped trim of metal that held the shirt on the rack.

"What is this?"

"Some kind of fishing hook," Killa suggested as he leaned over us.

Cameron stepped between our group and took the shirt. "This is a hanger, sometimes referred to as a coat hanger. It is like the clothes pins you used to hang your tunics on the lines."

People passed us, staring wide eyed like they had never seen people who looked like us.

"Are there no tribes here?" Catskill asked, eyeing a man who would not break his stare as he marched by us.

"There are tribal people all around the globe, but none that I know of look quite like you all. It's kind of funny." Cameron laughed as he handed Kateri the shirt. "You guys don't look like an ancient civilization who somehow made it to the future. You look different, like settlers with striking cheekbones."

"Settlers?" Killa questioned.

Cameron waved him off. "It doesn't matter, just find some clothes."

"Where should we look? This place is bigger than any market I have ever been to," Catskill said. He looked a little happier today, and I was glad to see him finally doing better. But I could not blame him. He had taken the life of our chief by accident and was protected by an outsider. It was a jarring situation.

"Grace and Carter will help you guys," Cameron explained as he moved over to grab my hand. "Annie will help you and Kateri, but I'll be right here to offer some help too." I nodded, and he lifted his wrist to stare at the small device strapped to it. "Meet back here in two hours."

Shopping was exhausting. We bustled through isles and rows of clothes. Kateri seemed to enjoy it. She was her usual chipper self, trying on things, and finding her size. Turns out, my hips were rounder than Kateri's by five inches.

"But I am a huntress, I am supposed to be stronger and more muscular than a healer." The woman only blinked at me as she held the yellow measuring tool in her hand.

"Sister, it is no competition. You are still so beautiful."

"How about no more measuring," Annie suggested.

The woman only nodded, and we took our leave from her changing station. Cameron interlaced his fingers with mine as we began to stroll slowly through the store. I watched a nearby couple closely, the way the girl giggled and clutched to the arm of the boy she was with. He was smiling so brightly at her, it made me want to try it.

"Cameron," I said, looking up at him.

Lazily, he glanced down at me with asserted brows.

I said, "I want to do that." I pointed at the couple.

"You want to hold my arm?"

I nodded quickly.

He shrugged. "All right." Casually, he lifted his arm and I clutched it. "Do you like it?" he asked.

I smiled warmly. "Very much so."

He chuckled, his smile brightening like the boy's did when the girl grabbed his arm. "Good."

We began walking again, and while clutching his arm, I

reached for a dark piece of clothing.

"That's nice, I think you'll look great in it," Cameron offered beside me.

"Really?"

He leaned over and kissed my head. "Absolutely."

"Cameron?"

We both snapped our vision toward the voice. A woman with straight hips and dark frames stood across from us, clutching a shirt.

"Garrith," Cameron responded as if he had seen a ghost.

"Fancy seeing you here." She approached us. "Who is this?"

"Garrith, please," Cameron said quietly. "Just let it go."

"Like the way you did our relationship?"

Relationship? Does Cameron know her?

"Cameron," I pulled on his arm, "what is she talking about?"

"You mean you haven't told her?" She laughed loudly. "You can't be serious, Cameron."

He looked uneasy, his shoulders dropped, and he looked down at me, his green eyes had lost all their joy. "This is my ex-girlfriend."

"Ex-girlfriend?" I repeated. "What is that?"

Garrith squinted behind her frames, and then she folded her arms like she was trying to understand my question.

"It means, I had a relationship with her in the past."

"A relationship." I paused, looking down at the floor. I noticed her shoes. I had not seen anything of the sort, but there was a platform beneath the shoe, like stilts beneath the heel that made her taller. "You mean she was who you were going to marry, as I was to marry Catskill?"

Cameron sighed. "Something like that."

"What is this?" Garrith finally asked. Her pinched face was even tighter now with an expression that made her look unpleasant.

Cameron lifted his wrist and tapped the device on it. "It was nice seeing you, Garrith." He turned to me and grabbed my hand. "Let's go."

"Hold on," Garrith called, walking closer to me. "Who are you?" She was almost as tall as Cameron. I shrank beneath her gaze as she peered down at me. Her dark lashes were clumped together by a black goop, and there was something like paint across her face. I wondered if this was the markings of her tribe.

I cleared my throat, "My name is—"

"Don't answer her." Cameron stepped between Garrith and I. "You need to leave. Now."

"It's a store, Cameron," she snapped at him. "I can shop where I please."

"Fine, but you don't get to question her."

"Who is she to you?"

"I am the one he loves," I responded for him.

Her eyes almost pushed her frames off her face as she stared at me.

"Are you alright? You are suddenly paling." I reached for her shoulder, but Cameron grabbed my wrist.

"This is my girlfriend," he said to Garrith. "I love her, and I don't want you messing with her or talking to her. Ever. We are done, Garrith."

She shook her head and looked between Cameron and me. "This is what you left me for? Her?"

"She is who I left everything for."

His response made her step back, and her eyes slid to my frame. Blinking in disbelief, she let out a defeated chuckle as Annie and Kateri approached. "I see now," her voice was softer, and she was looking down at my shoes. They were closed-toe, Cameron called them sneakers, and they were all white and a little too big for me.

"Sister." Kateri came over and grabbed my hand; she looked worried.

Annie was carrying a large bag with things Kateri had picked out, and she set it down as she stood beside Cameron. Garrith nodded, working her mouth to lick the front of her teeth. She looked like she would cry.

"For two years, Cameron, I tried. But it was pointless all along. You came back different. Someone else."

As she spoke, Grace, Carter, Killa, and Catskill came rushing over.

"And it was all because of her." She looked at me, tears threatening to fall. "We didn't fall out of love ... because you never loved me. For two years, I thought you were damaged beyond repair from Peru. But you were better off there than here with me."

"I already apologized," Cameron said coldly. "I don't know

what you want."

She continued to eye me from top to bottom in one slick look. "She's pretty. She glows like the sun during the harvest evening, or even the stars at night. She must be special. Some kind of guiding light over there." She whimpered instead of letting out the laugh she wanted to produce. A tear slipped down her cheek, and she wiped at it quickly. "You were certainly lost without her. But you look good, Cam. You look the happiest I've ever seen you. I'm glad you found what I couldn't give you." She glanced around our entire group. "You've got a family now. You've got a family and I'm not part of it!" She began to sob, but Cameron's cold voice cut her short.

"*Stop it*," he snapped. "You don't get to do that to these people. To *me*. No one's going to pity you, Garrith, so just leave."

She swallowed, bobbing her head quickly as she wiped at her tears. "I know. I'm sorry. I'd better go." She looked at me once more. "What is your name?"

I pulled my hand from Cameron's and reached for hers. Her slender fingers trembled in my hand as I clutched it. "My name is Sunstar de Achille, Chief of the Sand Ribbon Tribe, the guiding light to those who wander."

"Sounds like a long story." She smiled weakly.

"It is one my people will long remember even after I am gone. One that now you shall remember."

She chuckled, and I released her hand.

"I'll be seeing you, Sunstar." She looked back at Cameron.

"Cameron."

"Garrith." He nodded, and she turned on her heels, clicking and clattering away.

We all stood there in silence for a moment, trying to figure out what had happened.

Annie broke the quiet. "Sorry, Cam, we got here too late. We were across the store when you pinged us."

He nodded, lifting his wrist to tap his device, and I realized he had called to his guards with the little gadget.

"It's fine, let's just go." He glanced over at me. "I'll explain when we get home." There was a half-smile on his face as he took my hand. I nodded and followed him through the store as Kateri and the others followed us.

The drive was painfully silent. No one spoke until we arrived at Savannah's house. Cameron asked if everyone could give us some time alone. He took me into the bedroom I'd been staying in and sat on the bed, patting the spot next to him. I sat beside him. A thin smile was stretched across his lips as he looked down at the floor.

"I didn't tell you before because I didn't think I needed to."

"She was someone from your past?"

"Yeah," he said. "Before I came to Peru, she and I were involved. But we ended the relationship, and I went to Peru alone."

Cameron had never told me how he ended up in his tourist

accident. I listened to his heavy words as he regretfully spoke.

"A few days into the trip, we got in the accident, and you saved me. Then I returned home for two years, and Garrith and I started seeing each other again. But," his voice fell quiet for a moment. "I couldn't stop thinking about you. I didn't know I'd fallen in love, and when I realized it, it was too late for her."

I placed my hand on his knee, and watched his eyes find my hand. "Catskill was fortunate enough to find love elsewhere, but Garrith is not so blessed. It is no different for Killa. Elainnis has found love in another man, and Killa is left loveless for now. The matter of the heart is tricky. You do not direct it, God does."

He smiled softly as he took my hand.

"Sometimes, Outsider, following directions is not so simple. Sometimes they are hard to follow, and we end up making our own path, following one that is not intended by God. However, sometimes, even when we do follow the path of God, bumps and scrapes can happen. We must push forward if it is the will of God."

"Well—"

"Cameron?" Savannah knocked on the door.

He stood from the bed and opened it. "What's up, Mom?"

"Your father is calling."

He shrugged. "Let him leave a message."

"He says it's urgent. He found something for the project you've been discussing with him."

Cameron stirred. "Oh!" He whirled around, his eyes

blazing. "Sunstar, come with me. I want you to meet someone."

Thirty-One
Who Must Return?

"Who's this?" A woman with big blue frames and brown coils looked me over.

"Cassidy, this is my girlfriend, Sunstar. Sunstar, this is my father's assistant, Cassidy."

I nodded at her.

"Oh." She laughed as if something was humorous. "You are the next chief?"

"Cass doesn't think you're a chief." Cameron rolled his eyes.

I patted my chest twice and said, "It is true. I am the chief of the ribbon that lies hidden within the sand."

"Oh, I cannot wait for Mr. Taylor to meet you."

"Don't be cruel," Cameron snapped.

"Don't be unreasonable. Taylor Industries is not built on crushes and daddy issues."

"And they're not built on sleazy office flings, either," Cameron said bitterly.

Cassidy's eyes widened, and she glanced around the room before stepping forward. "How dare you?" she snarled.

"I could ask you the same. Does Betty know?"

Cassidy's face flashed red, and she pushed past me to a door which she unlocked and held open. "Wait inside," she said without looking at us.

"Come on." Cameron led me inside. "This is an office. It's like a space for working. Instead of doing work at home, we do work in offices here."

"Like chopping wood? You would do it in here?"

"Well," he pushed the door closed, "not exactly. Chopping wood would be done outside. Or in a factory of some sort. It depends if the lumber is being produced on a massive scale or—" he glanced down at me. "Never mind."

"A factory, I have heard of those."

He nodded as he retrieved a glass from a cart. "Water?"

I nodded and he held the glass beneath the clear jug of water.

"Is that pouring water through that thing?" I asked, pointing to the sleek black machine where the water streamed from.

"Yes. It's actually a water dispense."

"How fascinating." I stepped over to watch.

Cameron handed me the glass with a sigh. "I'm sorry about Cassidy. She's just kind of a glorified secretary because of her other ... responsibilities."

"Like what?"

"Why don't you take a seat," he said as he guided me over

to the wide chairs.

"Is this a table?"

"Kind of. It's a desk. Most people eat at tables and do work at desks."

I nodded, looking at all the frames. "These are different from paintings."

"They're photos," Cameron explained.

"Photos? They are similar to paintings?"

"Very. Except, photos are not interpretations. They are actual moments, frozen to be remembered."

"Really?"

He nodded glumly as his eyes looked over each photo.

"Who are these photos of?" I asked, leaning closer. There was a man with pale skin like Garrith's but he looked so similar to...

"That's my father, and his family."

"His family is not your family?"

A tightlipped smile spread over his face. "No. My mother is my family. She's all I've ever had."

That was why he never spoke of his family. He only had a mom. His father ran away, just like mine did. *But that means, this man is the one Savannah told me about.* The door opened to the office, and in stepped Cameron's father. He looked strikingly similar to Cameron, almost as if Cameron was his younger duplicate.

"Cameron, sorry I'm late. I know I said it was urgent, but I got tied up anyway." He stopped walking when he noticed me.

His eyes, they are green like Cameron's.

320

"Is this her?"

Cameron nodded and seemed to brighten a little. "Yeah. This is Sunstar."

I stood. "I am Chief Sunstar de Achille."

"No wonder Cameron fell in love with you. You're stunning," he said as he crossed the room to me. He towered over me; his gaze made me feel uncomfortable.

"John," Cameron said sternly, "back off. Or else I'm telling Cassidy."

John stiffened and glanced over at him. "Who told you?"

"I came to the office late a few days ago." Cameron only raised a brow, and a muscle ticked in John's jaw. He whispered something I could not hear as he walked around his desk to sit.

"So, what was so urgent?" Cameron asked.

"I found someone who's willing to make the design you had for the simple net and the possible piping. But they'll need to get out there and see it all for themselves."

"What is he talking about?" I asked.

"I've been discussing plans for your tribe with John, but it would be so invasive, I wasn't sure what you would think of it."

"I do not care about our privacy." I looked back at John. "I will give it up, if it means keeping the tribe alive."

"Well then it's settled." John shrugged. "That was easy."

"Wait," Cameron said. "Sunstar, if you're not planning to stay, how can we trust the plans will go through? That the tribe won't stop the construction? It will look bad on my father's business if we go out there and can't finish the work."

"You are right." I clasped my hands, fiddling with my thumbs. "As chief, I can enact a motion, but if I transfer leadership, the motion can be stopped."

"So give them an ultimatum," John suggested. He threw his hands open and shrugged. "Either they can take your help or not. If they say no, fine. If they say yes, then we go in and get things started with permits and all that."

"That would be a good idea," Cameron added. "If you call a council meeting, explain to them the plans, maybe they'll say yes."

"But you need to be prepared for if they say no," John said. "Both of you. My company isn't trying to make a difference, it's trying to make money. Business deals fall through, I don't care either way, but don't come back here all slumped-shouldered and regretful. You and your friends will have work to do when you all return."

"Work?" Cameron gasped. "You found them jobs already?"

"I've got their applications for their work visas right here." He held up thick parchment. "They'll need to fill them out and get them to me pronto. I know a guy who can expedite the process."

Cameron reached for the parchment, but John pulled away. "You and your group better return."

"We will," I answered.

John smiled at me, but it was not the same one Savannah wore, nor Cameron.

"Your smile," I said as he passed the parchment to

Cameron, "it is different from Savannah's and Cameron's. It is funny, the only thing they share is the same smile. Perhaps it is because they smiled about the same things without you."

John blinked at me, and the silence in the room was heavy and thick. Cameron's face turned into a hard frown.

"Sorry, I hadn't told her much about you."

"It is alright, Cameron. Savannah told me about your father."

"When?" Cameron asked, but before I could answer, John scooted forward in his chair and asked forcefully, "What did she say?"

"That you ran away because you thought it was best. Although it seemed to do no good, as did my father's disappearance."

"What is she talking about?"

The room suddenly felt uncomfortable. John rubbed a thick hand over his face, quickly hiding his eyes for a moment before the green orbs were unveiled again. The deep sadness in his eyes began to make me regret my words.

"Long story short, bad things happened to Savannah because she was with me. So, I stayed away from her, hoping it would help. Of course, it didn't."

Cameron sat still, staring at nothing.

"You're unhappy and guilty, that's why you've never loved Betty." Cameron shook his head. "I was *almost* like you, staying away from the woman I loved, suffering because I thought it was best. Thankfully, I had God, and my mother, and because of them, now I have Sunstar." Cameron raised his head to look at his father. "I forgive you, John, and I'm sorry I've held this against you for so long."

John nodded without looking at Cameron nor myself as a tear slipped down his cheek. We stood to our feet, Cameron took my hand, and we left John's office in silence.

When we returned to Savannah's house, Cameron gathered everyone into the living room. Kateri and Catskill came in first, they had been sitting at the dining room table when Cameron and I arrived home. Killa had to be awakened, he was taking a midday nap. I watched as Kateri and Catskill crossed into the living room. They had been chatting; they looked happy. I remember how wide-eyed we all were when we'd first arrived. But thanks to Savannah, we were able to relax and fit right in. I suppose if we did not have Savannah and Cameron, we would still be very wide-eyed. However, we'd gotten more surefooted. But I was afraid that might raise a problem.

Catskill sat on the couch with Kateri who wore a floral dress. The pink and red colors looked pretty against her copper-toned skin. Beside her, Catskill looked every bit a warrior in his white shirt and soft black pants. His shirt was almost too tight as it screamed for mercy across his chest and clutched fiercely around his biceps.

"You look worried, sister," Kateri said.

I ripped my eyes from Catskill's biceps to see Kateri smiling. "I am a little worried," I confessed.

"Did something bad happen?" Catskill asked.

I shook my head. "Something good, but it is complicated."

"Are you returning?" Kateri could always see through me with her brown eyes.

I looked off as Killa entered the room in a striped long sleeve shirt and grey pants.

He flopped into a big, cushiony chair as Cameron sat beside me. "Well?" Killa said, rubbing his face.

"Well, we've got good news, but it may also be bad news."

"On with it then," Kateri urged.

Cameron stood and began pacing the room. "We have a plan."

"*We* who?" Catskill interrupted.

"My father's company."

Everyone nodded.

"The plan is to create some kind of netting or strainer to catch all the debris that's been building while allowing the water to continue its flow. But they don't know how feasible it is since this is an ancient piping system."

"You are referring to the tribe—the puquois?" Kateri raised a brow.

Cameron replied, "Yeah, those."

"So we are returning, then?" Killa asked, slowly sitting up.

"We can," I added, "but we do not have to stay."

"We are risking our lives for what? You know the rules, Saloso," Catskill said angrily. "If one returns with supplies from the outside, it is to be burned and they are to lose the hand that carried the supplies into the tribe."

"I know," I said solemnly.

"And if there is great enough offense, your life could be taken," Catskill reminded.

I only sighed in response.

"And you still want to try this?" Killa asked.

I dropped my shoulders, glancing around the room. "We must not leave them to die."

"They were going to kill you!"

"It is our custom! They would have killed anyone else!"

"And anyone else would take their freedom and run with it!" Catskill snapped again.

"That's enough," Cameron said.

"Why? Why do you insist on returning?" Catskill asked, ignoring Cameron.

"You have a reason to run, and I will not ask you to return with me." I looked around once more. "I will not ask any of you to return with me. But I still have a duty to the tribe as the leader. I cannot abandon my duties just because it may inconvenience your new lives."

"She is right," Killa said after a moment of silence. "Saloso is still the rightful chief. If for nothing else, she needs to return to pass the power to someone else. It is only fair."

"When did the tribe ever care about being fair to you, Saloso?"

"It is not about them," I said to Catskill. "It is about me. I am the chief, and I am willing to do this as my final duty."

"Sister," Kateri said, "if this is your final duty, then I will return with you. I do not wish to stay, therefore, if you can promise me that this is not permanent, I will go with you. Catskill and I want to marry, but we cannot within the tribe because of who I am. This decision is more than about me now, so I need your word."

My dear sister, she had always been by my side, and she would be once again if I could do this for her. The secret meetings between Kateri and Catskill were proof enough that they were serious and had *been* serious. Despite Catskill's accident with our grandmother, Kateri still loved him. I could not take that from her. But I did not come to my decision because of her.

I looked up at Cameron. He was standing against the wall with his arms folded across his wide chest. He was quiet mostly, feeling like it was not his place to say much. Little did he know, all of this was for him.

"My sister," I finally said, "I give you my word, we will not stay. We will return here." I patted my chest twice and made the sign of the cross on my left shoulder. A chief's seal, an assurance that we will keep our word, or our dominant arm must be removed.

They all gasped, and Killa said, "You are serious then, we are actually going back?"

"But for how long?" Catskill asked.

"No more than three days. I will need enough time to convince them to one final council meeting where I can explain the details of Cameron's plan."

"That is fair," Kateri nodded. "Considering they may try to kill us as we return, getting them into a council meeting may prove to be a challenge."

"Alright," Killa said, "let us assume we can convince them to have a meeting, what if they do not like Cameron's plan?"

"My duty is to save my people, but the duty of my people is to have a desire to be saved."

"This is exhausting," Killa exhaled heavily, dropping back into the chair.

"And if they say yes, will that extend our stay?" Kateri looked suddenly nervous, her raised brows and alert eyes peered at me.

"If they say yes," Cameron finally spoke up, "my father will have a liaison who gets everything done on both ends and reports it back to Saloso."

"A liaison?" Catskill asked.

"A go-between." Cameron shrugged.

"Like Jesus?" Kateri asked.

Cameron's brows raised quickly, and then they lowered as he thought for a moment. "Yeah, like Jesus going to God on our behalf and stuff."

"Then it is settled." I stood. "We will return for three days, and no matter what happens within those three days, we are to return to Savannah's house afterwards."

Thirty-Two

The Samaritan Woman

"God is good," the sweating bishop said.

"All the time," we responded.

"And all the time?"

"God is good," the congregation replied.

The bishop was a large dark man who sweated more than Catskill when he hauled wood. Mr. Taylor needed more time to get a prospective plan in place for me to present to the tribe, and we ended up staying two full weeks in Savannah's home. Since deciding to become legal residents here in America, we were going to receive working visas from Taylor Industries, and then get our green cards. Cameron wasted no time in getting us prepared. He hired a private tutor who has been giving us lessons, preparing us for a General Education Diploma, since we didn't have any education or records.

We only had fifteen weeks to learn enough to pass the GED test. It seemed impossible since we knew so little, but our tutor made the classes somewhat enjoyable. Our GEDs will make us look more qualified on our working visas which won't be submitted until after our GED test results come through. For now, we are guests on extended vacations. Paperwork—not parchment—including who we are and where we came from is daunting but required as well. Considering our tribe has no records, no birth certificates, no form of identifying ourselves, it felt like we'd been given a second chance at life. Although, Killa wasn't too fond of the paperwork that gave us a second chance because Cameron wanted him to change his name. He said his name was a little too unusual for people here, and that 'Killa' could be what Cameron described as his middle name.

"Today, we have a guest."

I looked up from my gloved hands. Kateri insisted I wear them to match her this Sunday since we didn't match last Sunday. When we first visited Cameron's church last week, Kateri began to speak in the tongue of God, and Catskill passed out in the Spirit. Killa danced like the others in the church, and I could not stop weeping under the strong anointing. We had expected to be questioned, but the members here did not mutter a question to us at all. They simply welcomed us with open arms and invited us back. We returned this week for their invite, but the reverend of Cameron's youth was speaking today, and he wanted us to hear her.

"Reverend Bernie Lee has been a longtime friend of mine. She has her own church down in 'Bama, so when you all are down there, make sure you visit her."

"Amen!" a woman behind us yelled.

"Alright now, Reverend Bernie come on up here and give us the Word."

We all stood, and the thick woman on the keyboard began playing a gentle melody. I watched a tall woman stand from her seat in the front; a warmth began to radiate in my hand. Cameron's nervous grip pulled my attention from the platform to look at him. He offered me a shy smile before returning his gaze to the front of the church.

A tall, dark brown woman approached the stand. She wore a glistening gold robe with silver crosses on the ends of a gold sash that hung around her shoulders. Her hair was tightly coiled, and her black square frames sat neatly on her nose. She stepped onto the platform and hugged Bishop Nylin before taking the microphone.

"Good morning, church."

"Good morning," we all replied in unison.

"I'm glad to be here. It is the will of God who got me here. When the bishop called me and asked me to come preach during this anniversary program, I was going to say 'no' initially. I just wasn't up for traveling." She turned around to the bishop and said, "Sorry, bishop."

The thick bellied man laughed, waving a hand at her.

"But I'm here now," she turned to face us, "so let's give God a big praise!"

We all clapped, and someone began to sing up front as she opened her Bible.

"Dear Lord," she began a prayer, "today, let us feast on the Word You have prepared for these people. Let Your will be done in their hearts that they may receive this Word and grow from it, in the name of Jesus, amen."

"Amen."

"You may be seated."

We all sat down, and I caught a glimpse of Savannah. She was sitting on the other side of Cameron with a large black hat on, smiling at the reverend on the stand.

"Open your Bibles to John chapter four, I want to talk about something."

Bible pages began to rustle. We had never heard of a Bible, only scrolls, and we did not know how to read very well. However, Savannah gave us each a Bible, and when our tutor wasn't there, she taught us how to read with the Bible.

Paging the sacred Word, I heard Reverend begin again. "God changed my sermon today. I was going to talk about Jesus on the mountain, but this morning, God had other plans so forgive me if I stumble."

"That's alright, Reverend!"

"Go 'head!"

She looked up at the crowd and gave us a smile. "Now, this is a story I know a lot of you have heard about—the woman at the well." She paused, looking down at her Bible. "Let's start at verse eight. *For his disciples were gone away unto the city to buy meat.*" She stepped around the tall wooden stand. "In the next verse, we learn that Jews and Samaritans had no dealings, which is why verse eight is integral to this story. But jump back up to verse six, and it tells us that Jesus was *weary* from his journey." She placed a hand on her hip and looked around.

"Some of y'all have grown weary on your journey. You are so tired you just sat down by your own well. Can't get no water out; just sittin' by it because you've been working for the Kingdom. Working hard … you run down now."

A few people waved their hands in agreement, and there were a couple head bobs as Reverend Bernie spoke.

"So," she said, "jumping back down to eight, the disciples of Jesus had gone out to get meat. Sometimes, even the people closest to you don't know what you really need. They don't know that it's not food that you're hungry for, it's water you're thirsting for." She turned quickly and walked back to the podium. "For his disciples were gone away unto the city to buy meat! The very people that are supposed to be there to help you are gone! They've left, doing something else! Now you're there, tired and wearied, sitting by the well, too tired to drink! Y'all not hearing me."

I could feel a tingling in my belly, a heat that was neither hot nor sticky, just warmth radiating in my bones.

"Preach Reverend!" a man called out.

Reverend raised the mic and yelled into it, "Sometimes we get weary! And we get too tired to even help ourselves." She took another breath. "But God will always send a ram in the bush for you to realize you're not even thirsty for water! It is the Spirit inside you thirsting for God." Her voice trailed off as she stood at the end of the platform. People were standing—Kateri was standing—and clapping, and the piano player was back again.

"Look at verse ten." She waved us down as she crossed the

platform back to her Bible. "So, we know the woman just asked him in verse nine how can a Jew ask a Samaritan woman to get him something to drink. Now, listen to the Savior's reply: *If thou knewest the gift of God, and who it is that saith to thee, Give me to drink; thou wouldest have asked of him, and he would have given thee living water.*" She stood there shaking her head, and a collective praise began to ripple through the congregation. Even Savannah was clapping and nodding.

I glanced over at Cameron; he was leaning forward, staring at the Reverend. Her voice interrupted my thoughts and I looked back over at her as she began again.

"If you knew who you were talking to, you would be asking for the living water... See this sermon is for two types of people. The people who are like the woman at the well—they don't know who they're talking to. They don't know they're in the presence of the master." She leaned forward, trying to catch her breath. "The one who can supply your every need!"

"Yes, Reverend!" Praises to God rang out all over the building and there was an intense heat simmering through the church that no one seemed to notice.

"But the other folks in here," the reverend waved her hand around and the golden robes shimmied around her. "Y'all not like Jesus, but you are in the same situation. Y'all have grown tired, and you've sat down and reached out to anybody to get you something to drink. You're so desperate, don't even know you're asking someone you're not supposed to be speaking to at all!" She shook her head and the crowd grew wilder.

"You speaking to someone you have no business speaking

to. But glory be to God because He set it up like that so you can witness to even the most unlikely and their hearts can be changed. God can use you to draw in more just like them!"

Cameron erupted to his feet, clapping loudly and waving his hands. Savannah sat beside him, waving and dabbing tears from her eyes.

"See! We so stuck on tradition! We so stuck on what people look like! But we don't know what they're feeling like inside! That they are crying in the midnight hour to God, don't know if He'll answer them. But if you give them a chance, God could use you to change somebody. And see, here's the beauty in that," she waved her hand to quiet us, "when they get changed, they're gonna go back and get their friends."

I clutched my chest, waving a hand in the air. I felt so overcome by the Spirit, tears were falling again.

"Jesus did not get any water or any food, even when the disciples returned. Why?" Reverend asked. "Because Jesus had the *living water*! He had the water that could sustain for all eternity! See, what you don't understand … for y'all who are like the Samaritan woman, Jesus has what you need! You don't have to keep wondering. If He did not have it, He would not offer it!" She whirled around and ran to the other side of the platform. "And for those of you in a situation like Jesus, where you have the living water inside, but you've grown tired—hold on! Baby, you've got what you need right inside you!"

"You don't have to be weary! When the disciples came back in verse thirty-one, urging Jesus to eat, He refused it. Why?" She barked into the mic and glanced around. "Because

He was revived, rejuvenated with the living water! That living water is the Holy Spirit! You've got everything you need right inside of you, and you need to share that with the Samaritan woman!"

A woman was standing in the center aisle, and suddenly dropped to her knees, wailing and waving her hands.

"Let me tell you something." Reverend's voice was quieter now. "When you look into that well, and there's no way to draw that water out, when you ask someone and they can't draw the water for you, what do you do? You believe God, and He will quench your thirst with the living water!" She took a deep breath, wiped sweat from her brow. "That means, when you run into a brick wall, and when you don't have nowhere to go—when everything looks wrong, but you've been faithful to God … don't sit down by the well! Cry out to God and say FATHER!" She screamed, and I felt a rush of electricity jolting through my body. "Give me the living water to rejuvenate me so I can go out and continue to do Your will. So I can go out and offer this living water to others. And watch what He does."

Crossing the platform, Reverend Lee closed her Bible, and the pianist began to play gently. "Now," she said, "God needed someone to hear that. I don't know who and I don't know why, but I know this: The living water is available to everyone. Stop questioning, and don't grow weary, take the living water. Drink from the fountain of God and thirst no more. Y'all be blessed."

_____oOo_____

Reverend Lee left before Cameron got the chance to see her. He was a little upset, but he seemed to stir with joy as we rode home. Watching out the window as we drove, I was lost in my thoughts again. Tomorrow morning, we were getting on a plane from Mr. Taylor to return to the tribe; it made me wonder about my people in a different way.

For the longest, I was worried that my people would not accept the help we came to offer them, however, I have realized that this offering was not about their acceptance, it was about Cameron and me.

Our paths would not have crossed if that bus accident had not happened. At that moment, I became the Samaritan woman, and Cameron was in the same predicament as Jesus. He thought he needed aid, but Cameron already had what he needed, he just didn't know it.

My people did not recognize Cameron as one who could bring us life. It was thought that because Cameron was not like us, he could not help us. However, a conversation between the Samaritan woman and Jesus changed her sheltered perspective to receive teaching from a Jewish man.

One summer with Cameron changed my mind and others. I had always believed in the outside world, but only because I forced myself to. Cameron brought a different perspective, a new view on the world beyond the sandy borders, and the love I once faked for the outside became real.

"Sister? Why are you so quiet?" Kateri reached forward and squeezed one of my shoulders.

I turned to glance at her sitting between Catskill and Killa in a white dress with red fruits all over it. Her lips were painted red, and liner rimmed her eyes. Kateri had truly transformed, she loved it here, as I did.

"I am only thinking of the sermon," I replied.

She nodded. "It was so impactful, wasn't it? Too bad Cameron didn't get to see his old reverend."

"That's two contractions in one sentence, Kateri." Cameron adjusted beside me to see her. "Good job."

She pursed her red lips, trying to hide the gorgeous smile she wanted to show.

"Kateri," I said, staring at her lips, "can you paint mine? Your lips look quite fascinating."

She could no longer hide her smile and flashed it warmly at me. "Of course! As soon as we return to Savannah's, I will paint your face."

"Where are you learning these things at?" Killa squinted beside her.

She shrugged. "The tablets Mr. Taylor gifted us have all sorts of applications to try. I try them in my free time and find teachings of all sorts."

"Have at it," Killa leaned against the window. "We learn far too much already; I don't know how you have the time learn more."

"Killa used a contraction!" Catskill shouted.

"He did!" I squealed.

We were learning to read while learning to write and speak in the English language at the same time. The grueling lessons have been overbearing, but they seemed to be paying off.

Killa sat up straighter. He hadn't even noticed he'd used one.

"It is a shame we must return tomorrow," Kateri said, ruining the mood. "We were truly just beginning to enjoy ourselves."

"We do not have to go." Catskill shrugged.

"We do," I said solemnly. I caught their eyes, each person stared—including Cameron—as if I'd said something wrong. "During the sermon today, I read the entire story of the Samaritan woman. At the end of the story, she goes back to her people and tells them to come see Jesus, she brings them to Him, to the One who gives life."

Kateri folded her hands in her lap and sighed. "You are the Samaritan woman, returning to her people to give them a chance at life."

I smiled at Kateri. "Precisely."

Thirty-Three
The Outsiders

We stood in the private lounge of an airport, waiting for the jet Mr. Taylor promised us. We'd arrived in our Illinois clothes but took the time to change into our tribal attire in the private lounge.

When I stepped out of the bathroom, Cameron was waiting by the door. "Hey," he smiled.

"Hey," I answered.

"I wanted to talk to you about something," he said.

I slowed my pace and glanced up at him. "What is it?"

"Nothing bad." He shrugged. "Or I hope not."

"Are you ill?" I asked.

"No." He paused. "Let me set your bag down for you." He took my duffle bag and carried it over to the seats where Savannah and the others sat. Savannah was not returning with us, but she wanted to see us off.

"Listen," Cameron said, walking back to me. "I know there's a lot going on, and you've got so much schoolwork now and—"

"What is it, Cameron? Get on with it or I shall truthfully pass on."

He raised his brows and nodded stiffly. "Right. Close your eyes."

"Why?"

"I have a surprise I hope you'll accept."

Eyeing his weak smile a moment longer, I placed my hands over my eyes. I could hear him shuffling around quietly, and then Savannah gasped loudly. I dropped my hands and found Cameron down on one knee.

"I learned that in the Sand Ribbon for a man to take a woman as his wife, he presents her with an offering that she has to approve of. He does his best to provide an exotic animal, a dance, or something to impress her and capture her heart."

Wife ... the words echoed through my head as he continued.

"In my culture, the man does something similar. He presents the woman he loves with something invaluable; a ring that signifies the continuing love he will have for her. The ring is also symbolic of his heart. When a woman accepts a man's heart, they become one and share his heart." He chewed his lip, and tears began to swell in my eyes. "We are the bride of Christ. God gave us His heart through His son Jesus, and when we accept salvation—the sacrifice of Jesus—we accept the heart of Christ and share it with Him."

Kateri was standing now with her mouth covered, as Catskill and Killa watched intently.

"I love you, Sunstar, more than anything in the world. And I want to give you my heart. All of it. All of me. So, will you do me the honor in sharing my heart? Will you marry me?"

He opened the pink box in his hand; there was a silver ring with a big, glistening square rock on it. I blinked as the twinkling of the morning light winked off the ring.

"You are certain you will have me? Forever?"

"If forever could outlast eternity, it still wouldn't be enough time with you."

I clutched my heart and shakily opened my hand to receive it. Cameron chuckled and took my hand in his, he turned it over and slid the ring onto my finger. I stared at the heavy rock, and it began to blur as tears flooded down my cheeks.

"Congratulations!" Savannah yelled as she jolted to her feet to hug me.

Kateri came over with tears in her eyes. "Sister, you are getting married!"

Killa came and patted Cameron's back. "I gave him the information about the tribe's way of marriage."

"Thank—"

"You need to give it to Catskill," Kateri teased.

Catskill flushed red, glancing away as everyone laughed together.

"Excuse me," Grace's voice called behind me. He checked his tablet once more and then looked up at us. "Your jet has arrived, and we are ready for boarding."

Suddenly the joy from the room was sapped away. We all stood silently, as did Grace.

"Now," Savannah said, moving to stand in front of us, "you all have work to do when you arrive. Get it done and come home. Don't stay too long or I'll miss y'all way too much."

A light laughter rolled through the room when Carter stepped through the thick blue velvet covered door. "You guys have visitors," he said. "Can I let them in?"

"Yeah." Cameron nodded.

Carter disappeared, and before the door could close, it opened again. In walked the man who came to rescue Cameron and almost completely burned down our tribe. He also later rescued me, Kateri, Killa, and Catskill. His name was Fred, and he was followed by his team. Cassidy filed in next with Mr. Taylor following sheepishly behind her.

"We came to see you off," Fred said. "We've got a different job, so we can't go with you guys; but Carter, Grace, and Annie are more than enough protection. They'll be your team for this ride. I personally briefed them, and they know exactly what to do to find you and bring you home when you're ready."

I nodded at the tall, pale-skinned man.

"Mr. Taylor has also provided you all with a few electronics that are already on the jet. Please make good use of them and return them back to us," Cassidy said flatly as she eyed me. Her eyes roved over me from head to toe; I wondered if I looked like a chief to her. Her complete uncertainty of my chiefhood did not bother me as no one in my life had ever believed I'd be a chief, even the ones I was raised to rule over. But none of that mattered anymore. I had one job—to return and give everyone a chance at life. And then come home to marry Cameron.

He glanced down at me, trying to hide his nerves with a crooked smile. It almost made me laugh, but I suppressed the urge and turned my attention back to Mr. Taylor.

"I just wanted to tell you guys not to get comfortable there. I need you all back here and ready to work when you return," he said.

Savannah clarified. "When you all come home."

John glanced over at Savannah, his eyes slowly taking in the ageless woman. He was hopelessly in love with her; I hoped Cameron looked at me the same way Mr. Taylor looked at Savannah.

"All right." Annie and Carter stepped into the room. "The jet is all set. You guys can begin boarding now."

I spent the plane ride sleeping since my stomach could not settle, and the car ride meditating. Peru seemed hotter, but the toasting sun did not rage at us, rather it seemed like he welcomed us.

Traversing over the rough grounds, we walked in silence, everyone secretly afraid to approach the tribe. Fortunately, or possibly unfortunately, we arrived early enough to make it to the tribe just before dinner would be served, which meant tomorrow would be the council meeting. If I knew anything about the council, it was that they liked to take care of things quickly, and in this case, they would likely want us out before our three days were even up.

"Can we take a break?" Killa panted.

"Yes." I grabbed a tree to rest against. "Let us take a break."

"How much further?" Cameron asked as he pulled a water bottle from his bag.

"Not much." I turned to point through the bushes. "The tribe is just beyond this thicket."

Quiet yawned over us, stilling us as realization set in. We could very well die once we returned to the tribe. It was custom to kill the one who slayed the chief, and the slayer got to join the council or marry the next chief if she was not yet given away. Someone had killed Grey Hawk, and although they didn't know who had done it, we were now all aiding in the matter, which made us guilty as if we each had killed her.

"Do you guys remember what Bishop Dion taught us last week?" I asked. I glanced around, noticing Catskill and his jitters. He had become a nervous wreck again. I knew he was blaming himself, despite it being an accident. He hadn't said much since we left, and even before then, he had begun to clam up.

"He taught us about Esther, didn't he?" Killa asked.

I nodded. "Yes, the great Queen Esther whom God used to save her people."

Cameron looked over at me as he leaned against a tree. "If I perish, I perish."

I raised my chin and looked at the small group of my

people. "Those were the words from the queen, she was willing to put her life on the line to save her people. We have to do the same. God gave us this opportunity; He still wants to save our tribe, so we have to trust Him."

"You are right, sister." Kateri stood, she was wearing her healer's robe over her tunic that she'd run away in. She looked like the old Kateri again, however, I was not sure which version I preferred now.

"We must trust God. We must allow Him to use us as He used Esther to save those people."

"It's funny," Cameron said, stepping away from the tree, "High Priest Misty told me something about Esther just before the council meeting where Sunstar announced her decision to take the chiefhood. She said all of us could be used and put into palace-like situations." He slipped his bottle back into his bag. "When I was eight, I received a vision from God. I was told I needed to find a well to receive the living water. In the vision, I made it to the well, but I never reached in and got any water. When I turned around, there were hands reaching out to me for water."

"You did not give us physical water, but you are giving us another opportunity to have life," Killa said. "Without your help, our hands could not receive water to drink in the dream, it is the same now."

"Yes," Kateri agreed. "Water is life, and you have given us water because you did not need anything from the well or from us. You already had the water inside. You just didn't know it. God used us to bring the water out of you, and now you are sharing it with our people."

"And," I said, crossing through the grass to him, "you were in a palace-like situation, working for your father. Despite the negativity you may have felt, God strategically placed you there to be able to bring us a solution. God knew our time was running out, just like He knew the plans of Haman. And He set you up to be used to save us."

"For such a time as this." Everyone turned to look at Catskill. He took a deep breath, his shoulders bunching. Kateri rested a hand on his mighty shoulder, and when he raised his head, he looked every bit the warrior he used to be. "It is what Mordecai said to Esther."

"That's right." Kateri squeezed his shoulder, and he turned to her, smiling kindly. "He told her that maybe she was raised up for such a time as this."

Kateri pulled her gaze from Catskill to shift her attention to Cameron. "So maybe for such a time as this, you have been raised up."

Cameron's shoulders tightened. "It's possible."

"It is truth," I said, patting my chest twice.

"Then let us get on with it," Killa said loudly. "We might as well storm the place without fear. Besides, we are warriors, Catskill and I—"

"You are an injured warrior," Catskill corrected.

Cameron snorted, turning away to laugh, but Kateri could not hold in her laughter very well, and she burst into it, shedding a few joyful tears.

"Come now." I smiled. "We must hurry before it gets too

dark."

Gathering our things, we began the last truck through the thicket. Climbing over broken branches and prickly vines, we moved in silence towards our tribe. I heard movement beside me, and when I looked, Cameron had stepped beside me, reaching for my hand.

"You ready?" he asked.

I nodded. "I am ready."

We stepped into the clearing, crossing the coarse ground until the grass shriveled and turned into dirt. When the dirt had run out, and the blistering sun had begun to fall asleep, we arrived at the tribe. Silence snatched the muttering voices away. Big eyes stared at us, disbelief and fear washed over the very people I swore to protect. They looked as if I was a hungry animal looking for its next prey.

Inhaling slowly, I raised my chin and began making my way past the staring eyes. A woman grabbed her daughters, Amana and Rose, who were reaching for me. Cameron didn't let go of my hand, in fact, his grip grew tighter as we walked through the crowd, and through the tribe.

The council members often ate dinner in the chief hut or the council hut, but as we made our way to the chief hut, we realized they were not there.

"Come," I said to the others, "we must go to the council hut."

As we arrived, I clutched Cameron's hand.

"Are you alright?" he asked.

There was a small crowd of people who had followed us to

the hut, whispering and talking amongst themselves.

"I am alright."

"Sister." Kateri stepped forward and grabbed my shoulder. "We can do this."

I nodded and turned back to the door. *Lord, please hear me. I need You...*

Pushing open the door, the laughter stopped, and the smiles faded.

Thirty-Four

Sunny Frierson

Lady Falls stood slowly to her feet; her honey-gold skin wrinkled across her nose as if a putrid smell had just run across it.

"How dare you set foot here?"

Before I could answer, Commander Kumya shot to his feet and barked, "Traitors! They have returned to kill us too, and they even brought the one responsible for this crime!" He shoved his thick finger in Cameron's direction, but I stepped forward.

"Settle," I said calmly.

"Who are you to speak to me that way?" Kumya growled.

"I am your chief, Commander. You are sworn to protect me, however, I found I was running from you. Therefore, your life could be taken from you where you stand as you have broken the code you swore to abide by." I snapped my vision around the room. "I could remove every last one of you for violating your codes. Each of you swore to be my council, yet you rose against me. Such traitorous behavior should be dealt with."

"You have no power here!" Sinchi, a healer who likely replaced Kateri, spoke up.

There were five new people on the council, all inducted to fill the empty spots of all who'd left—plus one extra for elder Coya whom I released from her council seat at our last meeting.

"I have not given up my seat," I said, giving my attention to Sinchi.

His dark skin burned as he cowered on his cushion.

"I have not given up my seat, and I am not beyond the age limit. Neither have I broken any rules. I did return within the six months of travel time I initially took."

"You never presented a trophy, therefore, you are not our chief," Lord Hakan snarled.

"If a chief passes on, the next in line is immediately seated, void of all usurp mandates. You know our laws, or have you forgotten them?"

"This is an outrage!" Kumya shouted.

"Easy," Misty finally spoke. She sat in the chief's chair, her legs crossed, and she looked very comfortable. Her lips stretched into a smile, and she nodded at me. "Lord Chief, you have returned. It is your seat, please have it."

I raised a hand. "Tomorrow, I will have it once more. Tonight, you all shall sleep. I will see you at sunrise. Qispi," I called. He looked up anxiously. "Before sunrise, I will be waiting in my hut for preparation." I turned without another

351

word and left the council members to themselves.

Stepping back outside, the crowd that'd gathered began to disperse.

"Come," I said, "we will stay in the chief's hut."

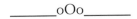

"That went well," Killa said as he snacked on a bag of chips. We weren't sure how they'd treat us, so we brought our own food just in case.

"It went as well as it could." I pulled my hair from its holder.

"And tomorrow? How will that go?"

"Tomorrow we will be leaving."

"Yes!" Kateri shouted. "I am so glad we do not have to stay any longer."

"This was your home only two or so weeks ago," Killa commented.

Kateri frowned, folding her arms. "It was my home; however, it was also my prison. I will always love this place." She reached out to touch the pelt on the floor, and then I realized Kateri was aching the most. Being free was beautiful but being free in a world you did not know was just as imprisoning as being in a world where everyone disliked you. Kateri was considerably happier with staying in Savannah's home, however, leaving behind all she knew was a bigger challenge for her than she'd allowed us to see.

"But," she said, taking a deep breath, "we have done our

part here. It is time for us to move on."

"I agree," Catskill said. "They would never accept us back. Things would never be the same. There's no reason to stay."

Killa shrugged, hating to admit how right Catskill was.

"Well…" Cameron toyed with his water bottle cap. "I will stay if you all really want to."

"We do not want to stay, Cameron. We are one family, including Savannah, we must return to her. We," I paused to swallow, "we no longer have a place here." I placed a hand on his leg, and he gave me a small smile.

"Tomorrow, I will go before the council alone."

"What?" The small smile Cameron had produced was raked away by anger and furrowed brows.

"It is better this way. Having all of you there would only make them more anxious. I must do this alone. You all can wait in the preparation room and listen in."

Kateri reached over and took Killa's chips. "Let her do it. She is right; I have sat in on those boring meetings. If the council feels threatened, they will look for every way to put us all to death on the spot."

Cameron sighed, dropping his head.

"It is alright, Outsider," I said carefully. "I will be alright."

"I know." He raised his head. "I just wanted to do this together."

"You are still my right side. I will leave that seat open for you."

He chewed his bottom lip before releasing it into a smile.

The next morning, we rose early and left the hut for the last time. I took nothing but my chief clothes, and my rod. Crossing the dewy ground, I stood in the middle of the tribe, taking it all in one final time. As I looked around, I wanted to consider staying, however, I had promised Kateri I would not stay. It felt like goodbye, it felt like the end. I suppose, at the end of things, even if they were not good things, there is always an emptiness left in the heart.

These were my people. This was my home. I grew up here, lost my mother and my father here. I discovered God here, fell in love here, and it was here that my life changed. Starting over seemed scary, as I stood there in the coolness of the morning, letting the clouds sweep their shadows over me. Logs that we sat on, an empty spit over burned wood. This was the gathering area. It was similar to the outside world. Dining rooms with a big table and chair, or even a living room with a fireplace, our worlds were more similar than they knew, and today I'd have to show that to them.

Taking a deep breath, I enjoyed the fresh scent of the earth, the way the morning dew made the dirt smell like rain. I took a step forward and decided not to look back as I headed to the council hut.

I stared at the images carved on it. So many women had done so many great things, and even if my tribe decided to forget me, I would never forget the efforts I made to save these people.

I placed my hand on my name, Sunstar de Achille, and I felt a bitter sadness swelling in my chest. "Cameron," I called with my hand still on my name.

He came up beside me and answered quietly, "Yes?"

"I've given things a lot of thought." I eyed the ring on my finger. "Today will be my last day as Sunstar de Achille."

He was silent, but I could feel his growing concern as it poured through his staring eyes.

"When I leave the council meeting, I will no longer be the one who guides the lost, she will have completed her journey. A new journey begins, and I want to start it with you, as your wife." I paused, tracing my hand over my name once more. "As Sunny Frierson."

Cameron's tanned hand traced over my name to land atop mine. "Then for now, I will call you chief Sunstar, and when you return to me from this meeting, you will be mine, and you will be Sunny."

Our hands fell from the hut, and I turned to face him. "Thank you."

He leaned down and pressed his lips to mine, enchanting me with his wonderous joy. He stood up straight and said, "You're welcome."

We walked around the back entrance and went inside the hut. Big dark drapes hung all around, Qispi sat on a dark cushion in the corner of the room in front of a bowl of water and paint. Kateri and the others were already inside, sitting on the stitched pelts that covered the ground.

Qispi stood when he noticed me and rushed over. "Chief

Sunstar, are you ready to be dressed?"

"Qispi," I said, "you have been so very good to me. I wish you the best."

He blinked, unsure of what I meant, but only nodded as he pulled me over to the cushion in the corner to paint me.

The designs of the paint were always done by the assistant. Qispi was chosen for me when I was still young. He was no older than I, but we formed a bond when we were children, and he was deemed to be my assistant. After being selected, Qispi and I stopped spending time together as he was being raised strictly to be at my every call for when I became chief.

Unfortunately, when my ride was over, so was his. I hoped that he would get the chance to work for longer—maybe the council would let him continue to serve as an assistant to Misty as they had been.

"Chin raised," he instructed. I followed his order. "Where did you run to?"

I opened my eyes to see his brown ones looking only at my chin. "What do you mean?" I tried not to move my mouth too much. Qispi was always quiet, it was the way of the assistant, to obey, not to speak.

"They searched as far east as they could before they began to run into tourists. The council feared you had escaped to the city."

"I left this place completely. You would not understand it." I paused. "I don't even understand it, but I went to—"

"The outside world, correct?"

"Correct."

I could see the others staring over Qispi's shoulder as we chatted.

"They do not want me to serve," he said as he began to paint down my neck.

"It is because of me. They do not trust you."

He nodded.

"I have hated my life," he said darkly. "It was hard being trained with never a break, just for you to run away."

"Hey!" Kateri snapped, but I raised a hand.

"I was so angry," he continued, although his face did not change, his words were filled with heartbreak. "I was so afraid they would kill me, but somehow, deep down in, none of that is what bothered me. It was that you got to be free, and I did not. But then I wondered, what would I do with freedom?" He painted me in silence for a moment, and I caught Cameron's eye. His brows had met in the center of his face, wrinkling his skin in a frustrated way. "Freedom, I would not know what to do with it, but maybe one day I will have it."

"Do you want to stay here?" I asked as he began to fan me.

"I ... I do not know how to answer. I have always been here."

"There is a way out, but you can only take it if you truly want it."

The only thing that echoed in the room was our breathing.

Finally, he lowered his fan and said, "Chief Sunstar de Achille, you are ready." He lifted my hat and set it on my head.

I leaned forward, bowing slowly as I rose again. "Qispi, I am ready."

He led me to the entrance; I took a deep breath as he rested the panther on my shoulders. "We are not all as free as you," Qispi said in my ear. "I am one who only takes orders, not gives them. I cannot freely give away the only bit of a life I have ever had for a chance at another that I may come to hate."

"It is a wise choice you have made," I whispered. "I will make certain that you will not be removed from this council." I stepped forward and he pulled the drapes back for me to step through.

Scowls. They all wore one, except Inti, who seemed amused by it all, and Misty. She was smiling as she sat beside Sinchi and Mayu, Kateri's apprentice. A younger woman with tanned skin sat beside Lord Hakan. I recognized her as his daughter, Nuna. As I sat, I found the former elder Coya's replacement, a tall thick man, Elder Rimak. And where Killa always sat was an older man, Lord Sky.

Misty made her way to the front; I nodded at her. She read from the scrolls, but I did not listen today. I was focused on trying to keep my heart from leaping out of my chest in anxiety. I was nervous, but I was a little excited to be finishing this journey. Sunstar's journey.

"Let us begin," I said as Misty sat.

With the new replacements, and leaving after the death of Grey Hawk, I wasn't sure of who, besides Misty, I could count on to believe in me. Elder Atik had once been someone dependable, however, I was not certain of her feelings towards me now.

"There are two orders of business I must address today," I

said. "My absence, and Qispi's role here."

A few scowls jolted into confusion at the last part about Qispi.

"What is this nonsense about Qispi?" Lord Hakan asked.

I raised my hand. "My absence shall be discussed first."

"Good," the commander said, "because your return is ridiculous! I should kill you where you stand," he snarled.

"Commander Kumya, I hereby sentence you to death."

Gasps echoed and the commander glanced around. "You cannot be serious!"

I lowered my gaze. "I am not serious. But if you threaten my life once more, I will rise from my seat to take your life myself."

"The way you took Lord Grey's?" It was Elder Atik who'd spoken, old and bald, sitting there glaring at me with tears in her eyes. At the first council meeting after returning with Grey's body, Atik was not sure what to believe. However, between then and now, someone had clearly fiddled with her ears.

"Settle," I said to her. "You are not far behind the commander." I turned my gaze from hers and back to the commander. "Do you understand?"

"Yes, Lord Chief."

"How can you sit there and make threats to a man with the surroundings of your name!" Nuna spat.

"I may issue warnings and threats to whom I please, and if I feel it so, I will issue one to you as well."

"You are not fit for that seat! You care not for life at all!"

Lady Falls was nearly shouting, but Misty cut in and snapped, "None of you are giving her a chance! Our chief, the rightful one, is sitting there defending herself against a council who has sworn to listen and support her. Has fear totally gripped our senses?"

"How can you defend her?" Elder Rimak said. He shrugged his big shoulders beneath the purple robe.

"I can defend those who are innocent, and even the guilty are defended by God. He protects them from death even when they are most deserving, every time they rise in the morning, or take a breath."

"You are not God!" Lady Falls cried.

I slammed my rod onto the platform I sat on and looked around the room. "I would like to discuss my absence now. Your feelings on my presence here matters not."

"How selfish," Nuna remarked.

"Qispi," I called, eyeing Nuna. He stood from the seat on my left and knelt beside me. "Strip Nuna and Lord Hakan." He nodded and stood. I motioned to the two warriors beside Kumya and they stood to help Qispi.

"You cannot do this!" Lord Hakan's dry voice cracked as he shouted.

"You have done poorly at raising your daughter; therefore, your house is not in order, one of the oaths you swore to upkeep. You have failed. And Nuna's behavior is not acceptable."

Nuna's eyes widened, and she stared down at her feet as the warriors escorted them out.

I let out a huff. "Now, I must discuss something."

Everyone looked nervous, uncertain of what I would do next.

"Our tribe is falling apart. Our water is running low. But I have found a solution. However, such solution would involve the outside world entering our tribe."

"Absolutely not," Lady Falls rejected.

"Hold on," Inti said, glancing over at Lady Falls. "After the last meeting, I took a stroll through our crops … they are dying. They are dry from no water and scorched by the sun."

"Inti, you cannot be serious?" Sinchi was appalled. "God has always provided."

"Maybe this solution is His provision."

"Or maybe you are just afraid," Sinchi snapped.

"I am afraid of dying, young healer," Inti admitted. "While I do not agree with the outside world intermingling with our tribe, I am willing to do what needs to be done to save the small bit of tribe we have left."

"It is true," the commander inserted. "The water sources are shrinking. The men were training a few days ago, and there was hardly any water in the well."

"It is the outside world we are referring to; we cannot just let them in. Everything we have done to protect ourselves from them, now we are just letting them in?" Elder Rimak fumed.

"Whether or not you let them in, it is up to you. The plan is to create netting, like the ones we use for big fish catches, but with finer holes. They will catch the rocks and drain the water."

"What do you mean, it is up to us?" Commander asked.

Misty raised a brow, and for the first time since I arrived at the meeting, I smiled. "I am here to announce my release of the seat to the Great Mist of the Sea."

"What?" Misty squeaked.

"You just became chief," Elder Atik said to me. "Why give it up?"

"Because I have found a new home where I belong. One where a predisposition is not imposed upon me. One where freedom and love resides. One where there is a real family waiting for me."

"So, you will abandon us?" Mayu asked quietly.

I shook my head at the small girl. "I will not leave you without someone seated in my stead. I have no place here, but I could not leave without finding a solution to our problem." I removed the folder from beneath my robes and handed it to Qispi. "High Priest Misty will look over the details. When, and *if*, she is ever ready, all she has to do is press this button." I extended a scraped box to them, and they all gawked at it.

Qispi retrieved the box and took it to Misty.

"Regarding Qispi," I said, "he will be the assistant to Misty."

"Why are you doing this?" Atik asked. "All your life you wanted to be the chief."

"That is true," Lady Falls agreed with a nod. "You have desired nothing more than to be chief. I do not understand why you would give it up."

"And you cannot take the blood of the chiefhood! Who

will bear us another heir—one who is meant for the throne?" Sinchi hollered.

"It is odd." I crossed my legs and propped my elbow on the stone armrest, my cheek rested against my fist. "All of you knew all I ever wanted was to be chief, yet almost every last one of you made it difficult for me to become chief at some point in my life."

"We had our doubts." Commander shrugged.

"I was but a child!" I snapped. "I was but a child ... wanting to do nothing more than prove that I was not Saloso. I was not the cry of the wild goose. But none of you would let me prove that, only Misty."

"Saloso, I believe I have—"

"I am not Saloso," I growled at Elder Atik.

She gulped, and nodded, slowly fixing her mouth to say, "Sunstar."

My ears tingled, and tears flooded my vision. "All along, you all knew my name." I swallowed thickly. "Well, it matters not, because even that will no longer be my name." Directing my attention to Misty, I nodded. "O Great Mist of the Sea, would you accept the chiefhood from me?"

"What about an heir?" Elder Rimak cut in before she could answer.

"It is time for a new bloodline to be born. It is time for a new beginning for our tribe. For too long, we have been sheltered and caged, too afraid of everything. A new leader will allow new risks. With Misty's ability to read, and her relationship with God, she makes the most suitable leader."

"But she does not carry our blood." Commander's face held a deep scowl on it.

"What is it if she does not carry the blood of the sand? You all followed her while she led in my seat when I was gone. Although Chief Grey was of the sand, she did not carry the same blood as me. Yet you all preferred to serve her than me." I paused, resting my cheek on my fist again. "It is not like the blood of Grande Chief Zasca did me well. One wrong move from my mother, and the blood pumping through my veins mattered not. You must not pick and choose when you will honor the tribe's traditions."

"I accept," Misty said as she stood.

Everyone gawked at her, but I smiled and stood to walk down the platform. "The guiding stick." I offered to her, but she shook her head.

"If we are going to break traditions, we must break all of them." She smiled down at me. "Keep it, so that you will remember us."

I nodded. "Then, I give my seat to you, Misty."

She smiled and said, "I will honor it."

Misty stepped aside and I walked through the tent, taking a final look at everyone as I moved to the entrance for the council hut.

"Chief Sunstar de Achille, daughter of Chief Nunca de Achille, descendent of Grande Chief Zasca, the one who guides the lost, and the Black Panther of the Sand Ribbon Tribe, you will not be forgotten," Misty called.

I turned and bowed as I stepped out.

Kateri and Catskill stood together, holding hands and Killa stood beside them with a towel and a bucket of water. "We thought you'd want to get cleaned up before we left."

I smiled as I came over to them. They gathered around, hugging me tightly.

"Thank you, all of you."

"Cameron stepped away to make arrangements," Catskill said. "You really handled yourself back there."

"I am proud of you, sister." Kateri took my hand.

I exhaled slowly. "Thank you. I was so nervous."

"You did fine!" Kateri laughed.

Kateri folded my chief garment after I changed; she wanted me to keep them as a memory. Cameron finally returned with good news that we were all set. Carter, Grace, and Annie had not left, they planned to stay the entire time instead of flying home yesterday. I glanced around the chief's hut once more, remembering who I used to be.

"Sunstar," Kateri called, "let's go."

I nodded and followed her out.

"Hold on!" a voice called behind us as we were leaving. We stopped, turning to find Misty and Qispi crossing the common area to us. "So, this is goodbye?"

I refused to cry and forced the tears not to fall. "This is goodbye, Misty."

She smiled at all of us and stepped to Kateri. "Your

role in this group is important. You will be to them what I was to this tribe. Remember your training."

Kateri squeezed Misty tightly and whispered, "I will not forget you."

"Catskill," Misty said as she stepped from Kateri's embrace. "She is a rarity, treat her as one. And forgive yourself, let what happened here stay here, understood?"

A flat smile formed on his lips as he pressed them together. Misty hugged him and moved to Killa. "Somehow, you got roped into this. That just means you were always part of God's plan. I wish you true love."

Killa laughed as they embraced.

"You have done well," Misty said as she came over and kissed my head. "Your mother would be proud of you. *I* am proud of you. You have defended the blood of the grande chief well. You will always be a chief here, and I will make sure your name is not forgotten."

"Thank you, Misty."

She shook her head. "No. Thank *you*." She squeezed me tight, holding me in a long brokenhearted embrace. The warmth almost reminded me of Savannah's hugs. I suddenly wanted to see her again while almost wanting to stay for Misty's sake.

She released me, dragging her hands down my arms to hold my hands a moment longer. Then, she stepped to Cameron. "In finding the well, you were able to bring life to us. We are indebted to you."

He laughed. "I told you, you know everything."

She smiled warmly. "It is the Spirit Who reveals all. Now, now," she waved a hand, "all is well with us. All be well with you. Take care of them for me, Cameron."

He nodded. "I will."

She hugged him tightly before stepping back. "Off you go now!"

Cameron grabbed my hand, and we both nodded as we turned to leave. After just a few steps, Cameron pulled me into him and wrapped an arm around my shoulders. "Let's go home, Sunny."

I looked up at him, his green eyes drowning me in joy. A new feeling of hope swelled in my chest, producing a genuine smile across my lips. "Yes," I said, "let's go home."

Epilogue

1 Year Later

"Merry Christmas, Sunny," I said as I leaned over to kiss her. It was our first Christmas as a married couple, but the second one we'd be celebrating together. Everyone made us stand under the mistletoe, despite how much I didn't want to. Even Sunny wanted to.

"You guys are so adorable!" Kateri squealed as she handed Sunny back her phone. "Now," she said, taking her own out, "take a picture of me and Kitten." She grabbed Catskill by his arm and pulled him under the mistletoe.

"All the romance is making me sick," Killa—whose name was now Ocean because he loved those comedy-crime movies—said as he passed by. He was still single, although it was by choice now. The girls at the sorting center loved him. He was strong and a hard worker, but Killa was focused on getting smarter to go to college eventually. He'd taken a strong liking to engineering and wanted to get into it. It was odd, because I thought with him being a pelt maker, he'd want to do that one day, but instead, he was interested in other things.

"On my count," Sunny said.

Kateri and Catskill were already kissing, and it didn't matter if she counted or not. They still weren't married or engaged. Catskill had told me he wanted time to see if things would work out between them in this new place. Apparently, things were really good for them. Catskill and I went ring shopping last week, and he was planning on asking Kateri to marry him on New Year's Day.

"Oh, come on!" Sunny cried, snapping a few pictures.

Kateri pulled away with a giggle as she retrieved her phone from her sister. "I cannot help it that he loves me so," she teased as Sunny rolled her eyes.

"Alright everyone," Momma stepped out the kitchen and waved her spoon, "dinner is almost ready so everyone head to the table." She disappeared back into the kitchen where Killa was helping her cook. Although Kateri was the only one who stayed with Savannah, Killa visited her almost every day to cook and chat.

Catskill ended up rooming with Killa since they had similar schedules. With Killa at the sorting center, and Catskill training to join the tactical team, they both woke up early, had long workdays, and were physically tired when they arrived home. But Catskill was going to move back in with Momma and Kateri and live there for a while once he married Kateri.

"Did we miss anything?" Carter said as he stepped into the living the room with Annie on his arm. Grace came stag as usual, but he was seeing some girl named Clora, and things were getting pretty serious between them.

"Merry Christmas," Sunny said as she hugged Annie. They'd been training together since Sunny didn't want to lose her fierceness or her strength. And, because Sunny didn't need a working visa and was gaining her citizenship through our marriage, she decided not to work at Taylor Robotics. Instead, she was able to snag a job at the public library as a part time librarian. She spent her days surrounded by books and knowledge, everything she's ever loved. It keeps her happy.

Kateri, on the other hand, didn't want to work, despite how good she'd gotten at her job. She was Cassidy's assistant until John felt she was ready to be a full-time secretary. She didn't hate the work, but it wasn't what she wanted to do. She wanted to become an herbalist, and design herbal treatments with her healing abilities.

"Merry Christmas. I brought dessert, and gifts are wrapped in the bottom of the bag. Grace's gifts are in there too," Annie said cheerfully.

"Perfect. I'll take them over to the tree and give the dessert to Savannah," Sunny said as she took the silver and red striped bag. Annie nodded and Sunny hurried off to take the gifts away.

"You just made it, dinner's about to be ready," I said to my guards.

"Good." Grace finally looked up from his phone. "I'm starving." He made his way past me to the dining room where Catskill and Kateri were sitting beside each other. I followed

Grace, Carter, and Annie inside—they sat across from Catskill and Kateri.

"Where are you going to sit?" The familiar voice made me turn around. It was Fred.

"Fred? What are you doing here?" I said as we hugged.

"I came to drop this off." He held out a small bag. "Gifts from your father. He sends warm wishes to you and everyone."

"Oh," I said, taking the little bag, "you're not staying for dinner?"

"No." He shrugged. "I've got to be on a plane in an hour. Just wanted to drop that off first."

"I see." I nodded. "I actually never really got the chance to thank you for bringing Sunny back."

He waved his hand before tucking it into his coat pocket. "Honestly, I was more interested in seeing who or what had hit that button. When I arrived, she said she knew you, and I recognized the big guy from our last visit."

"You mean Catskill?"

He nodded. "Yeah."

I'd almost forgotten that nearly three years ago, I was rescued by Fred who was met with the full force of the Sand Ribbon tribe.

"Well, whatever the case, I just wanted to say thank you." I extended a hand to him, and his thin lips pressed into a smile.

Taking my hand, he said, "Merry Christmas, Cameron."

"Merry Christmas, Fred."

He turned and disappeared out of sight while Killa and Momma made their way into the room with pots of food. As they made trips back and forth, Sunny finally returned, and everyone took a seat at the table.

"Before we start," Momma said, standing to her feet. "I want to pray, and Kateri has something she wants to read to you all."

We all stood in unison and waited quietly for Momma to pray.

"Dear Lord, it is Your birthday, and we gathered here to enjoy this meal. Give us your peace and grace and be with us as we celebrate the birth of the Savior. In Jesus' name, Amen."

"Amen," we all said collectively.

"Kateri," Momma said as we all sat down.

Kateri remained standing as she pulled out an envelope. Clearing her throat, she began, "Dear friends, I hope all is well. Hopefully, each of you are keeping the promises you made me before you left. The tribe is changing every day; however, we are learning to adapt with the changes. Elder Atik passed on last month, and a new baby was born into one of our families. There is a joy in the tribe. It's not quite as bright as Kateri's had been, but there is grand hope for this child. Maybe she can be the next chief. It is still too early to say.

"All is going well as far as the puquois go. We finally received our first permit, and can begin doing small things, such as inspections of the land's surface and the depth of the puquois. Everything is taking quite a while because, as you all know, for all of our lives, we lived hidden in the sand. Now, we are being made known, and it has not been easy.

"I hope that the new journey for all of you is going well,

and I hope to hear from you each soon. May God forever reign and let us always serve Him. O Great Mist of the Sea, the Chief of the Sand Ribbon Tribe."

We all sat in silence for a moment, each of us mulling over the letter. *You did it, Jesus,* I prayed inside. *You blessed us to bring them the living water.* But as I looked around at the dinner table, at my big new family, I realized they had brought water to us, too. I needed the Sand Ribbon people as much as they had needed me. If it weren't for that trip to Peru, I wouldn't have found these great people, I wouldn't have reignited my faith in the Lord, and I wouldn't have found the woman of my dreams.

I reached for Sunny's hand as Momma stood to begin carving the turkey. She glanced at me. "What is it, Cameron? Are you happy about the letter?"

I nodded and gently squeezed her hand. "I'm also happy about this."

"The birth of baby Jesus?"

I laughed and leaned down to kiss her forehead. "About the birth of our new beginning."

THANK YOU!

Thank you for reading! Enjoy more works by **A. Bean** and **TRC Publishing**!

Subscribe to our newsletter at therebelchristian.com to be notified of new releases, updates, and sales!

The End of the World
(Christian Apocalypse series)

Too Young
(Christian Children's Fantasy)

The Scribe
(Christian Historical Fantasy)

Withered Rose
(Christian Romantic Suspense)

I AM MAN
(Christian Science Fiction)

Cross Academy
(Christian Epic Fantasy)

ACKNOWLEGEMENTS

Firstly, I want to acknowledge Christ as my Lord and Savior, the Holy Spirit as my guidance, and God as my father. This was a tremendous story for me to write, however, when God gave me the vision for this story, I buckled in, and wrote it.

Secondly, I'd like to acknowledge Frank "Sonny" Frierson, Sr. You are dearly missed, grandad.

Finally, the late Reverend Bernice Lee, my grandmother. You were so extraordinary, and I loved listening to you preach as a child.

The Rebel Christian Publishing

We are an independent Christian publishing company focused on fantasy, science fiction, and YA reads. Visit therebelchristian.com to check out our other books!

The
Howler's Cry
Cross Academy Series: Book II
Valicity Elaine

Withered
Rose
Valicity Elaine

I △M M△N
Valicity Elaine

I △M LOST
Valicity Elaine

I △M BR○K≡N
Valicity Elaine

I △M FR≡≡
Valicity Elaine

I △M
C○MPL≡T≡
Valicity Elaine

The I Word
Valicity Elaine

PATCHES
Valicity Elaine